T0274458

ALL THE TRUTH I CAN STAND

ALL THE TRUTH I CAN STAND

A NOVEL BY

MASON STOKES

CALKINS CREEK
AN IMPRINT OF ASTRA BOOKS FOR YOUNG READERS
New York

Calkins Creek
An imprint of Astra Books for Young Readers, a division of Astra Publishing House
astrapublishinghouse.com
Printed in the United States of America

ISBN: 978-1-6626-8088-5 (hc)
ISBN: 978-1-6626-8087-8 (eBook)

Library of Congress Cataloging-in-Publication Data

Names: Stokes, Mason, author.
Title: All the truth I can stand : a novel / by Mason Stokes.
Description: First edition. | New York : Calkins Creek, 2024. | Audience: Ages 14 and up. | Audience: Grades 9-12. | Summary: "A gay teenager in 1990s Wyoming must contend with the violent loss of a loved one."--Provided by Publisher.
Identifiers: LCCN 2023045790 (print) | LCCN 2023045791 (ebook) | ISBN 9781662680885 (hardcover) | ISBN 9781662680878 (ebk)
Subjects: CYAC: Grief--Fiction. | Interpersonal relations--Fiction. | Prejudices--Fiction. | Gay men--Fiction. | Wyoming--History--20th century--Fiction. | LCGFT: Novels.
Classification: LCC PZ7.1.S753125 Al 2024 (print) | LCC PZ7.1.S753125 (ebook) | DDC [Fic]--dc23
LC record available at https://lccn.loc.gov/2023045790
LC ebook record available at https://lccn.loc.gov/2023045791

First edition

10 9 8 7 6 5 4 3 2 1

Design by Barbara Grzeslo
The text is set in Garamond 3 LT Std and Neutraface.
The titles are set in Neutraface and Brush Up.

For Matthew Shepard

History is not the past—it is the method we have evolved of organizing our ignorance of the past.

—*Hilary Mantel*

PROLOGUE

They took his shoes. Not that they needed to, since he wasn't going anywhere, what with his hands tied behind his back. His head was caved in several inches. His face was covered with blood, the only clean spots the tracks made by his tears. When they found him, the cop thought he was thirteen, not the nineteen he really was. He was that small.

I wasn't even there, but I can't stop seeing it. The butt of that pistol coming down, again and again, on his beautiful face.

But here's the thing. Those people who think they know what happened? They have no idea.

BEFORE

SEPTEMBER–OCTOBER 1998

CHAPTER ONE

The first time I saw him, he was riding a big fake horse. I was mostly interested in the horse. It was for the university's production of *Oklahoma!*, and my dad had gotten me on the stage crew. He was looking for a way to get me out of my bedroom—"back into the world," as he put it. He wasn't wrong. I was spending a lot of time in my bedroom. It was the only place where I could just be. You know, not have to pretend that everything was okay when it wasn't.

I helped make the horse. It looked good—fake, but in an obvious way, like you were supposed to know it was fake. I didn't notice the guy on the horse until he started singing. It was the first song from the show, the one where the male lead, Curly, is singing about what a beautiful morning it is, how the meadow shimmers in the early light, and the corn is as tall as the sky. His voice—light and soaring, like a swallow—pulled my attention from the horse to him.

He was wearing blue jeans and a plaid shirt, with a bolo tie around his neck. His hat was at least a couple of sizes too big, and he kept pushing it up so he could see where he was going. He finally got frustrated with the hat and threw it into the fake corn, stage right, and it was only then that I could see his face. It was small, like the rest of him, but there was something in his eyes that was big. Like he had something inside of him that was bigger than he was. His hair was dirty blond, and it glimmered in the stage lights. I guess people would have called him cute, which was going to be a problem for the production, since cowboys aren't really supposed to be cute. I imagine *rugged* is more what you're going for with a cowboy, and this kid was far from rugged.

But there he was, as Curly, riding his fake horse, singing about how everything was going his way. His hundred-watt smile made you want to believe that there was nothing out there on the shimmering meadow but beauty, and goodness, and *possibility*.

But there was something in his voice that made you doubt the smile, if only for a second. Just a hitch, maybe. The tiniest crack. But it was enough to suggest that he knew that beauty and goodness were as fake as the horse, that possibility was the last thing you should ever hope for.

"His name's Shane," a voice behind me said.

I turned to find a girl, older than me, maybe nineteen or twenty, long dark hair hanging like curtains around her face.

"What?" I said, flustered.

"Shane," she repeated. "The guy you've been staring at."

"I wasn't staring." My face felt hot. The girl raised an eyebrow.

"The horse," I said, trying to recover. "I helped make the horse."

"Real lifelike."

"It's not supposed to be lifelike. It's supposed to be, like, theatrical."

"It's definitely that," she said. "Very theatrical."

She was a big girl. Not fat, just big. Like every bit of her was necessary. Her skirt was shorter than most girls her size would risk. She was wearing a faded Hole T-shirt under an oversize army jacket, Doc Martens on her feet. Her jacket was covered with band pins: The Breeders. Sonic Youth. Sleater-Kinney.

"And what about you?" she said. "Are you *theatrical*?" Something about the emphasis she put on the word made it more than a simple question. I decided to dodge it.

"I'm on the stage crew."

Not knowing what to say next, I told her my name.

"I'm Ash."

"Jenna," she said. "We've been watching you, Ash. People are talking."

"What?"

"You've become the object of great speculation. No one knows who you are, or where you came from. But we have several theories."

My scalp started to itch.

"I don't go here," I said, resisting the urge to rub my head.

"Where exactly do you go?"

"Juniper High."

"Ah. That would explain things. So, you're what, sixteen?"

"Seventeen."

"And how does someone in high school find himself making horses for a college production?"

"My dad works here."

"What's he teach? Maybe I've had him."

"He's not a professor. He works on the grounds crew. And he's done some landscaping for Mr. Finster, the director. I'm basically here because Finster liked this thing my dad did with zinnias."

I looked back at the stage, where Shane was leaning on a fake fence, looking at a girl. The girl was pretty, with hair like Rachel from *Friends*, which didn't exactly fit in with the whole prairie aesthetic. She was a head taller than Shane, but the difference in height didn't matter, because he was singing again, and smiling, and that smile was bigger than the stage and brighter than the spotlights. It was such a stupid song—the one about a surrey with fringe on the top—but the girl was hooked.

"And what about you?" I asked, turning back to Jenna. "Are you in the cast? I haven't seen you on crew days."

"I'm just a hanger-on. I guess you could call me a theater groupie. The singing cowboy's a friend of mine."

Shane and the girl had gotten to that part of the song where he takes her in his arms and she leans her head on his shoulder, pretending to be asleep. I was suddenly struck by the desire to have Shane's arms around me, his voice whispering in my ear.

"He's good," I said, not knowing how to say the rest of it. The voice, delicate like a bird. The smile that lit up the stage. Something in his eyes that was bigger than all of it.

Jenna laughed and did that thing with her eyebrow. My face burned again.

"You're cute," she said. "Maybe I'll see you at the party tonight?"

"What party?"

"Oh. Awkward. No one told you? I'm sure that was just an oversight."

I wasn't so sure. I'd always heard what a bonding experience theater could be, but as the only high school kid in the production, I hadn't exactly bonded with anybody. I mean, the two guys I made the horse with talked to me, but they didn't really have a choice.

"I don't know," I said. "I'm not really a party person."

"Maybe you haven't been to the right parties."

She was probably right about that. Also, the appeal of spending another Friday night at home, pretending that I was okay by myself, was starting to wear off.

"I'll have to ask my dad."

"Or not. I'll send you the address. What's your email?"

Here was the problem with having a character from your favorite video game as your email address.

"Spacemama@aol.com," I said.

"Space Mama?"

"Space Mama. She's a character from *Rayman*. She's this lady in an astronaut costume that—"

"Spare me the details, Space Mama. I'll see you tonight."

. . .

I thought about not asking my dad, just taking off without saying anything, but I couldn't do that to him. Things at home had been pretty bad lately.

But I also couldn't tell him the truth. A college party couldn't have been what he had in mind when he urged me to get "back into the world."

He knew what college students were like. He'd found too many empty beer cans and used condoms in his carefully planted shrubbery.

"I'm getting a pizza with Ryan," I said. I used to be over at Ryan's almost every day, but I hadn't hung out with him in months. Dad had asked about him a couple of times, but I'd just said something about him being busy. Now, Dad slipped me twenty dollars and told me to have fun.

It took me forever to get ready because I couldn't decide what to wear. I figured the bigger the better. Anything to cover up my scrawniness. I ended up deciding on a pair of baggy jeans and a flannel shirt that gave the illusion of shoulders.

I spent another five minutes in front of the mirror trying to tame my hair. I liked the color, jet black, but it didn't really have a shape, apart from that bit that curled up on the side no matter how hard I tried to keep it down. The mirror reminded me that my nose looked like it belonged on someone else's face. It was too big for mine. I liked my eyes, though, which were almost as black as my hair. My mom said they looked soulful.

The party was in a run-down neighborhood on the other side of campus. The address Jenna emailed me led to a small one-story house with peeling paint and people crowded around a keg on the porch. I stood outside in the dark for what must have been fifteen minutes. The idea of trying to fit in with a bunch of college kids made me sick to my stomach. But the thought of going back home and spending another Friday alone was enough to get me up the stairs and through the front door.

The air inside was clotted with cigarette smoke, the people packed in tight. I thought about bolting, but the thrust of the crowd had already pushed me into another room, a living area with ratty furniture shoved up against the walls. I squeezed my way into a corner and tried to look like that was exactly where I wanted to be, but it's impossible to stand by yourself in a corner at a party and look like you're cool with it.

I finally spotted Jenna across the room, talking to some guy I'd never seen before. He looked out of place among all the theater people. He was older, maybe thirty. His hair was long and greasy, and his eyes kept darting around the room while Jenna talked to him. Eventually, she saw me, said something else to the guy, and joined me in my corner.

"Daddy approved?" she yelled. The music was loud, that pulsing pop stuff I hated, all driving bass and stuttery snare drum.

"Something like that."

"Cool."

"Who was that?" I asked, nodding toward the guy she'd just left.

"Just someone I'm talking to for an article I'm working on."

"You're a journalism major?"

"No. Veterinary sciences. I'm just writing for the campus newspaper as an extracurricular."

"You want to be a vet?"

"My parents want me to. I'm mostly just looking for ways to spend more time around cows."

I laughed.

"Really?"

"Yeah. My parents manage a ranch up near Sheridan, so growing up I spent a lot of time with cows. It feels weird not to have them around. People think cows are stupid, but they're actually very smart. They have these complex social structures. I'm currently working on a project about cow grudges."

"Cow grudges?"

"Yep. There's some research that suggests that cows can hold grudges against other cows. Like if one of them pushed another one away from the trough. The one that got pushed away will remember it weeks later and find a way to retaliate."

"How do cows retaliate?"

"Mostly ear biting. Also some strategic defecation."

I was pretty sure I didn't want to know what that involved.

"And this article for the campus paper. What's it about?"

"The local meth trade."

"Meth?"

"Methamphetamine. It's this drug that's become a huge problem in Juniper in the past couple of years—the whole state, really. I'm beginning to get a handle on some of the small-time dealers who move it, but I still don't know where it's coming from."

I knew Juniper was full of stoners—what college town isn't?—but the idea that it was the center of some sort of meth trade was crazy. That kind of thing only happened on the coasts, not here in "Wyoming's Hometown."

"Sounds dangerous," I said. "Snooping around drug dealers."

"It can be. But I'm careful. Anyway, too many lives are being ruined, and no one seems to care. Someone has to tell the story."

"And that guy? He's a dealer?"

"If I told you that," she said, smiling, "I'd have to kill you. Come on, let's get a drink."

She grabbed my arm and pulled me over to the bar, where people were ladling something that looked like cranberry juice into red plastic cups. Jenna poured one for herself and one for me. It looked safe enough, but the bitter taste at the back of my first sip let me know it was more than cranberry juice. I put it back down on the bar.

A new song came on, some up-tempo trancey thing, and people started dancing. I was bobbing my head slightly, which was my version of dancing, when I noticed a buzz in the crowd. The energy in the room had shifted somehow. And then I saw the source of the shift. It was Shane, dancing his way into the crowd. The other kids danced around him, toward him, with him, and he was at the throbbing center of it all, his face bright like a little kid at Christmas. I couldn't take my eyes off him. Every bit of him was in motion, all wriggling shoulders and hip thrusts. His hands seemed like they belonged to someone else, traveling over his body, caressing his chest, running their fingers through his floppy hair. At one point we made eye contact, and the hairs on my arms stood up.

"You like him," Jenna yelled into my ear.

"What do you mean?" I asked, still unable to take my eyes off Shane.

She put her hand on my arm and turned me toward her.

"It's okay," she said, her eyes kinder than they had been. "You don't have to be afraid. Not here. Not with these people."

I almost laughed. She made it sound so easy. Like there were places where you could just stop being afraid, even if being afraid was what kept you safe. If there was a gay rights movement, it hadn't made it to Juniper. Just the week before, I'd seen a guy downtown wearing a shirt that read: "In Wyoming we have a cure for AIDS. We shoot fags."

And now, just by watching me watch Shane, Jenna had seen something in me that I'd worked hard to keep hidden. If Jenna could see it, maybe everybody else could too.

"I don't know what you're talking about," I said. Her face tightened, her eyes growing cold again.

When the song was over, Shane rushed over to us and threw himself on Jenna, wrapping her up in a big hug.

"Girl," he said, "are you aware that you're the sexiest person in this room? Love the eyes."

He was right. She looked amazing. She was wearing a knee-length dress, made of this cool olive-colored material. It was kind of prim and proper, with a bit of lace at the neck and the sleeves, but the black choker she was wearing undid the primness. So did the white stockings that came up to her knees, giving her a sexy schoolgirl vibe. Her eyebrows were pencil thin, and her eyes were layered in mascara. She was beaming, all because of Shane.

He unwrapped himself from Jenna and turned to me.

"And you must be Ash," he said, flashing that megawatt smile. "I'm Shane."

He was even smaller up close than he was on the stage, a good four or five inches shorter than me, and I was only 5'7". But standing there in front of me, smiling, his blue eyes lit up by a lamp on the bar, he didn't seem small.

"Jenna's told me so much about you," he said.

"Really?" I asked, casting a side-eye at Jenna. "That's strange."

"What's strange about it?"

"Well, she doesn't really know anything about me. We only just met."

"You'd be surprised," he said. "This girl has magical powers."

I was about to tell Shane how good he was in the show, but a new song came on, and he yelled, "Oh my God! I love this song! We must dance!"

He grabbed Jenna's hand and pulled her back toward the center of the room. And there I was again, alone in my corner, wishing I was the kind of person who could have followed them and thrown my body up against all those other gyrating bodies, not worrying what I looked like.

Shane and Jenna were soon joined by Patrick, the hot guy playing Jud. The three of them were dancing together, but gradually it became clear that Jenna was an extra, necessary only to make it less obvious that it was the boys who were dancing together. Watching Shane on the dance floor and feeling my stomach lurch at how close he was to Patrick, I realized that standing alone in the corner was not going to get me closer to Shane, which was suddenly all that mattered.

I made my way through the crowd, and when I got to the three of them, I did the only thing I could think of. I started bouncing up and down like a crazy person. I'm sure I looked like an idiot, but maybe it didn't matter. Jenna was yelling "You go, girl!" and Shane looked surprised, like he was seeing me for the first time. Only Patrick seemed less than thrilled with my presence.

We kept dancing through the next few songs, and at some point I realized I didn't hate the music anymore. The thumping, the pulsing, the tension and release of drums and synths surged through my body, a kind of euphoria, connecting me to Shane, to Jenna, even to Patrick.

After another couple of songs, I said I needed some air and headed out to the front porch. The air wasn't the real reason. I wanted to see if Shane would follow me.

It had cooled down considerably, and the sweat on my neck gave me a chill. A couple of guys were tapping a new keg, and I moved to the other end of the porch, away from the glare of the porch light. I just stood there, staring out at the street, and waited, wishing I was the kind of guy who could do more than wait.

I was about to give up when the screen door swung open. I resisted the urge to turn around. The porch creaked, and there he was, standing beside me.

"Hey," Shane said, bumping his shoulder against my arm and sloshing the beer he was holding.

"Hey."

"Want a beer?"

"No thanks."

"You don't drink?"

"Not really."

"Probably don't smoke then either, right?" He put his beer down and pulled out a pack of cigarettes, offering me one.

"Nope."

He lit his cigarette, took a big drag.

"You're a good dancer," he said.

I laughed. "There's no way that's true," I said.

"Okay, well, maybe *enthusiastic* is the better word."

"Yeah. Enthusiastic hopping is really all I've got."

"It works," he said, taking another drag on his cigarette, his eyes still on the street.

We were quiet for a minute, and I was afraid he was about to go back inside. I needed to keep him talking.

"You said Jenna told you about me. What'd she say?"

"Nothing, really. Just that I should meet you."

"But why? College guys don't usually hang out with townies."

"She thinks I need to meet new people," he said. He took a drag on his cigarette. "Different people."

"And I'm different?"

He turned his gaze toward me.

"Jenna seems to think so."

"Different from what?"

He turned back toward the street.

"Different from the people I usually find myself with."

"What kind of people do you usually find yourself with?"

He took one last drag off his cigarette before flicking the butt into the yard. I watched its ember arc, die.

"The wrong kind," he said. I wanted him to look at me, but he kept his gaze on the street.

"How do you know I'm not the wrong kind?"

He laughed again, taking a sip of his beer.

"It's just a feeling I have. Jenna was right. You've got this whole 'boy next door' vibe going on."

"You mean boring?"

"No. Not boring. More like, someone you can trust."

Trustworthy. Didn't exactly sound like the kind of guy whose bones you might want to jump.

"She said something else," he continued, glancing toward me.

"What?"

"She said you were cute." He bumped my arm again. I was glad we were in a dark corner of the porch, so he couldn't see me blush.

"That's not really how I think about myself."

"Well then," he said. "You should reconsider."

I knew I should say something, that I thought he was cute too, but it felt like I had cardboard in my mouth, and I couldn't get the words out.

"We should get breakfast tomorrow," he said.

My heart fluttered. Was he asking me out? Like, on a date?

"Sure," I said, trying to keep the heart fluttering out of my voice. "That'd be cool."

I gave him my address and suddenly realized how late it was. Dad was going to be pissed.

"I have to go. Can you tell Jenna I said goodbye?"

"Sure. See you tomorrow."

And then he hugged me. His body fit perfectly into mine, and his hair smelled of lavender. The lavender stayed with me on the walk home. It seemed like it was coming from the flowers, the bushes, every tree that I passed.

CHAPTER TWO

I woke up Saturday morning with that itchy feeling you get when you can tell someone's looking at you. When I opened my eyes, there was Shane. I closed my eyes, thinking this must be a dream, but when I opened them again, he was still there.

"Your dad let me in. He said it was time for you to get your lazy ass out of bed."

"What time is it?"

"Ten thirty. Did you forget about our breakfast plans?"

I was suddenly aware of what my bedroom must look like to Shane. I didn't know how I hadn't noticed this before, but it was like a time capsule, full of action figures and LEGOs that I hadn't touched in years. There was the PlayStation poster that everybody had and—oh my God—faded rainbow-colored dinosaur sheets on the bed. I wanted to tell Shane that I was cooler than all this, but I wasn't sure I was.

"No," I said, wiping the sleep from my eyes. "I didn't forget."

"Get dressed," he said. "I know just the place."

. . .

His car was not what I expected, more of a truck really, a very used red-and-black Bronco that looked way more Wyoming than he did.

"Are you from Juniper?" I asked.

"Casper. But I've lived all over. I went to boarding school in Germany when my dad took a job in Belgium, and then I went to college for a while in Georgia, and then I came back to Casper. Most recently I was living in Denver, until I moved here in July. How about you?"

"Born and raised."

"You say that like maybe that hasn't been such a good thing. You don't like Juniper?"

"What's there to like?"

"Well, sure, the town's not much. But if you get just outside of town on the right night, it's beautiful. The stars and the moon so sharp, the air clean, the smell of sagebrush and pine trees coming off the Snowy Range. And this is my favorite time of year, when the winds are pushing the summer out and the fall in. Something about the altitude changes the quality of the air and the light. Everything's so pure."

"You sound like Curly singing about the corn. No wonder you're good in that part."

His eyes glimmered.

"You think I'm good?"

I tried, and failed, to keep myself from blushing.

"I think you know you're good."

"I do. But I want to know what you think."

"Well, you made me believe that everything was going your way."

"Isn't it?" he asked, and there was that smile again, brighter than stage lights.

We turned onto Main Street, the heart of the "Historic District." Downtown Juniper is picture-postcard charming, blocks of two-story brick-fronted buildings, old-timey storefronts and signs, dry goods stores, a pharmacy with a soda counter. It was almost too perfect, like it was working hard to keep up a front it couldn't quite maintain.

Like the rest of Wyoming, Juniper was in bad shape economically. The only good jobs were at the university, and if you weren't lucky enough to snag one of those—lucky like my dad—you were out of options. Tourists would come through town and wander the downtown streets, thinking they were seeing the real Juniper, but they weren't. They had no idea what it was like to live here, in a town that was always just on the verge of slipping off the map.

Shane took us to the Stagecoach, a diner that had been around for as long as I could remember. I almost suggested we go somewhere else. The Stagecoach used to be a regular Saturday morning hangout for me and Ryan and a couple of other guys. I didn't want to run into them with Shane. But then I decided I was just being paranoid.

The hostess greeted Shane like he was a long-lost son, and our waitress couldn't help flirting with him. He flirted back, telling her she was getting too thin. She beamed.

While we waited for our food to arrive, I tried to pay attention to what Shane was saying—something about *Buffy the Vampire Slayer*—but I was finding it hard to focus. All I wanted to do was look at him—those blue eyes, his cute little ears, the puffy lips—and the looking part of my brain was crowding out the hearing part. But I definitely heard what he said when I was about to dig into my huevos rancheros.

"So, what's it like being gay at Juniper High?"

I glanced around to see who else had heard him.

"Um," I said, leaning in, speaking quietly, hoping he'd take the hint. "I wouldn't really know."

"Wait," he said, red patches blooming on his cheeks. "You're not gay? I thought—"

"No. Yes. I mean, no. I am gay. It's just that nobody knows."

"Well," he said, smiling. "Not nobody."

"Right. There's you. And Jenna, I guess. Though I never actually told her."

"She's got excellent gaydar."

"She's kind of scary."

"Yeah," he said, laughing. "I know what you mean. The first time I met her, I was totally intimidated. She comes off all hard and tough. I think it's because she grew up with three older brothers. She had to fight for space. It's also why she's crazy good at reading people. Boys—especially straight boys—don't really talk about stuff. You just have to figure out what they're thinking."

"Yeah. That's the scary part. It's like she knows everything about you."

"But you know what? There's nobody I'd rather know my secrets than Jenna. Because once she knows them? She's like a mama bear. She'll do anything to protect you. And that tough outer shell? She needs that. She's been through some stuff."

"What kind of stuff?"

He looked down at his plate, fidgeted with his straw wrapper. When his eyes met mine again, there was a sadness there that wasn't there before.

"The kind of stuff nobody should have to go through," he said.

He shook off whatever he was remembering.

"Anyway," he said, his face suddenly bright again. "In my experience, if you're not a little intimidated by the girls you're hanging out with, you're hanging out with the wrong girls."

He pushed his plate and mangled straw wrapper to the side.

"But enough about Jenna," he said. "Let's talk about you. How long have you known you were gay?"

"I don't know. Maybe always? Or at least as long as I can remember. But for a long time I didn't believe it."

"What do you mean?"

"I mean, I knew I liked guys. But I couldn't imagine being gay, you know? It just didn't seem like me. The clothes. The music. It's not really my thing."

"But liking guys," he said, smiling. "That's your thing?"

"Yeah. That's my thing."

"Well, that sounds pretty damn gay to me. And that's the only thing that matters. All the rest of it—the clothes, the music, the hair—that's up to you. Your problem is the only gay people you know are on television or in the movies."

He wasn't wrong.

"What about you?" I asked. "Have you been out, like, forever?"

"What," he said, laughing, "because I'm so obviously queer?"

"I wouldn't have put it that way, but, yeah, I guess that's what I meant."

"Well, in third grade I dressed up as Dolly Parton for Halloween."

"Did you get your ass kicked?"

"No," he said, with a roll of his eyes. "I was too *fabulous* to get my ass kicked. But the older I got, the more I realized that being such a flamer was going to get me in trouble. I spent a lot of years trying to hide it. I watched the way I walked, the way I moved, the way I talked. But kids kept calling me a fag anyway. I can't tell you how many times I came home from school crying, unable to tell my mom what was wrong."

The idea of a younger Shane being bullied made me want to go back in time and beat the hell out of his tormentors.

"So what changed?" I asked.

"I guess I got tired of being afraid all the time," he said. I thought about what it would be like not to be afraid all the time.

"What about boyfriends?" I asked.

"What about them?" His smile was flirtier than it was a moment before.

"Like, do you have one?"

"Ugh," he said, hiding his face in his hands. "I'm not so good at boyfriends."

"Why?"

"I don't know. It just hasn't worked out."

I wanted to know more, but Shane was distracted by something, his eyes drifting over my shoulder, and then Ryan was standing at our table. I felt that clammy feeling you get when you're about to throw up.

"Hi, Ash," he said.

"Hi," I muttered, trying, maybe failing, to keep the anger out of my voice.

"I just wanted to say how sorry I was to hear about your mom. She was cool. I really liked her."

"Thanks," I said. If it was just the anger, this would have been easier. But seeing him there, I realized how much I missed him.

"I should have said something sooner. I'm sorry I didn't."

There was nothing to say to this. The silence was heavy. Ryan and Shane looked at each other and then back at me, waiting for me to introduce them, but I couldn't do it. The silence deepened, lingered, until Ryan said, "Well, anyway. I'll see ya," and left.

"Wait," Shane said. "Your mom died?" The look on his face had me on the verge of tears. He looked like *his* mom had died and that he was feeling it for the first time.

This wasn't really something I wanted to talk about, but maybe it would be better than talking about Ryan. I took a deep breath and swallowed the tears that were just on the verge of spilling.

"Yeah," I said. "Six months ago."

"I'm so sorry, Ash."

"Yeah. Thanks."

"Do you mind if I ask what she died of?"

I'd learned to dread this question. It made me remember what happened, and I didn't like to remember what happened. But something about the way Shane was looking at me made me think that maybe now, with him, I could talk about it. It was his eyes, I think, which radiated an empathy so deep that *he* seemed to be the one in mourning.

"Cancer," I said. The word was like a chunk of glass in my throat.

"She was first diagnosed five years ago, when I was twelve. I remember that day like it was yesterday. She and Dad sat me and my brother down and said everything was going to be okay, that she was going to beat this thing. She went through the chemo, and then the radiation, and it sucked, but she was able to joke about it, about how hair wasn't really that important. Just a bow on top of a package."

"That's fierce," Shane said. "She sounds amazing."

"She was," I said, and I let myself sit with that for a minute.

"By the time I was fourteen," I continued, "she was well, and we could all breathe again. But then a couple of years later, it came back, in her bones this time, and she and Dad didn't talk about beating it. They just got kind of quiet. And Christopher—that's my older brother—he and I got quiet with them, like if no one talked about what was happening, maybe nothing was."

I had to look away from Shane if I was going to make it through this next part.

"But then one night, Mom came in and lay down beside me on my bed. I could feel the pain inside her, the effort it took just to lie down. I couldn't help but imagine what was happening to her at that very moment, her bones being eaten away from the inside.

"'I'm just happy I've gotten you this far,' she said, and I started crying, and so did she, and that's when I knew what was happening.

"She died a month later."

Shane didn't say anything, just reached across the table and took my hand. I wanted to let him hold it, but I could feel the eyes of the other diners on us. I used the excuse of wiping a tear from my cheek to take my hand back.

"But it was like something bigger than her had died," I said, "some really important thing that was necessary to keep the rest of us going. Christopher stopped going to his classes at the community college and got a job bartending. Whenever he's not at work, he's usually holed up in his room, not saying a thing to Dad or me. Dad took time off from work, said he wanted to be home with us, but that was a lie. Being at home was torture for him because Mom wasn't there. At work he could pretend that everything was normal, but when he came home, I sensed his hesitation as he entered the house, like he was walking into someplace that was haunted."

I suddenly heard myself talking, and I worried that I was saying too much. But Shane's eyes, so full of care and concern, made me want to keep going.

"I guess I just kind of shut down. I could tell my dad was worried about me. He kept asking me how I was doing, but I didn't know how to answer the question. So I kept saying I was fine. I wanted him to stop worrying, which is why I agreed to work on the stage crew."

"And your mom didn't know about you?" Shane asked. "That you were gay?"

"I got close to coming out to her a couple of times, but I kept using her cancer as an excuse, thinking she had enough to deal with without me adding this to it. But I think she knew. Moms just know, right?"

"Yeah. Moms know. Mine certainly did, long before I ever said anything to her."

He took my hand again, and this time I let him hold it.

"Here's the thing you need to know, Ash. She knew, and she loved you. I guarantee it. She knew exactly who you were, and she loved you."

I'd been trying to believe this, but hearing Shane say it made it real.

"Thanks," I said, taking my hand back and wiping my eyes.

"Anytime," he said. "Seriously." My eyes burned, and I couldn't tell whether it was from the tears or from the way Shane was looking at me.

"We should get out of here," he said, pulling his wallet out of his pocket. He threw a wad of cash down on the check and noticed me staring at it.

"Yeah, I know. I'm an overtipper. You'd be surprised how many people will order the most expensive thing on the menu and still leave only a five-percent tip."

He slid out of the booth.

"Are you going to be at rehearsal later today?" he asked.

"It's just cast today," I said. I slurped down the last of my soda. "Stage crew isn't due back until Monday."

"You should come anyway. Jenna will be there, and we can hang out later."

My heart fluttered.

"Sounds great. And thanks for breakfast."

"My pleasure, Ash." Something about the way he said my name felt really good. I mean, he didn't have to, right? It's not like there was any confusion about who he was talking to. I was the only person there. But he chose to put my name on his tongue. I liked it.

CHAPTER THREE

When I got home, I tried to make a dent in my homework. I had an essay due on Sir Thomas Wyatt the Elder and a bunch of problems to solve for precalc, but I couldn't focus. All I could think about was Shane. When the clock finally hit 3:30, I left a note for Dad and biked over to campus.

In the darkened theater, they were running the scene where the creepy and brooding Jud is trying to get Laurey to go to the social with him, after she's turned down Curly's offer of the surrey. Curly, our nice-guy hero played by Shane, loves Laurey. The problem: so does Jud.

Though Shane was the star of the show, Patrick, who was playing Jud, stole a fair amount of attention. He was lanky but muscled, and his hands were in constant motion, like they were chasing each other. He was always clenching his jaw so that the muscles in his face quivered. Emma Martin, the girl playing Laurey, had this way of shrinking away from Patrick, like she was afraid of him, but you could tell that she thought he was hot. Which I'm guessing Shane did too, judging by the way he was dancing with Patrick at the party, and by the way he was leaning forward in the front row, his eyes locked on him.

The jealousy that had overcome me the night before came surging back, which was crazy. I had no claim on Shane, no indication that he even liked me, apart from a shoulder bump or two and a breakfast. But here I was, out in the world on what should have been a lonely Saturday, with so many things coursing through me. Jealousy, yes, but also hunger, and need. Maybe even hope. Watching Shane watch Patrick, I would've given anything to have him look at me like that.

When the scene ended, Shane got called up on stage to talk with Mr. Finster and the other actors, and Jenna found me in the back of the theater.

She was wearing a T-shirt that read "Celine Dion Is the Devil" and a red-and-black plaid skirt.

"What's your beef with Celine Dion?" I asked.

"If I have to hear one more time how her heart will go on, I swear to God, I will track her down and punch her in the throat."

"Yikes."

"What, you don't like her, do you?"

I thought about what Shane said about Jenna being someone you could trust with your secrets. Maybe this was a chance to test that. Because being gay wasn't my biggest secret. My biggest secret was that I loved *Titanic* and everything associated with it, including Celine's "My Heart Will Go On." Every fiber of my being told me I was supposed to hate that song. The dainty little flutes at the beginning. The cheesy lyrics. But, oh my God, that key change about three minutes in, when Celine throws her voice up in the air and we know Jack and Rose and their love for one another are all going down with the ship—tears and goose bumps every time. I had to leave the room if the video came on.

Maybe some secrets are just too embarrassing to share.

"No," I said, "of course not. Mass-culture drivel."

She didn't look entirely convinced, so I changed the subject.

"What do you know about Patrick?"

"You mean is he gay?" she asked, raising an eyebrow, "and thus a rival in your quest for Shane's affections? Are we admitting that now? Or are we still pretending that you don't know what I'm talking about?"

If I gave her this one, maybe I could keep the Celine Dion thing under wraps.

"We're admitting that now. But how'd you know? Am I that obvious?"

"Yes," she said, laughing. "When you look at Shane, it's like you're a kid who has just seen his first zebra. You know, like you had heard of such a thing, but you couldn't believe it existed until that very moment."

"Shane's a zebra in this scenario?"

"A zebra, a unicorn, a two-headed giraffe. Pick your rarity. Also, you couldn't take your eyes off him at the party."

"So? He's a good dancer."

"Well," she said. "If I'd had any doubts—which I didn't—the clincher was when you smelled him."

"I smelled him?"

"Shane said that when he hugged you goodbye, you sniffed his head."

Busted.

"It wasn't so much his head I was sniffing. It was his hair."

"Still, straight guys don't usually smell each other's hair."

"Their loss," I said, remembering the lavender.

"Anyway, you don't have anything to worry about with Patrick. He's straight. As in very."

"Does Shane know that?"

"I don't think he cares."

"What do you mean?

"Shane likes a challenge. He's pretty much been beating the odds his whole life."

I wanted to ask what she meant, but I had a more urgent question.

"Am I a challenge?"

She laughed.

"You most definitely are not," she said, still laughing. But then her face grew serious. "Which is why you're just what Shane needs."

I wanted to hear more about how I was perfect for Shane, but just then, Shane and Patrick joined us, and before I knew it, they were saying goodbye, something about getting dinner, leaving me and Jenna standing there like idiots, waiting for an invitation that never came.

"What just happened?" I asked.

"Abandonment," Jenna said. "It pretty much comes with the territory. Want to go back to my place for coffee?"

. . .

Jenna lived in a studio apartment on the edge of campus. There was a mattress on a raised platform, and under the platform was her desk, which was littered with newspapers and computer printouts. Low bookcases separated the sleeping/study area from a living area, where she had arranged a couch and a couple of chairs around a coffee table, all of which looked carefully chosen from vintage furniture shops. Band posters lined the walls. A couple I recognized: Sleater-Kinney, Bikini Kill. Others I didn't: L7, Bratmobile, Tribe 8.

"Would you consider yourself a 'Riot grrrl'?" I asked.

"Maybe at one point. But now the whole Riot grrrl scene has become so trendy. But I love love love Carrie Brownstein." She pointed toward a Sleater-Kinney poster. "She makes me wish I was a lesbian."

While she made the coffee, I studied the pictures she'd lined up on top of the bookcases. There was one of a much younger Jenna with short, spiked hair.

"Your punk phase?"

"I make no apologies," she said, pulling mugs down from a small shelf.

Another photo showed Jenna and four boys leaning on a fake fence in front of a forest backdrop.

"Are these your brothers?" I asked.

"Yep."

"Shane said you had three."

She was still for a minute. The coffeepot gurgled.

"No," she said, finally. "Four."

She handed me a cup of coffee and searched through a pile of uncased CDs. When she pushed play on Joni Mitchell's *Blue*, I laughed. This had been one of my mom's favorites, but it seemed far from Jenna's taste.

"I never took you for a folkie."

"I'm not. But Joni was, like, the OG punk. She was totally badass. Still is."

We sat on the couch, which wasn't nearly as comfortable as it looked. The coffee was stronger than I liked, but being there with Jenna, I felt somehow more grown up. Like maybe the next phase of my life was starting. The thing that had freaked me out about her at first, her ability to see right through me, was starting to seem like a good thing. Maybe I could be totally honest with her. I was beginning to get what Shane meant about scary girls.

"When Shane and Patrick ditched us, you said abandonment comes with the territory. What territory?"

"Being the gal pal of the gay guy. It can be risky. At first it's all, 'Oh my God, a man who listens, who's funny, who's not pressuring me for sex.' It's perfect. But eventually, he's going to need more than sparkling conversation. Let's just say it's not my first rodeo."

"That sucks," I said, remembering what it felt like when Shane and Patrick took off without me. "Why do you put up with it?"

"I'm surprised you have to ask," she said, laughing.

"What do you mean?"

"You know what I mean."

"Because of Shane?"

"Because of Shane," she said. "I remember the first time I met him—it was at a meeting of the Pride Alliance—I—"

"Wait, I thought you said you weren't—"

"A lesbian? I'm not. I just learned early on that gay people are more fun than straight people. Anyway, some of us had been meeting over the summer, and Shane showed up in July, just after he'd moved here. It's like he has some kind of superpower. People just love him, fully and immediately. He flounced in, flashed that smile, introduced himself, and it was all over. Everybody was totally crushed out."

I knew exactly what she was talking about.

"And ninety-five percent of the time," she continued, "he's the most amazing person I've ever met. Kind and sweet and supernaturally aware of what other people are feeling. As for that other five percent? That's just Shane chasing dick. You can't fault him for that.

"I mean, if he weren't gay, he'd be the ideal boyfriend. He listens. He doesn't try to make me into somebody I'm not. Like, this guy I dated last semester. He was cool at first. We liked the same music, and he was way hot. But after a while, he got all clingy and insecure. He'd freak out if I wanted to do something without him. He just wasn't fully cooked yet, you know? It makes sense. It's a scientific fact that girls mature faster than boys."

"Even gay boys?"

"Depends on the boy. Shane, for example, is a very old soul."

"And what about me?"

"The jury's still out on you. But you do seem cooler than most kids your age."

I had to keep myself from beaming.

"Anyway, it's not like my whole life revolves around Shane. That article I'm working on takes up a lot of my time."

"Any new leads?"

"Not really. The people who know things are good at not talking. But I just saw some new numbers from the Department of Health. Juniper teens are twice as likely to use meth as the national average. And the number of meth users in Wyoming has gone up sixty-five percent in the last year." She was talking with her hands, sloshing coffee on her lap. "The mortality numbers aren't out yet, but they're going to be ugly.

"As for you," she continued, putting her mug down and wiping her lap with a napkin, "you don't have to worry about Patrick. Shane's going to learn that he's barking up the wrong tree with that dude. You just have to be a little patient."

This was not good news. I sucked at being patient. The hour before lunch was always the most challenging part of my day.

"I don't know why you're doing this," I said.

"Doing what?"

"Being nice to me. Trying to set me up with Shane."

"Like I said, Shane needs to be with a different kind of guy. His romantic choices are usually bad ones."

She was staring at me, not saying anything. A cloud passed over her face.

"Also, you remind me of my younger brother."

"He's gay?"

"No. But he had this similar wounded-kitten vibe. Like he needed someone to take care of him."

"Had?"

"He died."

I didn't know what to say. I waited for her to say more, but she didn't.

"I'm sorry. My mom died recently."

"See?" she said, forcing a smile. "Wounded kitten."

CHAPTER FOUR

Watching Shane leave with Patrick had been a kick in the gut. If I'd known where they were going, I would have followed them, like some pathetic little puppy. It would have been embarrassing, but it couldn't have been worse than what I was feeling knowing they were together, somewhere, without me.

For so long, I'd walled myself off from this kind of disappointment, at least since I was twelve or thirteen. That's when Mom started asking me, like, every single day, "What's wrong?" Apparently, before that, I was this totally lively kid, the center of whatever group I was a part of.

But then puberty happened, and Ryan Strickland's neck became an issue. He sat in front of me in homeroom, and suddenly a neck I'd never given a second thought became the most fascinating thing I'd ever seen. The swoop of muscle and tendon. The pale sliver of skin that peeked out above the T-shirt. I had a strong desire to put my mouth on it. And if you're a guy who wants to put your mouth on Ryan Strickland's neck, you can't risk letting too many people really know you, especially in a town like Juniper.

So, I kind of shut down. I managed to make a few friends, gravitating to those kids on the fringes. Quiet types. Loners. We were the leftovers, those kids who didn't fit into one of the suddenly visible categories: the jocks, the rich kids, the beautiful people. We probably came off as scary, but we weren't interested in hurting anybody.

There was Brandon, a band geek who played the clarinet. Dustin, who had turned *Dazed and Confused* into a philosophy of life. Chuck, who was just kind of there. He barely said a word, but he seemed to like hanging out with us.

And then there was Ryan. He was cute in ways he didn't even know. He wore these thick, horn-rimmed glasses that were completely out of style. In fact, everything about him was out of style—his hair, which lacked product. His clothes, which weren't fashionably baggy. And that was the point, I think. When all the guys at school were trying to look like the guy from *Dawson's Creek*, Ryan just looked like . . . himself. And it worked. I'd find myself staring at him, especially at his lips, which were redder than most, almost like he was wearing a pale shade of lipstick.

The first PlayStation came out when I was fourteen, and Ryan's uncle bought him one on launch day. So his house became the place to be. It was *Rayman* that really hooked me. It was a side-scroller, so different from the first-person shooter games that were all the rage. It was so full of color and weird characters. Playing this game was probably the closest I ever got to doing drugs.

So, yeah, for a while, things were working. Sure, I wasn't the outgoing kid I had been. But I had a group of friends, and we had a way to spend the hours that stretched out after school.

But being a leftover is complicated. You'd think maybe this would be the place where a gay kid could be himself, but that's not how it works. Being on the fringe means you have to work that much harder to keep from falling off the edge of the acceptable. That means being able to trade, and endure, an onslaught of gay jokes. Calling each other "fag" or "faggot." Twisting each other's nipples and pretending you don't secretly love the contact. Describing, in ridiculous detail, the things you want to do with girls, even if the thought of actually being with a girl scares you to death.

It didn't help that I had developed a full-on crush on Ryan. It wasn't just his neck, or his lips. It was a connection I'd never felt with anybody before. Like we didn't even have to talk to know exactly what the other one was feeling.

There was this one time when the guys and I were sleeping over at Ryan's house. My sleeping bag was next to Ryan's. At some point during the night, he and I woke up with a jolt at exactly the same moment, like we had been sharing a nightmare.

"That was weird," he said, and somehow I knew exactly what he had seen in his dream. Because I had seen the same thing.

We didn't say anything more about it. Didn't need to. This was just another sign that we shared a bond that defied logic.

My crush was the worst kind, since, despite our almost mystical connection, there was no way he was going to feel the same way. He was madly in love with Amanda Turner, his lab partner in bio. But I couldn't help myself, and I worried that the other guys could feel the energy that radiated off me whenever I was near him, that they'd notice how I kept touching him, accidentally. So, I folded further in on myself. This takes a lot more work than you'd think. It's exhausting.

And anyway, it didn't work. I remember the moment when things changed. We were all at his house, watching *Home Alone 3*, because Blockbuster was out of copies of *Independence Day*. I was sitting next to him on the couch, which was where I always sat. But this time maybe I was sitting just a little too close. Maybe my shoulder rested against his. Maybe I let my leg brush up against his leg and stay there. Because suddenly he yelled, "Get off me, faggot!" and pushed me away. We'd called each other "faggot" a million times, but this time was different. This time he meant it. Maybe because he realized that "faggot" was no longer just a stupid slur we hurled at one another, but the truth about me. We made it through the rest of the movie, but I ducked out as soon as it was over.

After that, I was cut out of the loop. No invitations to game nights or sleepovers. No responses to my IMs. The one time I tried to talk to Ryan at lunch, he wouldn't even make eye contact with me. He just picked up his tray and left.

It was shortly after they dropped me that Mom died, and my dad felt so bad for me he bought me my own PlayStation, which meant I had everything I needed in my bedroom. I didn't need Ryan. I didn't need the others. I didn't need anybody.

But then I saw Shane on that fake horse, and everything changed. How was that even possible? That a guy singing about corn could suddenly make you aware of everything you'd been missing. The butterflies that come with attraction. The ability to imagine a life better than the one you're living. And for, what, twenty-four hours, I let myself believe that something might happen between Shane and me, even though I knew it couldn't. I mean, who was I kidding? Clearly Patrick was more his type than I was.

I logged on to AOL, my cursor hovering over the search box. But what was it I was searching for? "How to get a guy to like me?" "How to succeed at being gay?" "How to be hotter than the guy playing Jud?"

Thing is, I'd gotten too paranoid to risk any of these things. I'd had a close call with Mom once. I'd been searching "gay teen" and was engrossed in what I was finding when I heard Mom's shoes clacking toward my room. I managed to close the window just in time, but it spooked me.

I logged off and went back to torturing myself with images of what Shane and Patrick might be doing, when pebbles flicked against my window. Just like in a movie. And when I pulled back the curtains and looked outside, there was Shane, glowing in the light of a full moon.

"What are you doing here?" I whispered, opening the window. The cool, September night surged in, the air already so different from a few weeks ago. I was aware of my heart, beating much quicker than just a moment before.

"I've come to take you away," he said, louder than he needed to.

"Shhh! My dad and brother are asleep. Take me away to where?"

"It doesn't matter. Just away. Get dressed and meet me out front."

I threw on jeans and a hoodie and padded down the creaky hallway, carrying my sneakers. Outside, I found Shane on the sidewalk, his head tilted up, sniffing the night air.

"What's that smell?" he asked.

"Stink Lake."

"Oh my God! I've heard of that. I just never knew where it was."

"Yeah. It's just a block that way, in Stink Lake Park."

"Is that really its name?"

"Not officially. It's actually Ramie Park, but everybody calls it Stink Lake Park because, well, duh. It's especially bad in the summer. It's beginning to ease off, though. It's way better than it was just a few weeks ago. August was ripe."

"Charming," he said.

"Do you know what time it is?" I asked.

"Late?" He looked suddenly sheepish, like a little kid up past his bedtime.

"It's 1:00 a.m. What are you doing here?"

"I was out with Patrick, and then he went home, and I wasn't tired yet."

"What were you guys doing?"

"Nothing. We had dinner, and then we were at The Old Brick for a while, and then Lucky's."

The Old Brick and Lucky's were dive bars near the university. The Old Brick was also where Christopher worked, and the idea of Shane and my brother being in the same space turned my stomach upside down.

As did the possibility that Shane might be twenty-one. I'd been hoping he was on the low end of college age.

"Wait," I said. "How old are you?"

"Nineteen," he said, flashing a flirty smile. "My fake ID is amaaaaazing."

It must be, since he didn't look any older than me.

"Are you drunk?"

"Maybe a little?" he said. He lifted his right foot and put his arms out to his sides.

"Did you drive here?"

"No. I'm hoofing it. Hey, let's go smell that lake."

For a guy with short legs, he was speedy, and I had to run to catch up with him. We crossed College Avenue near the skate park and followed the path toward the lake. The stench got worse as we got closer to it. Luckily, Shane got distracted by the playground.

"Swings!" he yelled, running toward them.

I took the swing next to his and found myself matching his rhythm, giddy on the upswing, our feet pointing toward the sky. Eventually we stopped pulling and kicking, our arcs diminishing, until we were mostly still, dangling next to each other, our shoes tracing circles in the dirt.

"I'm sorry for being an asshole earlier," Shane said, staring down at his feet.

"What do you mean?"

"For running off and not inviting you to come with us. That was a dick move."

"I mean, I was pretty confused. You said we'd hang out."

"I know," he said, looking up at me. "It was so rude. It's just, I'd been trying to get Patrick to go out with me since rehearsals began, and when he finally said yes, I guess I forgot about other people."

"So, what, were you guys, like, on a date? I thought he was—"

"Straight? That's what Jenna kept saying, but I didn't believe it. In my experience, a lot of straights guys . . . well . . . aren't."

I thought about my own experience with Ryan, which didn't line up with Shane's theory.

"So, how'd it go?"

"It was fine at dinner. But later he was kind of an asshole."

"What'd he do?"

"I guess he kind of shoved me? He got pretty angry."

"He shoved you? Why?"

"I don't know. I'd had a couple of beers, and I sort of kept touching him. I guess he didn't like it."

"Yeah. That's the weird thing about straight guys."

"I know, right?" he said, missing my attempt at sarcasm. "In August, my family and I were up in Yellowstone, camping, and I slipped away to this bar in Cody. It got late, and I was talking to this one bartender, Stu. He and his friends were going up to some lake to look at stars, and they invited me to come with. It was cool for a while, just drinking beer around a fire. Stu and I were talking, and I was sure he was into me. Anyway, next thing I know, he punches me."

"Next thing you know?"

"What?"

"I mean, there must have been something between talking and punching. What'd you do?"

He dug his feet into the ground and twisted his swing so he was facing me.

"You think it was my fault?" He looked hurt all over again, like it wasn't Stu who punched him, but me.

"He shouldn't have punched you. But you have to be careful with guys like that."

"Guys like what?"

"Straight guys. I don't think you're supposed to be all flirty with them. I don't think they like it."

"I was just being myself," he said. "I liked him. I thought he liked me. So, yeah, maybe I touched him on the arm or the leg one too many times. If he's such a big, tough man, why is that so threatening?"

"I don't know. But it is."

He picked his feet up, and his swing twirled him away from me. I was thinking about that eagerness of his, his enthusiasm for everything. It was the thing that drew people to him, but maybe it was also the thing that got him in trouble.

He twisted himself back toward me and looked me in the eyes.

"I always end up with the wrong people," he said.

"Maybe not always," I said, holding his gaze and daring myself to be the kind of person who could make a moment like this happen.

Our faces were inches apart, and suddenly the night was loud, like someone had turned up the volume on every cricket, every frog, every buzzing streetlight. Shane took a deep breath and let it out. I smelled the beer on his breath, sour and musty. He made a noise, a soft grunt, like a pigeon. And then, whatever was about to happen . . . didn't. He just lifted his feet off the ground, and the swing twirled him away from me.

"Come on," he said. "I should get you home."

I followed him out of the park, neither of us saying anything. When he left me in front of my house, he reached up and mussed my hair. No kiss. No hug. Just a hair muss. Like maybe I was his little brother, even though being his brother was not at all what I had in mind.

CHAPTER FIVE

I spent Sunday helping my dad in the yard. The thing about having a landscaper for a father is that there's a never-ending series of projects. You'd think he'd get tired of digging and planting and mulching from his job at the university, but no. The weekend would come, and he couldn't wait to get his hands dirty again. Maybe it was a way to keep his mind off Mom.

By the time school rolled around on Monday, I was sore and bone tired. It felt good, though. Like I'd earned that feeling.

First period on Monday was conceptual physics, the only class I really cared about. It was physics, but without the math, which meant it was just mind-blowing theories about really, really small worlds (all that crazy subatomic stuff) and really, really big worlds (like, the *universe*). The teacher, Mr. Lindquist, was cool. He was this jowl-faced, walrus-mustached man who was so passionate about the subject. I found myself lingering after class or stopping by after I ate lunch, during his free period. He'd ask these ridiculous questions—What is time? What is nothingness? Is the future already scripted?—and then show me how physics could answer them.

Whenever I thought of Shane, it was like millions of subatomic particles were swirling around inside me, like some sort of quantum sandstorm.

. . .

At rehearsal Monday afternoon, I was backstage making picnic baskets for the big party scene. This involved weaving a lot of wicker, and it was calming, in a brain-deadening kind of way.

Jenna found me mid-basket. "I need a cigarette," she said, and I followed her outside. The days were starting to feel more like the nights. Even with the sun out, the air had a chill to it, and the wind made it feel twenty degrees colder than it was. Too cold for the faded David Bowie T-shirt Jenna was wearing.

"Guess who paid me a visit Saturday night," I said, declining the cigarette Jenna offered me.

"A certain singing cowboy?"

"Bingo."

"Was Patrick with him?"

"No, it was just Shane. He threw pebbles at my window."

"Very romantic," she said, taking a long pull on her cigarette before stubbing it out on the wall. "So, what happened?"

"We went to the park and played on the swings. And then I thought he was going to kiss me. And then he didn't. He just walked me home and mussed my hair."

"Sounds like a big night. Was he drunk?"

"A little."

"That explains it."

"Explains what?"

"If he was really drunk, he definitely would have kissed you. Being only a little drunk meant he thought about it, wanted to, but decided against."

"Why would he decide against?"

"What," she said, laughing. "Like you're so irresistible?"

"No, I'm plenty resistible. It just didn't feel like it in that moment."

She pulled out another cigarette, was about to light it, but had second thoughts.

"He was protecting you," she said, putting the cigarette back in the pack.

"Protecting me from what?"

Her eyes met mine.

"From himself."

The wind suddenly picked up, leaving us blinking in the cold.

"Why would I need protecting from him?"

She took the cigarette out again, lit it, and took a long drag.

"These things are going to kill me," she said, "but they make me very happy." She took another drag and just looked at me, like she was trying to figure out whether I could take what she was about to tell me.

"He's a mess," she said, finally, stubbing her half-smoked cigarette out on the wall. "He's carrying around a lot of damage."

I almost laughed. Shane seemed way less damaged than most people I knew. But Jenna wasn't laughing.

"What kind of damage?"

"Let's just say life hasn't been easy for him. Anxiety Disorder. ADD. Panic attacks. Depression."

I remembered Shane at Stink Lake Park, kicking himself higher and higher on the swing, carefree as a little kid. I couldn't make that person line up with what Jenna was telling me.

"But why?" I asked. "I mean, he's got everything going for him. He's smart. He's talented. He's crazy cute. He could have anybody he wants."

"Did he tell you about what happened in Cody?"

"About that guy who punched him?"

"Yeah. Did he tell you what happened after that?"

"No," I said, pretty sure I didn't want to know what came next.

"Shane filed a police report, saying the guy raped him."

My stomach lurched.

"What?"

"Yeah. He withdrew the complaint the next morning, said he was too drunk to remember what happened."

"But it still could have been true, right? I mean, maybe that actually happened?"

"Not according to the medical report, which found no evidence of sexual assault."

"Wait. How do you know this?"

I was suddenly hot all over, despite the cold wind, like maybe I had a fever. I didn't know what I found more upsetting. The possibility that Shane had been raped, or that he had lied about it.

"When Shane told me this story, something about it didn't make sense. So, I called up the Cody police department and identified myself as a reporter. I told them I was working on an article for the campus paper about the alleged assault. They sent me the report, and it was clear that Shane made the whole sexual assault thing up."

"But why would he do that?"

"Like I said, a lot of damage."

"You keep saying that. But what does it mean?"

"There's only so much I can tell you, Ash."

"Because you don't know? Or because you won't tell me?"

"I've already said too much. If you want to know more, you're going to have to ask Shane. But don't let him scare you away, okay? I mean, yeah, he's kind of a mess, but who isn't?"

. . .

Back inside, the rehearsal was just breaking up. The stage lights had dimmed, and people were grabbing their bags and hugging each other goodbye. Shane was on stage, by himself, just standing there in the dim light.

And then he started singing. No accompaniment, just him. It was "Somewhere," from *West Side Story*, a song I knew well because my mom used to sing it to me when she was putting me to bed. It's about trying to find a place where you fit in. Like, there's this magical "somewhere," a place of peace, and quiet, and belonging. I used to feel so safe with my mom singing to me, holding my hand when she got to the last verse, like it says in the lyrics. Take my hand, and we'll get there together.

But hearing Shane sing it, I was overcome by the sadness that lurks just beneath the lyrics. His voice was beautiful, but so vulnerable—fragile, like the dream of a better place. I felt the disconnect between the words, which are so full of hope, and the feeling, which is that hope will break your heart.

Others must have felt it too. During the second verse the theater got real still. People stopped packing up their things and just stood there, frozen in place, listening to Shane. When he let go of that last note, a note he had barely been able to hold on to, the quiet lasted, and deepened. There was no applause. Just a kind of hovering sorrow, as Shane walked off the stage into the darkness of the wings.

CHAPTER SIX

At school I was mostly able to keep my mind off Shane. Between learning about "The Great Die-Up" of 1886 in my Wyoming history class (bad winter, dead cows) and trying to understand terminal velocity in conceptual physics, my brain was pretty much occupied. Rehearsals were tougher, since Shane was right there, all the time, singing and being adorable, but even then I was kept busy with making more fake corn (Mr. Finster thought the fields looked a little sparse). No, it was the nights that were tough. I passed them waiting for pebbles to ping against my window.

When they still hadn't pinged by Saturday, I emailed Jenna and asked for Shane's AOL screenname. I spent the afternoon logging on to AOL, hoping to find Shane online, but he never was. I couldn't stop thinking about the kiss that wasn't, followed by the brotherly hair muss. I needed to know what was happening between us. I grew increasingly frantic, checking every ten minutes, getting my hopes up with every screechy dial-up sound, only to have them dashed. I finally decided I'd have to resort to something less technological and throw my own pebbles.

Jenna was online, so I IM'd her, asking where Shane lived. She said it was a ground-floor apartment on 8th Street, across from the Methodist church. It was just a couple of blocks from campus, only a ten-minute walk. I spent a few hours psyching myself up and finally found the necessary courage around ten o'clock that night. I told my dad I was taking a walk, which was not untrue.

Our neighborhood was so quiet, the moon throwing shadows of the trees onto the sidewalk. The houses were cute, the kind of houses that adults called "modest" to avoid saying "cheap." They were so different from the fake mansions that were springing up on the outer edge of town, just past the new Walmart.

Jenna didn't remember the apartment number, but she said it was on the right side, ground floor, around back. There was only one door it could have been, so I skipped the pebble-throwing stage and knocked.

It took a minute, but eventually the door cracked open, and Shane's face poked through. I delivered the line I had practiced on the walk over. Completely casual.

"Hey. I was just in the neighborhood and saw your lights on."

Only then did I realize there weren't any lights on, at least not any you could see from the street.

"What?" Shane said.

"It's me," I said, trying to recover. "Ash." I waved, like an idiot. "I've come to visit."

This was not going well. Who, other than little old ladies, says "I've come to visit"?

"Um, it's not really a good time," he said. "Maybe I'll find you tomorrow."

As he started to close the door, a voice boomed from inside.

"Who's your friend, Shane? Don't be rude. Invite him in!"

The door swung open to reveal a man standing behind Shane. He nudged Shane aside and pulled me in with a huge hand on my shoulder.

"I apologize for our friend here. He sometimes forgets his manners. I'm Cal. Come in, come in."

In the soft glow of the apartment, I got a better look at Cal. He was old, maybe in his sixties, and dressed all in black—black jeans, black shirt, black baseball cap. He had a caterpillar mustache and a sad little ponytail. He was tall, well over six feet.

"Shane," he said. "Get your guest something to drink. I don't believe," he continued, turning to me, "I've had the pleasure of making your acquaintance."

"Ash," I said, offering my hand, which his hand swallowed.

"Ash, Ash. That's a nice name. So, how do you know Shane?"

"I'm on the stage crew for the show he's in."

"Ah, *Oklahoma!* What a travesty of musical theater. Sure, it's got a few good songs in it, but the story doesn't make a lick of sense. I can't believe they're still putting that thing on."

"It's the second-most-produced musical in the country," Shane said, returning from the kitchen. His hand shook as he handed me a glass of water.

"What's first?" I asked.

"*Bye Bye Birdie*," Shane said. He seemed unable to decide where to be, moving from the living area to the kitchen and back again.

"Oh my God!" Cal shouted. "That's even worse! What a load of horse-shit! They need to ditch that old-timey stuff and do something more modern. *Chicago*. Now *that's* a show."

"Um, wasn't that set in the 1920s?" Shane asked.

"Ah, what do *you* know," Cal said. "Sit down, Ash, sit down. You too, Shane. All this flitting about's making me nervous."

The couch had seen better days. It was one of those brown scratchy numbers that old people have. I was hoping Shane would take the seat next to me, but Cal beat him to it, leaving Shane a small wooden chair across from us.

His apartment wasn't what I'd imagined. I guess I thought it'd be, well, gayer. You know, fabulous? But it was kind of bare, with nothing on the walls. Other than the couch and the chair, there was just a TV, a boom box, and a VCR on the floor in the corner. CDs and VHS tapes were scattered about. Unopened boxes were tucked under a table in the dining area.

I tried to make eye contact with Shane, to make all of this less weird, but his attention kept skittering around the room.

"So," I asked, "how do you guys know each other?"

"Oh," Cal said, "Shane and I go way back."

"But didn't you just move here?" I asked Shane.

"I knew him from his Denver days," Cal said. "I used to run some businesses down there, and one night we found ourselves at the same watering hole, place called Mr. Bill's.

"You were there with your little friend," Cal said, turning toward Shane. "What was his name?"

"I don't know who you're talking about."

"Sure you do. Little guy. Big eyes."

"Kevin?"

"Yes, that's it. Kevin."

"He's not my friend."

"Oh," Cal said. "My apologies. Anyway, Mr. Bill's is an interesting place. Ever been there, Ash?

"I'm seventeen."

"Oh, right, right. Anyway, that's where we met, and we've been thick as thieves ever since." His voice was raspy, his chest wheezing when he breathed. "Sometimes I act as Shane's chauffeur. I run a limo business, you see."

"I wouldn't think there's much call for limos in Juniper," I said.

"Oh, you'd be surprised, Ash. Juniper's not the sleepy little town it appears to be. Let me tell you, the stuff I've seen . . . I get paid for my discretion, you see. For being there, but not being there, if you know what I mean. Boy, I could write a book. But what about you, Ash? What's your story? You got a girlfriend? Good-looking boy like you."

"No. No girlfriend."

"A boyfriend?" Cal asked, a sudden glimmer in his eye.

"No."

"It's okay if you do. I've always found Juniper—hell, the whole state—to be a 'live and let live' kind of place. We mostly stay out of other people's business."

"Really?" I said. "Because you seem pretty interested in mine."

I regretted this immediately. I knew I shouldn't piss this guy off, but I couldn't help it. Everything about him made my skin crawl.

The change in Cal's face was subtle, just a slight hardening around the mouth. But it was enough to make the whole room feel different. Cal's eyes were fingers. I could feel them on my skin.

"I like you, Ash," he said, unleashing a big laugh. "You've got grit. Shane, you should bring this boy around more often."

"Maybe," Shane said, glaring at me. "His dad keeps him on a tight leash. Speaking of which, shouldn't you be getting home? Your dad will be worried."

Despite the casual way he spoke, there was desperation in his eyes. He wanted me gone.

"Yeah," I said, getting up from the couch. "It's getting late."

"Ash," Cal said, putting his meaty hand on my shoulder. "It's been a real pleasure. I sure hope to see you again." He leaned in close, and I caught a whiff of wet leaves, like he was moldy. He winked.

"Yeah, maybe," I said, turning toward Shane. There was so much I wanted to say to him, but what I really wanted was to touch him. To hold him. To offer myself up to him in whatever way he would allow.

But instead I mumbled a quick "See ya," and before I knew it, I was outside again, in the cooling night air. I could feel Cal's hand on my shoulder the whole way home.

. . .

When I got home, Dad was asleep, but Christopher's door was cracked. I poked my head in. He was lying on his bed, reading a comic book. It was *The Crow*, another in Christopher's long line of dark and messed-up stories about dead people who come back to life to seek vengeance on their killers. His room was a mess, way worse than mine. Clothes were draped over every surface. Stained plates littered the floor. The room smelled stale, a mix of dirty laundry and something harsher, something chemical. If Mom was still alive, she wouldn't have put up with this for a minute.

"Hey," I said.

"What do you want?" He didn't even look up.

"Do you know some guy named Cal?" I asked. Cal seemed like the kind of guy that might hang out at The Old Brick.

"Why do you ask?" he said, finally looking up from his comic.

"No reason. He's a friend of a friend." I wasn't about to put Shane's name in my brother's head. If he knew him—which he might, since Shane had been to The Old Brick with Patrick—he'd probably know he was gay, and I didn't need the guilt by association.

"Everybody knows Cal," Christopher said, sitting up. "That guy's half a fag. You should stay the fuck away from him."

"How do you know him?" I asked, trying to ignore how comfortably "fag" rolled off Christopher's tongue.

"That's none of your business. But listen. Whoever this friend of yours is? If he's hanging out with Cal, he's not somebody you want to be friends with."

Maybe he was right, but Christopher was the last person I wanted advice from. We'd never been close, unless you counted him constantly picking on me when we were younger. But more recently, there wasn't even that. I almost missed the bullying. At least that meant he knew I existed.

We had zero in common, no shared interests that might have brought us together. I asked Mom about this once. I wanted to know how two people raised in the same house, by the same parents, could be so different.

"Your dad and I had nothing to do with it," Mom said. "The two of you showed up, on day one, already exactly who you were."

So I stopped trying to figure it out. But I envied those kids with the cool big brother, the kind of guy who was more of a friend than an asshole. It's like there was an empty place where my brother was supposed to be.

I felt it again, that surge of hatred he could so easily call up in me.

"What do you care?" I asked.

"I don't," he said, lying back down and taking up his comic book. "Now get the fuck out."

Later, lying in bed, I kept thinking back to that moment when I was leaving Shane's apartment. It was like my body was being drawn toward his by some super-powerful magnet. All I wanted was to wrap my arms around him, to have his arms wrapped around me.

Maybe I wanted to rescue Shane. Maybe I wanted to be him. Maybe I wanted to let him inside me in a way that changed me completely—that turned me inside out. I didn't understand what was happening to me. All I knew was that Shane made every part of me hum like a streetlight.

. . .

I wasn't surprised when Shane pulled up in his Bronco Sunday afternoon, saying we were going for a drive. I wasn't even surprised when I agreed. Despite how weird Shane had acted the night before, I didn't even hesitate when he pulled up to the curb in front of the house, flashed that smile, and said "Come on." Dad wasn't around to ask permission, which seemed its own kind of permission.

It was a beautiful morning. Crisp and clean. Pale-blue sky, with just the faintest wisps of clouds. We followed Market Street west, passing under the interstate. The strip malls and fast-food restaurants eventually gave way to dilapidated warehouses and abandoned buildings. Where Market turned into 130, the plains unfurled and the sky opened up. It was nice to be reminded that, just a few miles from my house, the world suddenly got bigger, freer, more beautiful.

I waited for Shane to say something, to apologize, maybe, for last night, but he was quiet. At some point the silence got to me, and I asked him where we were going.

"Nature," he said. "I need nature." Then he was quiet again.

The lack of conversation gave me a chance to look at him. His profile was TV ready. High cheekbones, jutty jaw, his hair swooping down perfectly over dark eyebrows. He was wearing a denim jacket over a T-shirt, and the look was . . . well . . . straight. If I didn't know better—and if he never spoke or gestured in any way—I'd think he was just a smaller-than-average heterosexual cowboy.

The Bronco strained a bit as we climbed higher, entering Medicine Bow National Park. I hadn't been up there in years. It could have been a painting, with perfectly placed trees, and hills, and fenced-in pastures. Shane pulled us into a parking area near Mirror Lake, and I followed him up a trail that led into heavy woods. After a quarter mile or so, the woods suddenly opened up onto the lake.

"This is one of my favorite places in the whole world," Shane said, his voice a shock after so long a silence.

"It's beautiful," I said.

"I took a class once on romantic poetry, and we learned about something called the sublime. It's this feeling you can get in nature, a feeling of awe. It's like you're so overwhelmed by the sheer beauty, you might burst. But at the same time, it's kind of terrifying, like maybe whatever you're looking at will swallow you whole."

Something about the way the lake and the mountains butted up against each other created this amazing contrast, the mountains simultaneously rising out of the water and plunging back into it. Shane was right. Beautiful and terrifying at the same time.

He led us over to an outcropping of rocks. It had warmed up considerably since the previous night, and the rocks were hot to the touch. Shane took off his jacket, and then, without the least bit of self-consciousness, he stripped off his T-shirt, flopping back on the rock like a lizard in the sun. I was that kid who kept his T-shirt on in the swimming pool, but I didn't want to be the only one wearing a shirt on a hot rock in the warm September sun, so I took mine off and lay down next to him. All I could think about was my pale skin and my lack of muscle, but Shane didn't seem to notice.

We were quiet for a while.

"You must think I'm an asshole," Shane said.

I turned my head so I could see him. His eyes were closed, his chest rising and falling with his breathing. The flesh around his nipples was the color of wet sand.

"I don't know what to think. I mean, what was that all about last night?"

"Bad timing," he said.

I wondered if he knew how lame that excuse sounded.

"Yeah, I'm sorry for just showing up like that. I didn't know you'd have company."

I guess he heard something in the way I said "company," the disgust that lay just underneath it.

"Cal's complicated. You have to get to know him."

"I don't want to get to know him. Did you see the way he was looking at me?"

"He's basically harmless. As long as you stay on his good side."

"And if you don't stay on his good side?"

He opened his eyes and turned his face toward me.

"Then he's not so harmless."

His face was close to mine. I didn't want to say anything. I just wanted to lie there, so close we could feel each other's breath. But there were things I needed to know.

"Then why do you hang out with him?" I asked.

He turned away from me, and I felt the loss of eye contact like a cold wind. I turned my body toward him, wanting something I couldn't quite name. To put my hand on his chest, maybe, to feel his heart beating. But I just looked at him and waited for him to say something.

"Remember I told you I went to college in Georgia?" he said, finally.

"Yeah."

"Well, I was doing okay there. I was involved in the campus theater group, and I had my shit together, you know? But it didn't last. I started feeling worse and worse about myself, and the doctors couldn't get my meds right, and I kind of had a breakdown. My parents brought me back home, to Casper, and that was terrible. I was still depressed, and my dad and I were fighting all the time, and I just needed to get out of there. I'd heard there was a gay community in Denver, so that's where I went. But the people I met . . . well, they were the wrong people."

"Like that guy Kevin that Cal mentioned?"

"Yeah, Kevin. And he wasn't even the worst of the bunch.

"At first, Cal seemed like a way out of some of the trouble I was in. He kind of took me under his wing. I owed some people money, and he helped with that. And yeah, he looked at me the way he was looking at you last night, but nothing happened. But then the money thing became a problem. Turned out I owed Cal more than I thought, and he started pressuring me to pay up.

"But then I met this other guy, Brian. Older, but really nice. He didn't want anything from me, you know? He just wanted to help. He said he'd give me the money to pay Cal off and help me get back on my feet, but only if I agreed to go back to school. He was a professor, and getting a college degree was really important to him. I knew I couldn't stay in Denver, so I enrolled at the U and moved to Juniper.

"And I've been doing good." He sat up for the first time and looked me in the eye again. "I met Jenna, who's amazing, and I got cast in the show, and it seemed like I was starting over."

He paused, holding the eye contact.

"And then I met you," he said.

My eyes watered, like maybe I was about to cry.

"But I'm beginning to wonder if it's really possible to start over," he said, looking out over the lake. "Cal runs a lot of guys back and forth between Denver and Juniper, so he's always around. And these guys—well, they're the kind of people who are always looking for what they can get out of you. No matter how hard I try, I can't seem to shake the things I've done. It's like the past is never really past, you know?"

I sat up and was immediately dizzy—maybe from the blood rushing to my head, maybe from the sight of Shane, shirtless and glistening in the autumn sun. I wanted to fix him. I wanted to tell him that everything would be okay.

But I couldn't fix him, and I didn't know that things were going to be okay. All I knew was how desperate I was for his touch.

So many things fell away in that moment—doubt, fear, caution—and all that was left was need. Sharp, hungry need. I put my hand on the back of his neck and pulled him to me. He leaned in, his forehead against mine. He took a deep breath, and for a moment I worried what I smelled like. One of us made a sound like a kitten purring—it wasn't clear who. I felt a hunger inside me I didn't even know was possible, and when I kissed him, it was like I was trying to inhale him.

I barely even noticed the clouds rolling in, the purple-gray sky in the distance.

CHAPTER SEVEN

You know that feeling you get when you haven't slept in days? You're dizzy and lightheaded, and objects and people have a fuzzy line around them. That was me in the days that followed. It could be something as simple as Shane taking my hand, his thumb rubbing circles in my palm. Or the purring noise he made when he rested his chin on my shoulder. Or simply what it was like when our eyes met. Every part of me felt awake, all the time. I couldn't sleep, but that didn't matter, because I didn't want to. All I wanted was Shane.

I kept learning new things about him, and every new thing made me like him more. Once, when we were leaving his apartment, he said he had to do something first. He went over to the kitchen counter and tore a piece of paper out of a notepad and spent a few minutes scribbling something on it. After he folded it up, he rushed up the stairs to the apartment above his. He came down less than a minute later.

"What was that about?" I asked.

"Nothing. There's this old lady who lives above me. She never goes out, and nobody ever visits. I leave her little notes from time to time."

"Little notes?"

"It's this stupid thing I did when I was a kid," he said, looking sheepish. "I'd write these little poems and illustrate them with stick figure drawings and leave them in our neighbors' mailboxes. Turns out it's illegal to put unauthorized mail in people's mailboxes, so I switched to leaving little rocks—the prettier ones, like jade, or quartz. But with the upstairs lady, I didn't think she'd like rocks, so I'm back to breaking the law."

"Have you ever talked to her?"

"Once, when she was taking her trash out. Turns out she's really mean. I said something about it being a lovely day, but she just made a face and grunted."

What it came down to, I think, is that Shane was kind. And because he was kind, you knew he was never looking to hurt you, so it felt safe to tell him things, all the stuff you couldn't tell anybody else. The stuff you couldn't even tell yourself.

Like what an asshole I'd been when my mom was dying. I was just about to turn seventeen when she went into the hospital for the last time, and my birthday sort of disappeared with everything else happening. Nobody remembered it, and I was insanely angry. Shane said I probably got angry to avoid feeling sad. He said I should forgive myself. Easier said than done, of course, but he was right.

When we weren't together, we spent a lot of time on AIM, and I finally discovered the power of the emoticon. I'd always avoided them. They were so cheesy. But when Shane dropped his first 😘 into our chat, my whole body tingled.

But the best parts of those days were the long stretches of time when we would just hold one another. He was the little spoon, because, well, he was such a little spoon. He fit perfectly in my arms, like we were two pieces of a jigsaw puzzle. He'd fall asleep curled up against me, and I'd watch him sleep, monitoring his breathing, the rhythm of his heart.

And that hunger I felt on the rock? I still felt it. All the time. But the hunger was mixed with nervousness. Before Shane, I'd never even fooled around with another guy. I didn't know what I was doing. I didn't really know what I wanted. I mean, I'd seen stuff on the internet. Some pics on AOL. A whole bunch of "gay teen—first time" stories on an erotic stories archive. But the pics were more frustrating than helpful, thanks to our slow-as-a-turtle modem. How much time had I spent waiting for an image to load, worried that Dad or Christopher or Mom would be getting home any minute?

And the stories? I'd hoped to find information I could use, but that site turned out to be really creepy, since it was clear the stories were written by old guys. You could tell because of the language. It was all "supple young flesh" and "smooth hairless" this and "smooth hairless" that. Gross.

So, yeah, I didn't really know what I wanted. I just knew that I wanted.

But something was holding Shane back. He was two years older and, I assumed, more experienced. We'd be kissing, lying on his bed, and the moment would feel right. I'd put his hand on me, or slip my fingers just inside his waistband, and he would pull away. I didn't understand it. I mean, I knew he was turned on. But when I was desperate for more, he'd put the brakes on. And I'd find myself alone on one side of the bed, panting with a desire more urgent than a fire alarm.

After this happened a couple of times, I asked him about it.

"Is it me? Am I doing something wrong?"

"You're perfect," he said.

"So, are you just not attracted to me? You don't like me, like, that way?"

"I think you know I'm attracted to you," he said. His cheeks were red, and his lips were puffy and swollen from me sucking on them.

"Then I don't get it."

"I'm just not sure you're ready."

"I'm telling you that I am."

"We should wait," he said. "It'll be better if we take things slow.

"And anyway," he said, taking my hand to his mouth and kissing my knuckles. "What's the rush? We have all the time in the world."

And that's the crazy thing. It felt like we did. Being with him had changed my sense of time. Even though it'd only been a few weeks, it was like I'd known him forever. Mr. Lindquist would have explained this through Einstein's theory of relativity. Apparently, people used to believe there was a universal clock that everything ran by. But Einstein said that objects in space can be on completely different timelines, depending on their motion relative to each other.

This is what it was like being with Shane. He and I were living in a separate universe, where minutes were days and days were weeks. If you had told me that it'd only been two weeks since I first kissed him, I would have thought you were insane.

. . .

When I wasn't at school, I was either at rehearsal or Shane's apartment, and my dad started to get suspicious, wondering where I was all the time. I told him I was hanging out with one of the guys from the show.

"Is it that young man who came by the other morning? What was his name?"

"Shane."

"He goes to the university?"

"Yeah."

"You should bring him by the house. I'd like to get to know him."

I told Shane my dad wanted to see him. He was shockingly up for it.

"I'm really good with parents," he said, turning on that smile of his.

We arranged for him to come over Thursday, after rehearsal, which I figured was safe, since Christopher rarely got off work before two in the morning. My plan was to get Shane in and then quickly out. Just a quick "Dad, this is Shane, but he can only stay a minute, because if he stays longer than that, you might figure out he's gay, at which point you might figure out I'm gay, and none of us are ready for that yet, right? Anyway, see ya!"

It was a good plan, until I realized Dad had his own plan, which involved sitting Shane down and asking him questions. His was a real "getting to know you" plan, and it wasn't going to be quick.

"So, Shane, I hear you're in the big show. What part are you playing?"

"I'm Curly, sir," he said, and I saw what he meant about being good with parents. That perfectly placed "sir" was a stroke of genius.

"I don't know *Oklahoma!*. Is that a big role?"

"It's the lead, Dad," I said, "with all the best songs. Shane's got an amazing voice."

I was on the verge of gushing. Luckily, I stopped before adding that Shane was also an excellent kisser.

"So, what's his deal?" Dad asked. "This Curly fella."

"Well," Shane said, "he's in love with Laurey, and he's trying to get her to go to the box social with him, and—"

"What's a box social?" Dad asked.

"As near as I can tell, it's just a party where the girls bring picnic baskets, and the guys bid on these baskets, and whichever basket they get is the girl they get. It's kind of like an auction, but, like, you're buying girls? I guess that's how people did it back in the day."

"Not in my day," Dad said. "Ash's mom would not have put up with that for a minute."

"Yeah, it's weird. Anyway, Curly has a rival for Laurey's basket, this creepy guy named Jud. At the social, Curly ends up outbidding Jud, and Curly and Laurey get married. Jud shows up at the wedding and gives Curly a gun as a wedding present, and . . . well . . . I don't want to give away the ending. But things get pretty weird."

"Shane's really good in it, Dad. You should see him."

"I'll be sure to buy a ticket."

I shot Shane a look that said, "OK, we've charmed and satisfied him, let's get out of here," and he stood up, shaking my dad's hand. And we would have made it, if Shane hadn't asked Dad about a certain flower bed on campus that he'd admired, which got Dad talking about goldenrod and tricolor sedum, which was when the kitchen door creaked open. Christopher. Home when he shouldn't have been.

He shuffled into the front room and seemed surprised to find people in it. He was more of a mess than usual, his hair scraggly over his blinking eyes, brown stains on his shirt. He wobbled a bit before using the doorjamb to steady himself.

"Hey, Christopher," Dad said. "We were just talking about how hard it is to get the summer-to-fall transition right."

Christopher just stood there, blinking in the bright light of the room.

"Do you know Ash's friend Shane?" Dad asked. I was worried about how much of an asshole Christopher was going to be, so it took me a minute to notice Shane, whose face had changed. The smile he'd pasted on for Dad had disappeared, and in its place was something harder to read.

Neither Christopher nor Shane said anything. They just stared at each other. Finally, Shane got the smile working again and offered Christopher his hand to shake. "Nice to meet you," he said. Christopher just stood there, refusing Shane's hand, a slight grin on his face as he looked from Shane to me.

"How do you boys know each other?" he asked.

"That play Ash is working on?" Dad said. "Shane's the star of it."

"Is that right?" Christopher said, turning back toward Shane, who had finally lowered his hand. "You're a thespian?"

Shane laughed, like Christopher had said something funny, but Christopher wasn't laughing. His grin had hardened into something more threatening.

"I guess you could say that," Shane said, his smile slowly fading. I didn't know what was happening, and I didn't want to find out. What I wanted was to get Shane away from there.

"We should get going," I said, and without thinking I put my hand on Shane's arm. Just a light touch, the kind of thing I'd done loads of times before. Not something anyone would have noticed, really. But Christopher noticed. Realization—and then disgust—spread slowly across his face.

I glanced over at Dad to see what he had seen. He was oblivious.

"I won't be late," I said, pushing Shane out the door and onto the porch. We were halfway down the walkway when the door flapped open behind me, and before I knew what was happening, Christopher had grabbed my arm and spun me around. I could smell him, a mix of sweat, and smoke, and, just underneath, something harder, more chemical.

"So, you're a little faggot?" he hissed. "Just like him?" His breath was rancid. Drops of his spit landed on my face.

"Get off me!" I yelled, struggling to get away. His grip on my arm tightened. His fingers were claws.

"I fucking knew it! I'm just glad Mom died before she had to see what her precious little Ashley has become."

I lunged at him, ramming my head into his chest until we were both on the ground, flailing, me on top of him. I had him pinned under my knees, and I was punching him in the face, over and over again. Shane was yelling for me to stop, trying to pull me off him, but I had no intention of stopping. I wanted to kill Christopher.

And I might have if Dad hadn't suddenly appeared and jerked me away so hard my feet left the ground. He had me in a shoulder hold, squeezing tighter and tighter until I finally calmed down.

"What the hell is going on here?!" he yelled.

Christopher lifted himself off the ground, checking his face for blood.

"Fucking faggot just attacked me!" he yelled.

"Hey!" Dad yelled. "Language! Ash, what's this about?" His hold on me had become more of an embrace, and, for just a second, I thought about answering honestly. Saying I attacked him not because he called me a faggot, which I am, but because he said that Mom would have been ashamed of me if she knew, and I knew she wouldn't have been. I knew it.

But this urge toward the truth lasted only for a second. I pulled myself away from Dad, grabbed my bike off the fence, and tore down the street, Shane's cries of "Ash, Ash!" echoing in the night.

· · ·

I didn't know where I was going, until I did. The theater on campus. I wanted to be someplace dark and quiet.

It was an open secret among theater kids that the stage door never fully clicked shut. You could get in by slipping your fingers into the gap. Inside was empty, with only a soft spotlight focused downstage. The set was arranged for the first scene—the horse, the corn, the fence—but it looked eerie in the dark, not at all the beautiful morning promised by the song. I sat down and leaned against a bale of hay, in the shadows, and listened to the room, so quiet, but full of noise once your ears adjusted to the silence. The hum of exit lights and fans, the soft buzz of the PA system that someone had forgotten to turn off.

I'd never punched anybody before. Not even Christopher. When we fought, it was mostly slaps and pinches, maybe the occasional fist to the bicep, but never a punch. It sounded less impressive than it did in the movies, more of a soft thwack. And it hurt. Bone on bone. My right fist throbbed.

Maybe what I'd done was stupid, but it wasn't wrong. I could tolerate Christopher calling me a faggot. But when he said that thing about Mom, that was something I couldn't let go. And I guess I kind of snapped. Believing that Mom knew I was gay, and was fine with it, had helped me get through those dark days when I was full of regret over things not said. And then Christopher said what he said, and it made me wonder if I had been wrong all this time, imagining a mother who would still love me if she knew the truth, when maybe she would have been as disgusted as Christopher was.

But I wouldn't have snapped if I wasn't already on edge. Whatever had just happened between me and Christopher happened because there was something going on between Christopher and Shane. I could see it on Shane's face the moment Christopher entered the room, and I could see it in that creepy grin Christopher gave me. The two of them sharing a secret made my flesh crawl.

Something scratched at the stage door, and its hinges creaked as it swung open. I stayed perfectly still, trying to calm the sudden beating of my heart. Soft footsteps echoed from the wing, and a voice called my name. It was Shane.

He entered the stage, just a dark blur against a darker background, before moving into the soft spotlight up front. I stayed hidden and quiet in the dark, just watching him. The soft reds and yellows of the light caressed his hair.

"How do you know my brother?" I asked. My voice sounded small in that huge space, but it was enough to make Shane jump.

"Jesus!" he yelled. "You scared me to death. Where are you?" His eyes, accustomed to the spotlight, couldn't find me in the dark recesses of the set.

"How do you know my brother?" I asked again, getting up from the bale of hay and walking toward him.

"From The Old Brick."

"And you knew he was my brother? And you didn't say anything?"

"No. I didn't make the connection until Christopher showed up tonight. I swear."

I wanted to believe him, but something about this didn't make sense. The way they acted back at the house, Christopher's sudden anger, none of that was just a bartender and a regular running into each other.

"I don't think you're telling me the truth," I said.

He turned away, looking out over the empty auditorium. Seeing him there, in the soft haze of the spotlights, I was reminded that he was an actor. Maybe "Shane" was just one big performance that never ended.

I had to get out of there. I was just a few steps from the stage door when he said, "I met him through Cal."

I turned and walked toward the dim spotlight.

"How does Cal know my brother?"

Shane walked over to the lip of the stage and sat down, dangling his legs over the pit. I did the same, keeping several feet between us.

"How much do you know about your brother?" he asked.

"Not much," I said. It was scary how true that was.

"Do you know he deals?"

How ridiculous is it that my first thought was: what, cards? Like he works in a casino? But I quickly realized Shane meant drugs.

"What, like pot?"

"Yeah, pot. But other stuff too."

"Like what?"

"Whatever you want. But these days mostly meth."

I didn't believe him at first. Christopher was too lazy to be a dealer. But an image from earlier that night floated past me, Christopher blinking in the light of the living room, steadying himself against the doorjamb. The faint chemical scent that leaked off him.

"What's this got to do with Cal?" I asked.

"He's what you might call a facilitator. He doesn't deal, but he has a way of hooking people up with what they need. He knows people who can get you pretty much anything you want."

"And he hooked you up with Christopher?" I asked, trying to steady my breathing. I was still struggling with the idea that my brother was dealing drugs. I mean, sure, he was a jerk, but why would he involve himself in something like that?

Shane nodded.

"And what was it you wanted?"

He took a deep breath and released it.

"Meth."

I didn't know what to say. I didn't want to say anything, because saying something would have made all this real. But I had so many questions.

"What does it do?"

He stared off into the dark auditorium, and it took him a minute to answer.

"It makes you feel better than you've ever felt in your life. But the high doesn't last. You just keep chasing it and chasing it, and you catch it, but then it's gone again. And you can't not chase it. It's the only thing you care about."

"Do you smoke it?"

"Yeah, you can smoke it. Snort it. You can also inject it." I tried to fight off the image, a needle puncturing Shane's flesh, searching for a vein.

We had been staring into the darkness of the theater. Conversation was easier without the eye contact. But now his eyes were on me, and I turned to meet them.

"I'd been so good, Ash. Ever since I left Denver. That's where this all started. And I figured moving here was the best way to make a clean break. But then Cal hooked me up with your brother, and I was right back in it."

His jaw clenched, like he was trying to swallow something that didn't want to go down.

"And then Cal fronted me that cash, and let's just say he's not someone you want to owe money to. I ended up doing some things I never in a million years thought I'd do. But here's the thing. Once you start doing stuff you never thought you'd do, you just keep doing it. You get deeper and deeper, and after a while it feels like there's no way out."

His face was in constant motion as he talked, the muscles and tendons under his skin alive and dancing.

"Have you done drugs recently?" I asked.

"You mean, since we met?"

"Yeah," I said. I needed to know whether the Shane who meant so much to me was real.

"No. I haven't used since we met." It was fifty-fifty whether I should believe him. I decided to believe him.

"So, you're good now. You're okay."

"Yeah," he said, looking out over the rows and rows of seats. "I'm okay."

And I believed that too.

"Does Jenna know?"

He managed half a smile.

"What do you think?"

"I'm guessing she figured it out without you saying a word."

"Yep."

"Was she pissed?"

"You could say that. She's actually the reason I'm clean now. She said if I didn't stop, she was done with me. She also said she would disembowel anyone who brought drugs within twenty feet of me."

"Good for her," I said. But something else crossed my mind. Did Jenna know my brother? Did she know he dealt? And was this why she had taken me under her wing? Was I just a way for a college journalist to get to another piece of Juniper's meth trade?

I brushed the thought away. If it was true, I didn't want to know.

Instead, I thought back to that moment when I was almost out the door, when I was walking away from all this.

"Why'd you tell me?" I asked.

He turned toward me, and his eyes met mine.

"Because I'm trying to start over. And you're a part of that. I don't think this works without you."

I scooched over until my hip butted up against his. I took his hand in mine and leaned my head against his shoulder. I could smell the lavender in his hair.

"Well, I'm here now," I said. "You don't have to worry about all that other stuff anymore."

I wonder if Shane heard how ridiculous those words sounded. Or maybe he let himself believe them. I really hope he believed them. I hope he had at least one moment when he thought he would be okay.

CHAPTER EIGHT

When I pulled up to the house, Dad was sitting on the stoop in the glare of the porch light, armed with whatever Christopher had told him. Maybe it was the harsh lighting, but he looked old. Like, suddenly old. There was a slackness in his face, more cracks and lines than I had noticed before.

He slid over to make room for me, and I sat down beside him. I didn't know what to expect. My father was a quiet man. It was hard to know what he was thinking.

"You need to put something on that," he said, gently touching a place just above my right eye. I winced.

"You should see the other guy." I waited for him to laugh. He didn't.

"Dad, I—"

"No, wait," he said. "I've been working on this speech in my head, and I need to get it out before it gets all turned around."

The night air was full of Stink Lake, but I was glad we were outside. Whatever he was about to say needed space. The rooms in our house felt so small sometimes, like there was room for us, but not for everything we'd been through.

"Ever since your mom died," he said, "I haven't had a clue what to do with you boys. I've just been making it up as I go along, and I don't think it's working. I mean, the three of us are living in this house together, and it's like we don't even know each other anymore. And everybody says, oh, that's just the way teenagers are, they don't tell you anything. But I don't think that's what's happening here."

He cleared his throat, like he was trying to dislodge something.

"I think this is my fault," he said. "I think I've done something that's made you boys stop talking to me."

He hadn't said this many words in a long time.

"It's not anything you've done, Dad. It's—"

"No, wait. Let me finish. Because here's what I really want to say. You can tell me anything, Ash. Anything. And nothing you say will change the way I feel about you. I promise."

The muscles in my face started to twitch. I took a deep breath and fought off tears.

"What did Christopher tell you?" I asked.

"He told me a lot of things. But I'm more interested in what you want to tell me."

My heart was pounding in my chest. Telling the truth is scary. People rarely do it, and when they do, it changes everything.

"I guess Shane's, kind of . . . like . . . my boyfriend," I said. Shane and I had never used that word, but in that moment, that's what I decided was true. Shane was my boyfriend.

"So, you're . . ."

"Yeah," I said. I couldn't look at him. I just stared down at my feet, waiting for whatever was going to happen.

He put his hand on my shoulder, heavy and warm.

"Thank you for telling me," he said. "I'm proud of you."

"You're proud of me? For being gay?"

"For having the courage to say it." He took his hand away, and I missed it immediately.

"But why didn't you say something before? Did I ever say anything, or do anything, that made you think I wouldn't be okay with this?"

"It's not like I thought you'd kick me out of the house or whatever. But, I mean, look where we are, Dad. How many gay guys do you know in Juniper? Zero? How many fag jokes have you heard? Believe me, I've heard them all. And yeah, I figured you'd be okay with it, but . . . this town, you know?"

I was suddenly aware of the rhythmic bleating of a frog, and I made myself focus on it to calm down.

"But then I met Shane, and he's just so comfortable with himself. I want to live like that. I think he can help me."

Dad was quiet for what felt like forever. I couldn't look at him. I was afraid I'd see him crying or trying not to cry. I wouldn't have been able to stand it.

"You're a good kid, Ash," he said, finally. "I love you, and I only want what's best for you. I want you to be happy. And safe. Which is why," he said, putting his calloused hand on my neck and turning my head toward his, "I don't want you to see Shane anymore."

"Wait, what?"

"I'm sorry. But he's not the kind of person you should be around."

"What are you talking about?" I asked, pulling away from him. "You met him! You liked him!"

"He seemed nice. It's just—"

"What did Christopher tell you?"

"That doesn't matter. I just don't think—"

"What did he tell you?!" I screamed.

"Lower your voice," he hissed, glancing over at the neighbor's house. "He said Shane's heavy into drugs."

"And you believed him?"

"Why would he lie? He's just looking out for you."

"He's never looked out for me a day in my life!" I yelled. My fists were clenched. I was tempted to tell Dad that it was Christopher who was heavy into drugs, but that would have just made things worse.

"He said some other things too," he said. "About Shane."

"Like what?"

"It's not something I'm going to repeat. But the bottom line is this:

you're not to have anything to do with that boy. You can keep working on the stage crew, but that's it."

"You can't do this!" I yelled, getting to my feet.

"I can."

The tears I fought off earlier were coming back, but I didn't care.

"You wouldn't be doing this if I was dating a girl!"

"It's got nothing to do with that," he said through clenched teeth. "It's my job to keep you safe, and that means keeping you away from people like Shane."

"What does that even mean?! People like Shane! He's a good person! He's good to me!"

"We're done talking about this. I expect you to do as you're told."

"Yeah, well, good luck with that!" I muttered, slamming the door on my way into the house, slamming my bedroom door even harder.

I put my headphones on and popped a CD into my Discman. Hüsker Dü. The early stuff, loud, fast, and angry.

I paced back and forth, my ears blasted by a wall of guitar. Eventually, I wore myself out. The music wasn't helping. It made me want to punch things when what I needed was a quiet space to think. I threw my disc player on my desk and got undressed for bed, knowing full well I wouldn't be able to sleep. In the dark, I could hear the blood rushing in my ears, the beating of my heart. I did a breathing exercise I learned on an AOL grief forum after Mom died, when I was having trouble sleeping. Long inhale. Hold it. Long exhale. Wait. Long inhale. Hold it. Long exhale. Wait. Gradually my blood and my heart slowed to match my breathing.

It wasn't fair. Dad was so cool about the gay thing, but then he shut down the only part that mattered, actually dating someone. And yeah, parents are supposed to protect their kids, but what did he know about Shane, really, apart from what Christopher told him?

Dad had never acted like this, I guess because I'd never given him a reason to get all "my way or the highway." And yeah, maybe if Shane was still doing drugs, Dad would be right to keep me away from him. Hell, he probably wouldn't have needed to. I would have stayed away on my own. But Shane was a good person who had simply gotten mixed up with the wrong people, and he made some mistakes, but now he was better. And the last thing he needed was for his boyfriend to cut him off.

So, yeah, that wasn't going to happen. No matter what Dad said.

. . .

As soon as school let out on Friday, I biked to campus, so eager to see Shane that I almost collided with a gaggle of thick-necked football players outside the stadium. When I got to the theater, the first thing I noticed was that the fake horse had shrunk. Either that, or Shane had gotten bigger. Turns out it was the latter, only the guy on the horse wasn't Shane. I scanned the mostly empty theater and found Jenna, sitting off to the side.

"Where's Shane?" I asked, taking the seat beside her.

"How should I know?" There was something in her voice I hadn't heard before. She always had an edge, but this was different.

"I just thought you might know where he was," I said.

"Isn't that your job? As the *boyfriend*?"

And then I knew. That thing she'd told me about being abandoned by the gay guy when he gets a new boyfriend? It was happening again. And this time it wasn't just Shane's fault, but mine.

"I'm guessing you haven't seen much of Shane lately," I said. "And maybe I've had something to do with that."

"What, because the two of you disappeared into Gay Sex World, or whatever? He at least told me about that, how you put the moves on him up at Medicine Bow."

I could have told her she was wrong about Gay Sex World, but that wouldn't have changed the fact that she was right about everything else.

"Anyway," she continued, "I don't know where he is. Why don't you tell me? And tell Mr. Finster while you're at it. Because this guy? He blows."

On stage, Shane's understudy was still on the horse, which looked in danger of collapse. This guy was rugged, like an actual cowboy. He was a foot taller than Shane, and his shoulders were linebacker broad. He looked like the kind of guy you could climb like a tree.

"He certainly looks the part," I said. "Makes Shane look a little . . . dainty."

"Wait until he opens his mouth," Jenna said.

When he started to sing about what a beautiful morning it was, he sounded like a karaoke version of that guy from Metallica, all deep-throated, macho rasping. When this guy sang about how high the corn was, it sounded like he wanted to mow it down with a tank.

"Yikes," I said. "Can we get out of here? Go someplace where we can talk?"

I bought us a couple of Cokes from the drink machine in the lobby. I followed Jenna out of the lobby and down Fraternity Row. Kegs were being unloaded from trucks and rolled into the houses up and down the Row. Being around so many soon-to-be-drunk frat boys sent a squiggle through my stomach.

"I'm an asshole," I said. "I'm really sorry."

"Don't worry about it. I probably overreacted. I tend to do that. My therapist says I have abandonment issues. Anytime someone bails on me, I tend to freak out. Anyway, it's not you who should be apologizing. You don't owe me anything."

I was oddly hurt by this. I wanted to be a person who owed her something. I'd thought maybe I was.

We took one of the paths that sliced up the central lawn on campus. The buildings surrounding the green were made of rough-cut sandstone, heavy, muscular. They reminded me of bulldogs, with their wide shoulders.

"Did you know," Jenna asked, "back in the day, the president of the university used to graze his livestock here? They should definitely bring that back. This place would be a lot cooler with cows."

"Speaking of which," I said, "how's your cow-grudge project going?"

"My partner and I are kind of stuck. We've documented cows being assholes, but we've yet to establish cause and effect. Like, did another cow piss them off, or are they just having a bad day?

"Anyway," she said, "where's our golden boy? Missing rehearsal isn't like him."

"I don't know," I said. "I saw him last night, but I haven't heard from him today. Have you tried calling him?"

"I've been doing that thing where I refuse to call him until he calls me. Being passive-aggressive is usually the best response in these situations."

I finally had a chance to give her the raised eyebrow she was always giving me.

"What?"

"Just call him already."

"You call him."

"I don't have a cell phone."

She rolled her eyes and took out her phone, jabbing at it. It rang for a while before going to voicemail. Shane's voice sang a long and melodic "Heeyyyyyy, wait for the beep!"

"Hey! Dickweed!" Jenna said. "Call me!"

"Where did you see him last night?" she asked, putting the phone back in her pocket.

"He came over to meet my dad, and then we ended up at the theater."

"How was he?"

I could still see it, the way his face got tight when he talked about meth.

"He told me about the drugs," I said.

She cocked her head to the side.

"Really?"

"Yeah. But he said he hasn't done anything since he met me."

She smiled, and for a second I thought it was because she was happy that Shane had found someone who made him forget about drugs. But it wasn't that kind of smile.

"What?" I said.

"It's just that I've heard it all before."

"From Shane?"

"No, not from Shane. But from pretty much everyone I interviewed for my article. Yeah, it's great that Shane is clean. But staying clean is really, really hard. When Shane first moved here, he was in pretty bad shape. On his good days, he was so charming. But then it was like he'd turn into somebody else. He'd get so depressed. Said he felt completely hopeless and totally alone. He didn't have any energy, and you couldn't get him to eat anything. And I'm sure he wasn't sleeping. Like, for days. Which made him really anxious and paranoid. But then he'd bounce back. It was like someone had flipped a switch, and he was okay again. But he'd fall right back into a deep hole."

"It sounds like he's manic-depressive," I said. I'd learned about this in health class, the huge ups, the bigger downs.

"No," she said. "I mean, he might be, but that wasn't what I was seeing. I knew exactly what was going on. This was classic tweaker behavior. With meth, there's this intense euphoria when you're using, and then a massive depression when you're coming down. And then withdrawal, where your body's nothing but one big craving."

She was quiet for a moment, and she had this faraway look, like she was seeing it all again.

"Anyway," she continued, "I confronted him, told him he had to stop, and that I'd help him. And he said he would. He promised. And he did stop. In part because I told him I'd never speak to him again if he didn't. Luckily, he didn't call my bluff."

"What do you mean?"

"I wouldn't have been able to cut him off. That first night I met him? At the Pride Alliance? We spent, like, the next seventy-two hours together, straight. Nonstop conversation, you know? I'd never felt that in tune with another person. It was like we were twins who had been separated at birth. We couldn't get enough of each other. So, yeah, when I said I'd never talk to him again if he didn't quit using, it meant something. But I don't think that was really it."

"Really what?"

"The thing that got him clean. I think it was the show. Theater's like another drug for him. You've seen him up there. It's like he's floating just off the ground. I figured as long as he was in the show, everything was okay. But now . . ."

"You don't know that he's doing drugs again," I said. "Maybe he's just sick."

"Yeah," she said. "Maybe he's sick. But I wouldn't count on it."

She threw her can in a recycling bin.

"Meet me at High Plains tomorrow morning," she said. "Ten o'clock."

"For what?"

"We're going to find him."

CHAPTER NINE

High Plains—short for High Plains Coffee and Pastry Emporium—was a favorite hangout for college kids, who liked to riff on the "High" part. As in, "Dude, I'm so high. Get me a muffin." I ran into Jenna on her way out of the shop. She thrust a coffee and a muffin into my hands. "Here," she said. "We have to roll."

I followed her to her car, a beat-up Honda with bumper stickers pasted all over it, mostly for bands, but some political stuff too. One read "If you cut off my reproductive choice, can I cut off yours?"

"Cool," I said, gesturing toward the stickers.

"They hold the car together," she said.

Getting out of the house had been tough. Dad was suspicious when I told him I had to meet a friend who was helping me with a project for school. It took everything I had to keep him from driving me downtown himself and making sure I wasn't meeting Shane.

"You still haven't heard from him?" Jenna asked, taking a left on Elm.

"Nothing. He didn't respond to the email I sent last night. And I kept checking AIM, but he was never online. You?"

"He never returned my call," she said. "I tried him again this morning. Still nothing. We should check his apartment."

When we got there, I noticed that Shane's Bronco was missing and that his apartment's window shades were down. Whenever I'd been there during the daytime, he'd always had them up. Said he craved the natural light.

Jenna rang the bell and then pounded on the door. When Shane didn't answer, I was relieved. I didn't want to know what it meant if he had been home this whole time, avoiding Jenna's calls, avoiding me. Maybe he had just gone to visit his parents in Casper.

I turned to leave, but Jenna grabbed my arm.

"We have to go in," she said.

"Why? He's not here."

The look she gave me chilled me to the bone, and I knew immediately what she was afraid of finding inside.

"Do you have a key?" I asked.

"No. But I know a trick."

The trick involved Jenna shoving me through a narrow window around back. She said this was how Shane got in when he locked himself out, which apparently happened a lot.

I didn't want to do it. I couldn't face the thought of finding Shane passed out, lying in a pool of his own vomit. Or worse.

The window was over Shane's bed, which was just a mattress on the floor. I'd spent hours there, looking up at the shaft of light with Shane in my arms. Despite the chilled air, a trickle of sweat ran down my back. I slid the window aside and pulled myself up on the ledge. Jenna pushed my feet up, and then through. I didn't have time to steady myself, just tumbled into the darkness, and onto the mattress. It was mercifully empty, just a tangle of sheets and blankets. Lying there, I called Shane's name, even though I knew he wasn't there. I sensed the absence immediately. I turned on the bedroom and kitchen lights and let Jenna in through the front door. We surveyed the room, the boxes no more unpacked than they were the night I met Cal.

"You check the bathroom," Jenna said. "I'll check the kitchen."

"What am I looking for?"

"Anything that might tell us where he is."

The bathroom showed all the signs of someone who sucked at cleaning bathrooms. An open can of shaving cream, a dirty towel on the floor, toothpaste stains in the sink along with the scattered stubble of a recent shave.

I pulled a drawer open, revealing condoms and lube. My mouth went dry. The stuff Shane wasn't doing with me he was doing with someone else. Or had done with someone else. Or was planning on doing with someone else. I slammed the drawer shut and opened the medicine cabinet. There were more varieties of skin cream than I knew existed, the hair gel that made Shane smell like Shane, and a bottle of prescription pills. I took the bottle into the kitchen, where Jenna was sniffing around in Shane's mostly empty refrigerator.

"Look at this," I said, handing Jenna the bottle. "What's Fluoxetine?"

"Prozac. It's for depression. He should really be on Zoloft instead. It's much better, fewer side effects. Prozac turns your large intestine into a waterslide."

"What happens if you take this and do other drugs at the same time?"

"Depends on the drug. With meth, it doesn't really matter what you take with it. It's plenty toxic all by itself."

I looked around the kitchen, drawers and cabinets open, dirty dishes in the sink.

"There's nothing here," I said. "What do we do now?"

The fear of finding him passed out, or worse, was being replaced by a different fear. That we might not find him at all.

"There's this guy we should talk to," she said. "Skeezy little creep of a guy, but he might know something."

. . .

As Jenna drove, I asked her about the guy we were going to meet.

"His name's J-Town," she said.

I snorted. "What kind of name is J-Town?"

"A ridiculous name for an even more ridiculous person. His real name's Jared Townsend. White guy who thinks he's a gangsta."

"How do you know him?"

"He was one of the guys I talked to when I started working on my article. His name came up in a couple of the early interviews."

"He's a dealer?"

"Yeah. And not a good one. This dude's elevator doesn't quite go to the top floor."

We crossed the railroad tracks and headed into Juniper's so-called wrong side of town. The houses were small, run-down, and they were pushed right up to the front of their lots, separated from the crumbling sidewalk by metal fences.

Jenna turned into a trailer park. It wasn't one of the nicer ones that were cropping up in other parts of town, places with names like Sunny Meadows and Mountain View. This was just a dirt road lined with run-down trailers.

"I think it's this one here," she said, parking in front of a trailer with loose siding, rust stains under the windows, and paint peeling off the turquoise paneling. Approaching the front door, I saw the bottom corner of one of the window blinds fall back into place. Just as Jenna was about to knock, the door swung open, revealing a little dude, shading his eyes from the sunlight.

He was barefoot, wearing a soiled tank top and baggy jeans halfway down his hips, the sun bouncing off his pale skin. He had a scraggly beard and dark hair that swept up, the kind of hair you see in a black-and-white movie. This guy was bone skinny, but there was something intimidating about him. Like he was coiled tight, ready to spring. A thick chain hung around his neck, with "G Thang" monogrammed in gold. He took a drag on his cigarette.

"Hey, girl," he said, giving Jenna the up-down. "Do I know you?" He did this weird little swagger, a slight rotation of the hips.

"I was here once, back in the spring," she said. "I'm Jenna. This is Ash."

"You and me hooked up, right?"

"We did not. I'm a reporter. I was working on an article."

"Right, right, right. How'd that turn out?"

"Still working on it. But that's not why we're here. We were hoping you might help us find a friend of ours. Someone you might know."

"I know lots of people," he said, retreating into the darkness of the trailer. "Come in the house!"

It took a minute for my eyes to adjust. Dust hung in the air, lit up by the tiny rays of light fighting their way through closed blinds.

J-Town flipped a switch and the fluorescents on the ceiling flickered on, making everything look washed out, though it wasn't like J-Town needed help looking washed out. His skin was the color of ashes, and it reminded me of seeing my grandfather laid out in a casket.

J-Town stubbed his cigarette out in an ashtray, and his hand started shaking, like the cigarette had been the only thing keeping it still. I stole a look around. Beer cans were littered across just about every surface, in between ashtrays that needed emptying. A dirty white sock lay on the counter in the tiny kitchen. Something rustled in the corner, which turned out to be a cat, burnt orange, missing half an ear.

"Sit down, sit down," J-Town said, pointing to a couch full of burn marks and gashes.

The cat crept out of the kitchen and jumped onto my lap, nudging its head into my chest. I didn't want to touch it. Petting it would have been like petting J-Town.

"I like my girls big," J-Town said, leering at Jenna. "You look like you got a wild streak. I bet me and you could have some fun."

"I would snap you like a twig," she said, barely concealing the contempt she felt for him.

He flinched, but then the leer returned.

"I'm willing to risk it," he said.

"This friend of ours," Jenna said. "His name's Shane. Have you seen him?"

"I don't always know the names. What's he look like?"

"He's short," Jenna said. "Even shorter than you. Dirty blond hair. Cute."

"What makes you think I know him?"

"Might be one of your customers," Jenna said. J-Town didn't say anything for a minute. His eyes bounced around the room, his right hand dancing on the chair's armrest. His knee wouldn't stop shaking.

"I don't know what you're talking about," he said, finally.

"Dude," Jenna said. "That article I'm writing, it's about the meth trade. Remember? I know you're a dealer."

J-Town's hand stopped dancing, and his eyes landed on me.

"Who's this faggot?" he said.

"I told you," Jenna said. "His name's Ash. He's cool. You don't have to worry about him."

He kept staring at me. The cat fled back to the kitchen.

Jenna snapped her fingers in front of his face. "You need to focus, okay? You need to pay attention to what I'm saying. We're trying to find Shane. We think he might be in trouble."

"What day is it?" J-Town asked.

"It's Saturday," Jenna said, a harder edge in her voice. It was all she could do to keep from punching this twerp.

"I don't know anybody named Shane," he said.

"Are you sure?" Jenna asked. "We think you might have sold him something. You don't have to worry about us. We don't want to get you in trouble or anything."

Every muscle in his face tensed.

"You don't want to get me in trouble? Is that some kind of threat?" He stood up and moved toward Jenna, his hands clenched at his sides. I stood up, ready to do whatever I'd have to.

"Bitch, I don't know you!" he yelled, his spit hitting Jenna in the face. "And I sure as fuck don't know this dude," he said, pointing at me. "So you better watch what you say to me. Like I said, I don't know any Shane. Short or cute or whatever the fuck. You need to look for him someplace else, y'know what I'm saying?"

We just stood there, frozen.

"I ain't playin'," he said, taking another step toward Jenna. "Get the fuck out my house!"

He was trembling. It seemed like the slightest touch might make him explode.

We got the fuck out of his house.

. . .

We were parked at the Loaf 'N Jug. Jenna hadn't said anything since we left J-Town's, just gripped the steering wheel and blasted the stereo. The music was fast, angry, and female.

"I hate that tweaking little motherfucker," she said, finally, turning the music off. "He's the worst kind of asshole. Has been since the day he was born, probably. But then you put him on meth, and it's like adding this huge bucket of crazy."

"Is that what meth does? It makes you all twitchy and paranoid and aggressive?"

"Pretty much."

"And that's what Shane was like back when you first met him? That's how you knew?"

"With Shane it's different," she said. "He doesn't get aggressive. At least, not that I've seen. He just gets paranoid, and sad. The sadness is the worst part. I'd take a twitchy J-Town over a sad Shane any day."

She rummaged around in the center console, flipping through cassette cases. She popped out whatever we'd been listening to and inserted a new tape. Hole blared from the car's tinny speakers. Jenna and I just sat there, not talking, waiting for Courtney Love to go from a growl to a scream.

Without me wanting it to, my mind wandered back to the suspicion I'd had earlier. That maybe Jenna was just using me as part of her investigation into Juniper's meth trade.

"Do you know my brother?" I asked.

"Who's your brother?"

"His name's Christopher. He tends bar at The Old Brick."

"Tall, skinny guy? Hair like yours? Looks half-asleep most of the time?"

"Yeah," I said. "That's him."

"I mean, yeah, I know him from The Brick."

"Shane told me Christopher's a dealer."

She didn't say anything for a minute, just looked out her window.

"I didn't know that," she said finally. "Makes sense, though. A lot of stuff moves through The Brick. Being a bartender would put Christopher right at the center of it. It's weird, though. You'd think his name would have come up in my interviews. A lot of these lower-level guys are too stupid to be discrete."

"Maybe Christopher's not a lower-level guy," I said.

"Does your brother strike you as a higher-level guy?"

I tried to imagine Christopher excelling at something.

"He does not."

"And he and Shane know each other?"

"Yeah."

She was quiet for a minute, thinking.

"What kind of scumbag is he, your brother?"

"What do you mean?"

"I mean, what's he sell? The occasional nickel bag to frat boys? Or is he more serious than that?"

"According to Shane, he mostly sells meth."

"Of course he does. Motherfucker. And where is he now?"

"I don't know. Probably still asleep."

"Well, I think it's time we woke his ass up."

She pulled us out of the parking lot and cranked the stereo up. Courtney was fighting her way through a wall of guitars.

. . .

Dad was raking the front yard when we pulled up.

"I want you to meet my dad."

"Why?"

"To prove that you're not Shane."

"And why would I need to do that?"

"Because he said I can't see Shane anymore, and he probably thinks I was meeting him this morning when I met you. You're the perfect cover. Just follow my lead."

I introduced Jenna as someone who works on the campus paper, someone I had to interview for a homework assignment. High Plains got too crowded, I said, so we were going to finish the interview here. He appeared to buy it, told us there were cranberry muffins in the kitchen.

"You shady little fucker," Jenna said, as I led her into the house.

In the kitchen we found the muffins, but we also found Christopher, sitting at the table, still in his bathrobe, rattling a spoon around a coffee cup.

"This is Jenna," I said. He looked up, grunted, and went back to stirring his coffee. His eyes were cloudy from sleep, or from whatever he'd been doing the night before.

"We're looking for Shane," I said. "Maybe you've seen him?"

"Why the hell would I know where that little pussy is?" It sounded like he had gravel in his throat.

"Maybe because you're his dealer?" Jenna said.

If she'd hit a nerve, he didn't show it. He just smirked and took a sip of his coffee.

"I don't know what you think you know, but whatever it is, it's bullshit." He was so calm, like nothing we could say could hurt him.

"Anyway," he said, "you're not supposed to have anything to do with that loser, right? What would Dad say if he found out?"

"What would he say if he knew you dealt drugs?"

He put his coffee down on the table, his eyes suddenly razor sharp. Whatever lack of concern he'd been fronting was gone.

"Don't you fucking dare," he growled.

"Dad!" I yelled.

Christopher leaped from the table and jammed me up against the wall, his hand against my throat. His breath was rancid, full of coffee and cigarettes.

"Yeah?" Dad yelled from the yard.

"You're going to tell us about Shane," I hissed. "Or I tell Dad everything."

"You don't *know* anything," Christopher sneered, pushing me harder against the wall.

"Doesn't matter. I'll just make stuff up. I bet most of it will turn out to be true."

"Or maybe we'll just call the cops," Jenna said, taking her phone out of her jacket pocket. "I wonder what they'd find if they snooped around in your bedroom."

It took him a minute, but he eventually released his grip on my throat.

"Never mind!" I yelled to Dad.

"When did you see him last?" Jenna asked, pocketing her phone.

"Yesterday afternoon," Christopher said, sitting back down. "Around three o'clock."

"What did he want?"

"What do you think he wanted?"

"And you sold it to him?" I asked.

"I run a business," he said. "I aim to please."

"Was he with anybody?"

"Just his driver."

"Cal?"

"Yeah, Cal."

"Wait," Jenna said, turning toward me. "How do you know Cal?"

"I met him at Shane's. How do you know him?"

"I was in his car once."

"Where were they going?" I asked, turning back to Christopher.

"How the fuck should I know? And I don't really care. He's not my concern. And he shouldn't be yours, either. I'm serious, Ash. That kid is messed up."

"How did he seem?" Jenna asked.

"Gay," Christopher said. "He seemed really fucking gay."

I was on him before I knew what I was doing. Jenna pulled me away and shoved me up against the wall.

"I'll ask you again," Jenna said, her hand hard against my chest. "How did he seem?"

There was a glimmer in his eye, and the smirk was back.

"Not good," he said. "But he was on his way to feeling a whole lot better."

CHAPTER TEN

Sunday was hard. I still couldn't find Shane online, and Dad was lurking, so I couldn't risk calling him from the house. I kept biking over to the Kum & Go on Elm, where there was a pay phone. I knew he wouldn't pick up, but I couldn't stop trying.

Jenna said all we could do now was wait. If he was with Cal, as Christopher said, there was no telling where he might be. He could be back in Denver for all we knew.

I tried focusing on my precalc homework, which involved solving rational inequalities. This made me want to rip my own head off and throw it out the window.

I got myself to school on Monday, though I don't remember much of anything that happened there. What I do remember is walking into the theater later that afternoon, sitting next to Jenna, and waiting for the beefy understudy to stride out on stage and butcher the songs. The stage was set for the scene in Act II when Curly and Jud get into a bidding war for Laurey's basket. Finster had this idea to incorporate video projection. While Curly and Jud were bidding, Laurey would circle them with a video camera, capturing images that would be projected onto a huge screen at the back of the stage. They hadn't tried this in rehearsal yet, so there were a lot of people on stage working out the tech.

The tech crew finally cleared the stage, leaving just Finster, Patrick, and Emma Martin. One of the tech guys shouted something, and the screen at the back of the stage came alive, full of crazy, confused images as Emma swung the camera back and forth.

"Where's our Curly?" Finster yelled. "Let's go!"

I expected to see the understudy walk on stage and ruin this scene with Patrick, which is why, when Shane emerged from the wings, I gasped and grabbed Jenna's arm.

"Nice of you to join us, Shane," Finster said. "If you ever pull a no-show like that again, you're done. Understand?"

Shane didn't say anything, just nodded. I wanted to run up on stage and wrap him in my arms. I needed him to acknowledge me, to look out into the audience and see me there. If I stared at him hard enough, maybe he'd feel it, and our eyes would meet. But he stayed focused on Patrick.

Emma pointed the camera at Shane, and his face appeared on the screen. It was a close-up, and it reminded me of being on that rock with him, my face inches from his. The video feed was in black and white, making it look like he was in an old movie. I could tell he wasn't well. He had dark circles under his eyes, and his cheekbones were more prominent than usual, like maybe he had lost weight.

The houselights came down, leaving just Shane and Patrick in the center spotlight. Finster called for action, and Emma started circling, panning from Shane's face, to Patrick's, and back to Shane's, while the two men stood motionless, just glaring at each other. Offstage, a voice called for bids on Laurey's basket. Other voices shouted out dollar amounts. Eventually, Shane and Patrick joined in, bidding against each other as Laurey's price went up, and as Emma and her camera circled quicker and quicker.

Eventually, the offstage voices faded, replaced by the prerecorded murmurings of a string section. The strings got louder and louder, until they were so loud they hurt. It wasn't pretty, this music. It was all jagged sawing on violins and cellos, abrupt, fractured, dissonant. The music reached a crescendo, and Shane and Patrick started circling each other. White strobe lights flashed on stage.

As Shane and Patrick continued circling, Emma's camera strayed from their faces and found bits and pieces of their bodies. A shoulder, a neck, a waist, all jumbled up in some sort of weird painting. The strings continued to build as Shane and Patrick got closer and closer to each other, until they were standing face to face. Suddenly, Patrick threw his arms around Shane in a wrestling hold, and Shane responded by slipping from Patrick's grasp and wrapping his arms around Patrick's chest. The strings faded and were replaced by the low hum and throb of industrial music, the kind of thing you'd hear in a dance club on goth night. As the music got louder and louder, Shane and Patrick grappled with each other, but the grappling was beautifully choreographed, a series of poses and movements. As they fought—hands slipping off chests, arms circling waists, neck sliding against neck like birds mating—Emma's camera continued to capture bits and pieces: an eye, half a face, a strip of flesh made visible by a shirt caught in the struggle.

Eventually, and despite their difference in size, Shane threw Patrick onto the stage, but it was more like he lovingly placed him there, lowering Patrick to the ground like an injured bird. With Patrick on his back, Shane hovered just above him, their legs entangled, while Emma positioned herself behind Shane. Her camera threw Patrick's face onto the screen, a face that was hard to read because it told more than one story. Yes, there was loss there. Jud had been bested by Curly, both physically and in the contest over Laurey's basket. But the loss was complicated. It wasn't just that Jud had lost Laurey to Curly. He had lost something far more valuable: the ability to keep hidden what it was he really wanted. And what he wanted was Curly. His hunger crackled off the screen, as Shane floated just above him, like a lover. The music stopped mid-beat, and the stage went dark, and I was certain—even though I could no longer see them—that Shane and Patrick were kissing. Because that's the only thing that could have happened next.

. . .

We found Shane backstage, by himself. He was sitting on the floor, leaning against a prop cabinet, his knees hugged tight to his chest. He looked so small, like you could fit him in a backpack. He looked up as we approached, but then quickly looked down again.

I wanted to scream at him, to say how messed up it was for him to have disappeared like that, but I couldn't stand seeing his shame. I didn't want to make it worse.

"That was amazing," I said.

"Thanks." His voice was small, exhausted. He looked thrown away.

Jenna didn't seem worried about making things worse.

"How fucking dare you!" she yelled. "You can't just disappear like that! We looked everywhere for you! Do you have any idea what that was like? What we were thinking? What *I* was thinking?"

She was shaking. Shane stood up and moved toward her.

"I'm sorry," he said. "I'm so sorry."

"You *know* me," Jenna said. "You know everything! And still, you go and pull shit like this?"

Shane wrapped his arms around her. She resisted at first, but then she collapsed into him, sobbing.

I just stood there, not knowing what to do or say. Something was happening, and I wasn't part of it.

Jenna pulled her chin off Shane's shoulder, wiping her eyes. Shane pushed a strand of her hair back where it belonged and kissed her forehead.

"I'll never do that again," he said. "I promise."

"Don't make promises you can't keep."

"But I'm going to keep this one," he said. "I promise." He was smiling now, trying to flirt his way through Jenna's anger.

"We'll see," Jenna said, sniffling away a last tear. "But I have to say, that was maybe the hottest box social I've ever seen. And mad gay."

"That was all Finster's idea," Shane said. "His theory is that Laurey's just a decoy. The real romance is between Curly and Jud. Think about it," he said, some of his energy returning. "Curly and Jud want to have sex with each other, but they can't, because, you know, society. So, they need a girl, Laurey, that they can fight over, which gives them an excuse to wrestle. And through Laurey's camera, we see that they're not really interested in Laurey. What they want is each other. But since they're both so homophobic, and because they're living in this incredibly homophobic culture, desire turns into violence. Or violence turns into desire. It's all very messy and complicated."

"Well it worked," Jenna said. "I was totally convinced that Patrick wanted to fuck you. I mean, that Jud wanted to fuck Curly. Whatever. What was it like having him look at you like that?"

Shane glanced at me, but quickly looked away again.

"It's just acting," he said. "It's not real."

"Patrick's good," Jenna said, "but he's not that good."

They were okay again, Jenna's anger already a thing of the past. But mine wasn't. My whole body was clenched tight, ready to explode.

"Can we go back to the other thing?" I asked, trying to keep my voice calm.

"What other thing?" Shane asked. He still wouldn't look at me. Or couldn't.

"You," I said. "Disappearing. Not answering your phone."

"Yeah," he said, unable to meet my eyes. "The past few days have been kind of weird for me, and I needed some time to myself. I just needed to get away from people, you know?"

"Where'd you go?" Jenna asked.

"I went up to Casper. My parents were out of town, so I had the house to myself." His fingers were busy picking at his pockets, and I was reminded of J-Town, his hands in constant motion.

"Was that before or after you saw my brother?"

Shane's jaw tensed. His hands were finally still.

"What do you mean?" he asked, finally looking me in the eye.

"Christopher," I said. "You know, my brother, your dealer? He said you paid him a visit."

"I wouldn't believe anything your brother says. He's an asshole, and a homophobe."

"He's definitely both of those things, but why would he lie about selling you drugs?"

"To get you to think what you're thinking now!" he yelped, his voice suddenly loud, echoing off the stage walls. "That I'm some sort of druggie loser! I told you, that's not who I am anymore. I'm done with that shit."

I don't know what hurt more, the fact that he was doing drugs again, or that he could so easily lie about it to my face.

"Let's go get a coffee somewhere," Jenna said. "We've had enough drama for one evening."

Shane looked hurt, like I had betrayed him. Maybe I had. After all, what did I really know? Maybe he *was* in Casper. Maybe Christopher *was* making shit up. My brother certainly had a motive: his hatred of me.

"I don't think so," Shane said. "I'm wiped. I'm just going to go home and crash."

He stood up and gathered his bag.

"I'll find you tomorrow," he said. "Promise." He kissed us both on the cheek and flashed that smile of his, but for the first time I could remember, it failed to work its magic. It was like someone had turned his wattage down.

And then, just like that, the stage door clanged shut behind him, and he was gone. I wouldn't see him again for four days.

CHAPTER ELEVEN

It was just like before. He didn't show up for rehearsals. He didn't answer his phone or email. He was never online. He wasn't at his apartment. Jenna said there was nothing we could do. That you can't ever really save another person. It was up to the person to save himself. I hated hearing this, but it was probably true.

I honestly have no memory of what happened at school that week. I'm guessing I went to class, did my homework, but I don't remember any of it. Rehearsals were busy. Saturday was opening night, and we had lots of last-minute tweaks to the props and the sets to deal with. Jenna stopped coming. Said there wasn't any point without Shane.

The understudy—turns out his name was Lincoln—was thrilled with Shane's disappearance, though he tried not to show it. He pretended to be worried about him, but I heard him talking to the sound guy about this being his "big break."

Lincoln genuinely believed he was an amazing actor, but he delivered his lines like he was reading the words off the back of a cereal box. The true rock bottom of his performance was the fight scene with Patrick. When Shane played it, you genuinely believed that these two men wanted to kill each other and have sex with each other at the same time. But with Lincoln, there was no tension, no spark.

So, the show was off the rails, and Finster was freaking out. There was some talk of cancelling, but the other actors protested. They wanted their moment in the spotlight, even if it involved the worst Curly ever.

Which is why I was lying in bed, around ten thirty Friday night, thinking about how there's nothing worse than bad musical theater, when suddenly pebbles pinged off my window. I looked out, and there was Shane.

All it took was him standing there in the darkness, looking up at me, and I didn't care that he had disappeared without a trace for four days, leading me to think things I couldn't even say. It was like he was an electron and I was a proton, and the laws of the universe were drawing us together. I opened the window.

"Meet me at my apartment in half an hour," he whispered.

I didn't hesitate. Sneaking out wouldn't be a problem. Christopher was at work, and Dad always crashed early at the end of the week. I'd be able to sneak back in before he was any the wiser.

"Okay," I said.

. . .

When I arrived, Shane was waiting for me on the stoop, so eager he was bouncing on the balls of his feet. My stomach tightened when I remembered what Jenna had said about the euphoria that comes with meth use.

"Close your eyes," he said.

"Why?"

"Just close them."

I closed my eyes, and he took my hand and led me inside, making sure I didn't stumble on the step.

"Now open them."

His living room had been transformed. There was still the sad couch, the chair, the unopened boxes, but now they were surrounded by colored lights, and balloons, and streamers. A huge banner was duct taped to the wall: *Happy Birthday Ash!* Shane put a pointy hat on my head and another on his. He pushed a button on the boom box, and the Beatles' "Birthday" filled the room. He started bouncing around, which made the CD skip. When I refused to join in, he grabbed both my hands and spun us around, all the while singing those ridiculous lyrics. When the music finished, he kissed me.

"Happy Birthday, Ash," he said.

I didn't know what to say, but I thought I should probably start with the obvious.

"It's not my birthday."

"I know that, dummy."

"My birthday was back in March."

"I know that too."

"Well then maybe you can help me understand what's happening?"

"This is the party you never had. The one you missed. You know. When your mom was sick."

The bones in my face knew what he was talking about before the rest of me did. So did the tear suddenly streaming down my cheek. He remembered that my seventeenth birthday got lost in the turmoil of Mom's slow death.

"Thank you," I said. I wanted to say more, but it got all jumbled up with everything else I was feeling. I mean, he'd disappeared for four days, which made him an asshole, but then he turned up and did this sweet thing for me. "Thank you" was as coherent as I could be in the moment.

"You're welcome," he said, erasing the tear from my cheek with his thumb. "Come on. There's cake!"

He led me to the kitchen. The cake was lopsided, with writing on it that looked like it had been done by a third-grader. It seemed to spell out "Hopping Bouncy Ass," which I guessed was Shane's attempt at "Happy Birthday Ash."

"It's beautiful," I said.

"Not one of my better efforts, but you know, 'the thought that counts' and all that."

"It's a very thoughtful cake. I love it."

I was about to thank him again, but something stopped me, some barely conscious sense that maybe I was an idiot, so quick to forgive, all because he threw pebbles at my window and made me a lopsided cake.

He must have seen the change in my face.

"What's wrong?"

"You can't do this," I said, taking the stupid hat off. "You can't just disappear for days, and then blow up some balloons and think everything's going to be okay. It's not okay."

He reached for me, but I shook his hand off and took a step back.

"No," I said. "Do you have any idea what's been going through my head these past few days? What I've been imagining?"

He reached for me again, and again I stepped back, but he kept coming, until he had me wrapped tight in his arms.

And I forgave him, without him having to say another word. With his arms wrapped tight around me and his body warm against mine, I would have forgiven him anything.

. . .

Moonlight poured through the window, bathing his bedroom in a soft glow. We were spooning on the mattress, his back to me.

He'd led us there from the kitchen, and for a while, we didn't say anything. I was playing with his ear—more specifically with this adorable little bump he had on it. Ever since I first noticed that bump, I couldn't get enough of it. It was so . . . Shane. When I finally spoke, it was barely a whisper, my mouth against his ear.

"You have to tell me the truth. I'm okay with whatever you tell me, but you have to tell me." My hand was on his stomach, and he put his hand on top of mine.

He took a deep breath and let it out.

"You were right," he said. "About last week. I didn't go to Casper. I was with Cal."

My heart sank.

"Were you doing drugs?"

"Not at first. We were just drinking. Hit a couple of bars. But then, yeah, we found some meth, and there went two days—gone. I pulled myself together for rehearsal on Monday, but just barely. I was exhausted. So tired. When I got home that night, my body just shut down. And the next morning I was so sick."

He shuddered, like his body was remembering.

"I hate myself for letting this happen again," he said.

I hugged him tighter and kissed the back of his neck.

"And where have you been since Monday?" I asked, not sure I wanted the answer. "With Cal?"

"No," he said. "This time I really was in Casper. I told my mom I was sick and needed to come home for a few days. It was rough, Ash. It was like I fell into this really deep, dark hole. I couldn't sleep, and the chills were so bad I was shaking. Mom thought I had the flu."

"Wait, so you haven't done anything, since, what . . ."

"Since Sunday. I've been clean for five days now."

A wave of relief shot through me.

"And you feel okay?" I asked. "The chills, the withdrawal . . ."

"Yeah. I'm better now. Just tired. That'll pass in a day or so."

"That's great," I said. "Really. But . . ."

"But what?"

"How could you just leave without telling anybody?"

"I wasn't really thinking. I just packed a few things and took off. All I knew was that I had to get out of here."

"Finster was pissed. You left us with Lincoln. He's a train wreck."

"Yeah," he said, chuckling. "I saw Finster earlier today. After screaming at me for fifteen minutes, calling me the most irresponsible actor he's ever worked with, he said he was willing to let me back in. I guess that's how bad Lincoln is."

"Wait, so you're going on tomorrow night?"

"I guess. Assuming I can remember any of the words."

"You'll remember the words," I said, pulling him more tightly against me.

"It's after midnight," he said, detaching himself from me. "You should get going. Does your dad know you're here?"

"Not exactly."

"What's that mean?"

"He's forbidden me from seeing you."

"What?"

"Ever since that night when I punched my brother. He said you're a bad influence."

He was quiet for a minute, and when he spoke again, his voice was softer, barely there. Like maybe he was talking only to himself.

"Maybe he's right," he said.

"No. He's not right. You've done some things you shouldn't have done, but you're not a bad influence. Or if you are, you're only a bad influence on yourself. Not on me."

Our faces were just inches apart. I could smell the cake on his breath.

"You're sweet," he said, kissing me lightly on the lips. "But you should go. I don't want to make things worse between you and your dad."

"I want to stay here," I said. "I want to spend the night."

I said this without thinking. I didn't want to leave his bed. Shane had resisted doing anything more than kissing and cuddling, but surely he couldn't resist tonight.

He didn't say anything for a minute.

"I don't know . . . your dad . . ."

"I'll deal with him tomorrow. I'm in trouble either way."

It took him another minute, but he gave in.

"Okay," he said. "You can stay."

He got up to go to the bathroom, and when he came back, he got undressed and slipped under the covers. I did the same, my heart beating like a drum. At first, we just lay there on our backs, not touching, staring up at the shaft of light that pierced the window. I was trembling. When Shane finally spoke, it startled me.

"It's because of you, you know."

"What is?"

"Me going to Casper. Me getting clean. I wanted to be the person you think I am."

I wrapped him up tight in my arms, kissed him on the neck. Jenna said you can't really save another person. Maybe she was wrong.

"It's like you remind me of who I am," Shane said, "or who I was. You're different from the other guys I've been with. You're sweet, and you're honest, and you're not trying to use me for something. And I'm different when I'm with you. And when I remember that other me, I want to punch myself in the face. I can't believe the things I did. I want to stay like this. I want to be better."

There were so many things I could have said. How lucky I was to have met him. How he was the one rescuing me, not the other way around. How I hadn't had a moment's peace since my mom died, until this moment, lying there in that bed with him. But those were just words.

I rolled over until I was on top of him, my face hovering just above his. The feel of skin on skin was almost more than I could take. I kissed him, deeper than I ever had. I wanted to put every single bit of him in my mouth. I kissed his ears, his neck, his collarbone, each nipple in turn, as I worked my way down his chest. I could feel the energy coiled in his body. There was something rippling under his skin, trying to make its way to the surface. But when I got to the waist band of his boxers, something changed.

"Stop," he said, putting his hand on mine.

"What's wrong?" I asked, my voice as desperate as the rest of me.

"It's just not a good idea."

"It's the best idea I've ever had."

"Come here," he said, pulling me up so that my head lay on his chest.

"Is it because I'm younger than you?" I asked. "Because, yes, I am younger than you, but I'm not, like, *illegal* younger than you. I looked it up. Age of consent in Wyoming is sixteen. And I'm seventeen, hell, almost eighteen, which makes me, like, almost nineteen. So, we're basically the same age."

He laughed. "It's not that. It's just . . . I want to take this slow." He was stroking the side of my head, just like my mom used to do when I was upset as a kid.

"Yeah, I know. You've said that before." My voice had more of an edge than I intended.

"It's just that I really like you," he said. "Like, a lot. And that's new for me. And it's scary. In the past, none of this meant anything. Sex was just sex. I would jump into bed with guys at the first opportunity. But that never led to anything real, and I usually hated myself after."

He pulled gently on my earlobe, which I found strangely relaxing.

"I want things to be different with you," he said.

He kept tugging on my earlobe. I never wanted him to stop.

"I really like you, too," I said, and I forgave myself the lie. I was so far beyond liking him.

. . .

Saturday morning, the day of the show's opening, I woke up first, which meant I got to look at Shane. He was half out of the sheets, his upper body and one leg catching the sun streaming through the window. I stared at his face, trying to find proof of what he'd said the night before—that he hadn't done drugs in five days. He looked better than he had on Monday. His eyes were less puffy, and the hard edges were gone from his face.

He opened his eyes, blinking in the morning sun. When he saw me, he smiled.

"Good morning," he said, his voice ragged. "How'd you sleep?"

"I liked it."

He laughed.

"You liked it? Sleeping?"

"All of it. Sleeping. Waking up with you. The whole thing. I can't wait to do it again."

He laughed again and butted his head up against me, like a goat.

"What's the plan for today?" I asked.

"I have to be at the theater at four," he said, stretching, "and you have to go home and face your dad."

"Yeah, about that. I'm not going to do that."

"So, what," he said, laughing. "You're just never going home?"

"No, I'll go home. Just not until after the show. If I go home before then, he won't let me leave, and I'll miss your big debut."

"You have to at least call him. He'll freak out when he realizes you didn't come home last night. Like, call-the-cops freak out."

"He won't expect me to emerge from my bedroom before noon. And he goes to the farmers market around ten. I'll call then and leave a message on the machine, tell him I'm with Jenna. He seemed to like her."

"It's your funeral," he said. "Speaking of Jenna, we should find her and get breakfast. I need to try to make her not hate me."

. . .

At first, Jenna refused to come out of her apartment. She just kept yelling "go away!" out of her window. I couldn't blame her. The first thing Shane did after promising not to disappear again was to disappear again. And Jenna hadn't had the birthday party and a night in bed with Shane to help her get over it.

When Shane finally convinced her to come out, she refused to get in the car with us. She said Shane was a narcissist with no awareness of other people's feelings, and having breakfast with such a person was not her idea of a good time. But then I reminded her that it was Saturday, which meant the special at Lillian's was Belgian waffles topped with strawberry ice cream.

"You don't even have to talk to him," I said. "You can just sit there and eat waffles."

She made us sweat for a minute, but eventually she caved.

"Fine. But he's buying."

It took forever for our food to come, which was excruciating, since Jenna wasn't talking, and Shane was talking too much. I guess he was trying to make things normal again. When our waffles finally arrived, Shane was telling a story about the time his pants fell down during a production of *Grease*, but Jenna wasn't laughing. She just kept jabbing at her waffles like she wanted to hurt them. When she finally looked up, her eyes bore into Shane like lasers.

"Tell him," she said, interrupting Shane mid-sentence.

"Tell him what?" Shane asked, still laughing about the pants.

"Tell him the real reason I'm pissed at you."

Shane flinched. His mouth hung open, like he'd forgotten how to close it.

"That's not really my story to tell," he said, looking down at his waffles.

"You've made it your story to tell. So tell it."

When he spoke again, his voice was barely audible above the clatter of the restaurant.

"She had a brother who died of a drug overdose," he said, his eyes still on the waffles.

"A meth overdose," she said. "Tell it right."

"A meth overdose," he said, finally looking up. He looked like someone expecting to be punched in the face.

"And he knows that," she said, her voice shaking, "and he still pulls this shit. Disappears for days, probably doing every drug he can get his hands on, and I have to sit there and wait for him to turn up dead. Just like I did with Jesse."

Her jaw was clenched, her cheeks red.

I waited for Shane to defend himself, but he didn't say anything. He just got up from our side of the booth and sat beside Jenna, wrapping his arms around her and leaning his head into her neck. She took a deep breath, and she surrendered, sinking into him.

I wondered how many times she could be hurt by him, and then fall for him all over again. I wondered how many times I could.

But then her body stiffened, and she threw Shane's arms off.

"No!" she shouted, her voice piercing the restaurant noise. "I will *not* do this again!"

She pushed Shane out of the booth and stood up, knocking a glass of water over with her bag.

"I'm done," she said. "I am so over this." She turned and left.

. . .

We were in Shane's truck heading west out of town, out past the airport. He said there was something he wanted to show me. He hadn't said anything about Jenna since we left the restaurant, and I had the feeling he couldn't. Like maybe he was too ashamed.

It was nothing but wide-open prairie out there, broken up by the occasional fence. I thought he was taking me to the wildlife refuge that was out that way, but about halfway there he pulled over to the side of the road and turned the car off.

"This is it," he said.

"What is it?"

"This."

All I could see was exactly what I'd seen for the past several miles: a whole lot of nothing. Even the sky was empty.

"I don't see anything," I said. "It's just prairie."

"Exactly," he said. "Come on."

We got out of the car, and I followed him down a faint path. After a while, we came to a spot where the elevation changed slightly, a rise of just a couple of feet. If this place had a view, I guess this was it. Shane stopped and just stood there.

"Listen," he said.

I listened and heard nothing. The quiet was heavy, like a blanket. Shane lay down on a bed of soft grass, and I lay down beside him. He reached for my hand. For a while, he didn't say anything, and I knew I shouldn't either.

"I come out here sometimes to clear my head," he said, finally. "It's so quiet here. Barren. It's not beautiful, not like Mirror Lake." He squeezed my hand at the memory of the two of us on that warm rock. "It's the opposite of beauty," he continued. "The whole world is just . . . stripped down.

There's nothing but sky, really, the biggest sky I've ever seen. I think that's what I like about it. The sky's so big that it makes me feel utterly insignificant."

I knew what he meant. When Mr. Lindquist talked about the origin of the universe, I felt so small, like I was just a speck in a history that stretched back fourteen billion years. In the grand scheme of things, I was no bigger than the subatomic particles that made up every piece of me. You'd think this would be terrifying, but it wasn't. The smallness made me feel safe, somehow. Like I wasn't alone, and never would be.

"I want to disappear into a greater whole," Shane said. "Not some sort of religious thing, just something larger than myself. Sometimes, when I'm here, I think it's just on the verge of happening, and I try to let myself go. But it never happens. I always come back to myself. Just me. Nothing else."

We were quiet for a long time after that. I can still feel what it felt like, holding hands under a warm October sun. It was the kind of thing you never want to end. The kind of thing that has to.

CHAPTER TWELVE

I had squirrels in my stomach. I was in the same seat I'd been in countless times before, next to Jenna, waiting for Shane to take the stage, but it was different this time. There were other people there. Lots of other people. The box office had announced a sellout, not just for opening night, but for the whole two-week run. I guess people can never get enough of old-timey, feel-good prairie musicals. They didn't know what they were in for with Finster's strange vision.

"I'm surprised you came," I said.

"So am I," Jenna said.

The squirrels were mostly because of Shane. I was so nervous for him. But the squirrels also had something to do with not knowing what to say to Jenna. About her brother.

"I'm sorry about Jesse. That must have been really hard."

"Still is."

"Do you want to talk about it?"

"What is there to say? He was a depressed kid, and then he found drugs and discovered how good it could feel to feel good, and he started looking for ways to feel that way all the time. Weed, coke, meth. Eventually heroin. But it was meth that gave him the feeling he couldn't live without.

"We tried to get him help. My parents put him in one rehab place after another. He'd get clean and promise never to use again, and then he'd start lying about where he'd been, and stuff would start disappearing from the house—money, jewelry—and then he'd end up in the emergency room.

"And I had to watch him die. I don't mean just the last time, when he OD'd in his bedroom. I mean every second of the months before that, when we had to watch this beautiful kid turn into a corpse. Gray skin, less and less flesh on his bones, no life in his eyes. His jeans more often than not reeking of piss, or worse."

She pulled her head back, like she could still smell it.

"And then I started to imagine the same thing happening to Shane, and I just . . ."

I felt a shudder go through her.

"Jesse was my responsibility," she said. "He was the youngest, and it was my job to keep him safe. And I failed. And now the same thing is happening all over again with Shane."

She took a deep breath, let it out slowly.

"I hate that he's putting you through this," I said.

"That's the thing, though. I don't even get to stay mad at him. Because it's not his fault. And it wasn't Jesse's fault. This drug? It takes everything. Including the ability to give a fuck about the people you're hurting."

"So . . . you're not done with him?"

She chuckled, like the question was ridiculous.

"I can't be done with him. It's like it's not even possible."

The houselights went down, and my squirrels started acting up again. I didn't know if Shane was going to be able to do this. Given what he'd been through in the past two weeks, there was a good chance he'd simply walk out on stage and collapse.

"How much do you want to bet," Jenna asked, "that half these people make a run for the exits during the big gay sex scene?"

I took Jenna's hand. She must have been nervous too because she let me. Lights upstage gradually cast a glow over the corn, and lush strings swelled from the speakers. Shane's opening lines were crucial. As Finster put it, that first verse has to assure the audience that everything is going to be okay. Without that assurance, he said, nobody will care when everything falls apart.

Shane and his horse appeared, stage left, lit by a spotlight. The strings faded, and the silence that followed was ominous. Just when I thought the silence was going to last forever, Shane filled it. In the purity of his voice, the shimmering meadow and the impossibly high corn were absolutely real.

"Our boy's going to be fine," Jenna whispered, squeezing my hand.

The next hour went by in a blur. And then came what Jenna called the sex scene, with Jud and Curly using the fight as an excuse to grope each other. As near as I could tell, no audience members fled, but there was a lot of creaking in the hall as people shifted uncomfortably in their seats. Shane was better than I had ever seen him, as if he needed the audience before he could fully inhabit the role. And Patrick was so scary. That image of Jud's face on the screen, tortured with repressed desire for Curly, sent chills through me.

And then that damn ending. It had never made sense to me. It's Laurey and Curly's wedding. They're dressed all in white, and the whole town is celebrating this beautiful, perfect couple. And then Jud shows up with a gift for Curly, a peace offering, I guess. It's a gun. He approaches Curly tentatively, holding the gun out in front of him. Curly takes it, admires it, running his hand along the shaft as Laurey looks on nervously.

And then? Curly shoots Jud dead. While Jud's body lies center stage, the town holds a rushed trial, in which the judge says it would be cruel to lock a man up on his wedding night, and so declares a verdict of not guilty. This had always struck me as wrong, wrong enough to make the whole show fail in its final moments. Why did Curly shoot Jud? Why did the town let Curly get away with murder?

But this time I saw something I hadn't seen in rehearsal. Maybe I hadn't been paying attention, or maybe Patrick was holding something back. But now I saw it, just the smallest thing. While Curly is admiring the gun, Jud raises his hand toward Curly's face. The movement is barely detectable, but it's there. Curly looks up, sees Jud's hand, and shoots. Not because he thought Jud was going to strike him. Jud's motive wasn't violence. You could tell by the look on his face, the slight quiver of his hand. Curly shot Jud because Jud wanted to touch him, like a lover.

And this is where the special effects crew really showed their stuff. Jud's chest explodes in blood, which splatters all over the happy couple's white wedding outfits. They're like a modern painting now, white streaked with violent slashes of red. They remain blood-splattered during the trial scene, and they're still dripping with red paint during the final song, when Curly reprises "Oh, What a Beautiful Mornin'." But the morning's not beautiful, maybe never will be again. Jud's body lies heavy on the stage, and Curly's face registers, for the first time, what it is he's lost. Laurey sees it too, and you can see her world crumbling. And that's when it hit me that maybe Finster was a genius.

But the audience? They didn't like it. There was some half-hearted applause, the polite kind that people offer up because they feel bad for the actors. But mostly there were boos. I looked around at people's faces, which were scrunched up with disgust. Something had been taken from them: some beloved version of life on the prairie, where good people are rewarded, bad people are punished, and everything is happily resolved through the sacred union of a man and a woman. What they got instead was a newly married couple covered in blood and tainted by the stink of something perverse. This was not what the audience had come for. It was not what they thought they deserved.

. . .

Backstage, we found Patrick pacing back and forth, still amped up from the performance. At first, it looked like he was talking to himself, but then we saw Shane, slumped down against the wall.

"But look what we did to them!" Patrick said. "We fucked up their entire world. It was so cool!"

"They hated it," Shane rasped. Whatever voice he'd had in the show was gone now. "They hated *me*."

"They didn't hate you," Patrick said. "They hated that their feel-good moment turned into a blood-soaked love triangle with two dudes at the center of it. That's what they were booing. It's like Finster said. We were 'queering their heterosexual expectations.'"

"It's so easy for you," Shane said, standing up, more energy in his voice now. "The big handsome straight guy 'queering heterosexual expectations.' What about me? I queer heterosexual expectations every time I open my mouth. So, yeah, maybe we're both queer at the end. But you're queer and dead, which makes you safe. I'm the fag with a gun. The one they hate."

"You're getting worked up over nothing," Patrick said, walking away. "It was great art. Great art fucks shit up. Get used to it."

Shane leaned back against the wall, whatever energy he had, gone. He and Jenna stared at each other. It was strange to see them suddenly shy, neither knowing what could be said. Shane finally broke the silence.

"I'm—"

"Don't," Jenna said. "Just . . . don't."

He looked so broken. I couldn't stand to see it. I guess Jenna couldn't either.

"Come here," she said.

Shane pushed himself off the wall and into her arms. They held each other for a minute before Jenna pushed him away.

"You were amazing," she said.

I was distracted by the stage blood that covered him. A shiver coursed through me. I shook it off.

"It's true," I said. "You were so good. They wouldn't have been booing if you hadn't totally killed it."

A hint of a smile bloomed on his face. I held my arms out to him, and he folded himself into me. I wrapped him up tight. I felt his warm breath on my neck, and I kissed him on the ear. Something in his body shifted. I thought it was because of the kiss, but then he continued to tense, like maybe he was trying to get me off him.

Someone called my name, loud, the shout echoing through the theater like a gunshot. I looked at Shane, his face stricken, his eyes focused on something behind me. I turned around. It was Dad.

"Get away from my son!" he yelled. "Right now!"

I'd never heard his voice like that. It sounded more animal than human. He walked fast toward me and grabbed my arm.

"You're coming home. Right this minute. And all of this," he said, gesturing toward the props, the curtains, toward Shane. "This is done. Do you understand? This is *over*!"

He pulled me toward the stage door. I resisted, but it didn't do any good. My feet barely touched the stage. I looked back and caught a glimpse of Shane. Sheltered under Jenna's arm, he looked like he could have been her child.

. . .

On the drive home, I tried talking to Dad. He said he didn't want to hear it. Veins popped on his arms as he clutched the steering wheel. His face was beet red.

When we pulled up in front of the house, he turned off the ignition, but he didn't get out of the truck. We sat there for what felt like forever. He seemed to be trying to calm himself, like he didn't trust himself to use words yet. When he finally spoke, his voice was quiet.

"First, you're grounded. You're not to leave the house except for school."

"For how long?"

"Until I say so."

"But—

"No. No buts."

He said all this without looking at me. Maybe because he couldn't.

"Second, I want you to tell me where you were last night."

"What do you mean?"

"I'm not an idiot. Your bed hadn't been slept in."

There was no use denying it.

"I was at Shane's."

"You spent the night there? With him?"

"Yeah."

He gurgled, like he was trying to dislodge something from his throat.

"Did you . . . did you have sex with him?"

I knew how uncomfortable he was saying those words. I could have let him off the hook by telling the truth. But I didn't.

"That's none of your business," I said.

He finally looked at me then, but it was like he didn't even recognize me.

"Maybe you're right," he said, facing forward again. "But let me tell you what *is* my business. Not knowing where my son is. That's my business. Not hearing from him for over twenty-four hours when all he had to do was pick up the phone. That's my business. Not knowing whether he's alive or dead. *That's* my business."

Whatever calm he had manufactured was gone now, and I realized, much later than I should have, that he was terrified. Angry, sure, but mostly he was scared. He didn't know what was happening. He didn't know what to do. And he was frightened.

"I'm sorry, Dad. I really am."

"That doesn't matter now. The only thing that matters is what happens next. You're not to see him."

"But he's not who you think he is. I swear." My voice was ragged, pleading. "You need to give him a chance. You need to give *us* a chance."

"He's a drug user."

"Not anymore," I said, realizing too late that this was probably the world's worst defense.

"I need you to tell me you understand," he said.

There was no use fighting. I'd tell him what he needed to hear and wait for things to calm down. There was no way I was going to stay away from Shane.

"I understand," I said.

"Okay. Now get to bed. It's late."

I didn't realize until I got to my room that my shirt was covered in stage paint. Jud's blood, from when I had hugged Shane. I stripped it off and threw it in the back of my closet, where it seemed to glow in the dark.

CHAPTER THIRTEEN

I woke up Sunday morning with a raging hard-on. I'd spent the night dreaming about Shane. The way he looked, shirtless on a rock. The way he felt, skin against skin, in tangled sheets. The way he smelled after a long rehearsal, like peat. I'd just started to do something about it when I heard a shuffling outside my door. I froze. Paper rustled. Then more shuffling. Then silence. I waited it out, eager to get back to business, but the mood was broken. I sat up in bed, which is when I noticed something on the floor by my door. It was a pamphlet: "Safer Sex for the Curious Gay Teen." Scrawled in the corner: "Let me know if you want to talk. Dad."

Oh, sweet Jesus.

I flipped through the pages. A pencil drawing demonstrated how to put on a condom. A paragraph explained something called frottage, which I had never heard of, but which sounded hot. There was lots of stuff about HIV and STDs. Near the back, a couple of pages detailed sexual practices that I didn't know existed and couldn't imagine participating in.

No, thanks, I didn't want to discuss this with my dad.

But then I thought about what it meant that he had given this to me. If his primary moods last night were anger and fear, the delivery of this sex pamphlet suggested something else. Concern. A desire to help. I threw on a T-shirt and took the pamphlet to the kitchen, where I found Dad sitting at the table. He looked like a third-grader who hadn't done his homework and who knew he was about to be called on.

"Morning," I said.

"Morning," he said.

Maybe that was enough, a quiet moment of gratitude for the sex pamphlet, and now we could return to our regularly scheduled programming and pretend that none of this had ever happened. But then he started talking.

"I picked that up from the Health Center on campus, after you told me that you were . . . you know . . . and I kept meaning to give it to you, but didn't, and then after last night, with you and Shane, I thought, well, I guess I better. Not because you're going to have sex anytime soon—that would be difficult given that I'm locking you in the house—but at some point, maybe, you'll leave the house again, and you'll want to . . . you know . . . and I thought, well, you should be prepared. Not that you're not prepared, I mean, maybe you know all that stuff already, maybe you and Shane have been doing things . . . right . . . but still, a refresher course couldn't hurt."

He must have realized he was rambling because he stopped suddenly and took a breath.

"I'm just saying that I want you to be safe. It's a dangerous time . . . for kids like you . . . and I need you to be safe. Because I love you."

What was there to say after all that? Short and sweet seemed the safest strategy.

"Thanks."

"Is there anything you want to talk about?" He still looked like the frightened third-grader.

"No. I'm good." But then I thought again about what it meant that he had put himself through this. I owed him something in return.

"Though I guess I should tell you. Shane and I haven't . . . done anything . . . yet. We haven't had sex."

You've never seen a person look so relieved.

"That's good to know," he said. "I'm proud of you, Ash. You knew that it would be better to wait."

"Um, not exactly. I wanted to. It was Shane who said we should take things slow."

"Huh," he said. And this next thing cost him, but he said it anyway. "Maybe Shane's not all bad."

"Does this mean—"

"No. It doesn't. You're still grounded. For as long as it takes. And if I catch you with him, or trying to be with him . . . well, it would be a long time before I could trust you again. And that lack of trust will have consequences. Do you understand?"

"I do."

"Good. Now eat some breakfast and get dressed. You have work to do."

. . .

The work turned out to involve the removal of a tree stump from our front yard. The tree was long gone, but Dad had never gotten around to removing the stump, and I guess my lockdown offered him the perfect opportunity.

"How long is this going to take?" I asked.

"Somewhere between three and twelve hours, depending on the root system. But you've got nothing but time, right?"

Dad handed me a shovel and told me to start digging. The trick is to dig down far enough to expose the roots, at which point you use a pick-axe to sever the roots from the stump. Eventually you get to the taproot, which is when you use a saw. This was going to suck.

As I started to dig, I consoled myself as I often did when Dad gave me jobs like this: maybe this kind of labor would give me the ripped body that makes you a successful homosexual. It hadn't happened yet, but I remained hopeful. Meanwhile, I thought about Shane. What was he thinking, after seeing me dragged away by my dad? Was he planning some sort of rescue attempt? And more important, had he recovered from being booed by an auditorium full of people? I had to let him know that I was going to be locked down for a while, but I couldn't even IM him.

When I'd tried to log on earlier that morning, I discovered that Dad had taken the modem. And since leaving the house wasn't an option, at least until school the next day, I had to find a way to call him. I hatched my plan as I hacked my way through the roots.

"Dad!" I yelled, when, several hours later, I had finally uncovered the taproot.

"What is it?" he asked, emerging from the house.

"I'm beat. Can't move my arms. Could you maybe do this last one?"

I must have looked pitiful standing there, my arms hanging like sausages in a butcher's window.

"Fine. Go get some water."

Once inside, I could hear him sawing away at the taproot, which gave me what I needed to call Shane. Christopher had picked up an afternoon shift at The Old Brick, meaning that as long as I could hear the saw, I was safe. I went into the kitchen and dialed Shane's number. He picked up on the first ring, but he didn't say anything, just let the silence hang.

"Shane? It's Ash."

"Oh, hey! Sorry, I thought it might be someone else. What's that noise?"

"It's my dad. He's sawing a taproot."

"What?"

"A taproot. We're removing a stump."

"That's weird."

"Listen," I said. "I only have a minute. I'm grounded. I'm not going to be able to see you for a while."

"How long?"

"I don't know. Dad will cool down eventually, but it's not going to be quick."

"Are you okay?"

It wasn't until he asked the question that I realized I wasn't. I held my breath to keep the tears from coming.

"Ash?"

"This just blows," I said.

"I know, but we'll figure something out."

I was about to respond when I realized that something was different. The sawing. It had stopped.

"Shit. I have to go, he's made it through the taproot."

"Wait—"

"Ash!" Dad yelled, opening the front door.

I hung up, just in time to position myself with a glass of water at the counter.

"What?"

"Come help me lift this puppy out of there."

. . .

I spent the rest of Sunday recovering from the stump. I went to bed early and fell quickly asleep, exhausted. When I woke the next morning, I felt rested, but hollow. It sucked, knowing I wouldn't be able to see Shane. It was scary how dependent on him I'd gotten in just a few weeks, but it felt good to need somebody like that. Like I was fully present in my life for the first time in a long time. And a two-minute phone call every time Dad made me dig up a stump wasn't going to cut it.

I showered and made the long, cold bike ride to school, heading straight for the library. With our modem confiscated, the computers in the library were my only digital connection. I found one in the back corner angled away from foot traffic. I logged on to AOL, and my heart jumped when that familiar voice announced, "You've got mail!" It was from Shane, sent the night before.

> Hey, stump boy!
> I'm hoping you're ok and that your dad didn't bury you in the hole where the stump used to be. I'm sorry for getting you in trouble. Thinking about you.
> IM me when you can.
> Miss u 😘
> Shane

It's amazing what words on a screen and a ridiculous little kissy face can do to your pulse.

. . .

After first period, I got a library pass from study hall and went back to the computer in the corner. I logged on and saw that Shane was online.

SpaceMama: hey!

Shane6296: hey

SpaceMama: im so glad ur on

SpaceMama: miss u

I waited. Nothing.

SpaceMama: hello?

SpaceMama: Shane?

Shane6296: sorry im here

SpaceMama: r u ok?

Shane6296: sorry

Shane6296: just a bit down

SpaceMama: whats wrong?

Shane6296: its nothing dont worry about it

SpaceMama: i want 2 worry about it

SpaceMama: what is it . . . maybe i can help

Shane6296: remember when i told u sometimes it feels like i can never really escape the past?

Shane6296: i keep dragging all this shit around with me

Shane6296: the last few days have felt like that

SpaceMama: but whats going on?

SpaceMama: did something happen?

I stared at the screen, but nothing changed for what felt like forever. This was what I'd always hated about IM'ing. You couldn't tell if the conversation was still happening. Maybe the other person was typing feverishly, and you just needed to wait. Or maybe he'd found something better to do, someone better to talk to.

SpaceMama: hello?

SpaceMama: r u still there?

Shane6296: im here

SpaceMama: so what is it? u can tell me

There was another long pause.

Shane6296: its just something i gotta deal with

Shane6296: g2g

Shane6296: ☺

Shane6296: ttyl 😘

When the computer made the door-closing sound, all I was left with were those emoticons, pretending one thing, hiding another.

. . .

I checked back in during lunch. Shane wasn't online. I even risked another logon after school. I didn't really have the time, since my dad usually beat me home, and I knew he'd be on the lookout, just waiting for me to violate my lockdown. But I couldn't not check. I needed to hear from Shane, especially since it was obvious that something was wrong. When I logged on, he still wasn't there. I shot him a quick email begging him to tell me what was happening.

The rest of that Monday was hard. Minutes passed like hours. It seemed like the day would never end, and when it finally did, I was grateful for another night's sleep.

I rushed to school Tuesday morning, found my computer in the library, and logged on. Still no Shane.

I checked my buddy list. Jenna was online.

SpaceMama: have u seen Shane

MiSsWoRld: not since saturday nite. Why?

SpaceMama: he was kind of weird when we IM'd yesterday

SpaceMama: and i haven't heard from him since then

SpaceMama: do u think this is like last time?

SpaceMama: should we go looking 4 him?

MiSsWoRld: did you see the review?

SpaceMama: what review?
MiSsWoRld: the campus paper
SpaceMama: no what did it say?
MiSsWoRld: oklahomo
MiSsWoRld: limp-wristed curly
MiSsWoRld: queer bloodbath comic rather than tragic
SpaceMama: ugh do u think thats why he disappeared?
MiSsWoRld: maybe
MiSsWoRld: lmk if you hear from him

I logged onto AOL again at lunch, and then again before I left school. Still nothing. I stopped at a pay phone on the way home, dialed Shane's cell, but it went straight to voicemail.

The rest of that Tuesday was as bad as the day before. I fell quickly asleep, which is why it was weird that I woke up in the middle of the night. And it wasn't one of those gradual, groggy wake-ups. I was suddenly sitting bolt upright in my bed, as awake as I'd ever been. My heart was racing. I checked the clock: 3:15. Maybe something had woken me up. I rushed to the window, hoping to find Shane throwing pebbles. Nothing.

I tried to get back to sleep but couldn't. I threw on sweats and a hoody and went out on the front porch. It was cold, but I made myself sit there. I needed to figure out what I was feeling. Because it wasn't simple. I was still missing Shane like crazy, but now this other feeling was beginning to worm its way in. Anger. And it was different from the anger I felt when he disappeared the first time, and then the second. This anger felt like it was wrapped around my whole body. It felt permanent.

I went into the kitchen, dialed Shane's cell, and took the phone into the pantry, so I wouldn't wake up Dad and Christopher. It rang and kept ringing, and for a moment I thought he was going to answer, despite the fact that it was three thirty in the morning. When it went to voicemail, I was relieved, since I didn't think I could say what I had to say to an actual person.

"Hey," I whispered. "It's Ash."

The whispering reminded me of being in bed with him, his back against my chest, my arms wrapped around him.

"I'm sick of this," I said, and with that, everything came pouring out. "It's messed up. You just disappear, and you don't call, you don't even send me a message, just something saying you're okay. And yeah, I know about the review, and I'm sorry, but still, that's no excuse. I can't take it anymore. I thought you cared about me, at least enough to pick up the damn phone, but I guess I was wrong about that. So, that's it, Shane. I'm done. We're done. And don't worry about calling me, about trying to fix this. It's too late for that."

I was out of breath, shaking in the dark of the pantry.

"Have a nice life," I said, before slamming the phone down.

. . .

I must have slept for a couple of hours. I woke up groggy and took a shower, hoping the hot water would wake me up. I kept replaying that voicemail over and over in my head. If I thought that breaking up with Shane would make me feel better, I was wrong. I felt worse. If I was going to be miserable either way, why not be miserable *with* him?

I grabbed a banana and my bike and headed to school. The wind had gone from cold to bitter, and I had to blink the tears from my eyes. When I got to school, I found myself heading toward the library, out of habit, but I stopped myself. Why check my account? There wouldn't be anything there, and even if there was, what would it matter?

I went to homeroom, and then Wyoming history, trying to focus on what was going on around me, but I couldn't. By lunch I couldn't take it anymore. I went to the library and logged on. Jenna was on.

MiSsWoRld: where have u been?!?!

SpaceMama: sorry

MiSsWoRld: I saw Shane last night

Even just seeing his name on the screen made my stomach flinch.

SpaceMama: where?

MiSsWoRld: the pride alliance

SpaceMama: how was he?

MiSsWoRld: i don't know . . . maybe a little drunk. he'd been at the brick for a few hours

MiSsWoRld: we all went to the college inn after and had pizza

MiSsWoRld: he wanted me to go to lucky's with him after that, but I was beat

MiSsWoRld: have you heard from him today?

SpaceMama: no

SpaceMama: i dont think im going to

MiSsWoRld: why not?

I didn't want to tell her. Typing it would make it too real. But she deserved to know.

SpaceMama: i kinda broke up with him

MiSsWoRld: WHAT?!?!?!?!?!?

SpaceMama: i called him at like 3 am

SpaceMama: i left a message

MiSsWoRld: YOU BROKE UP WITH HIM ON A VOICEMAIL?!?!?!?!

The screen was still. Was she done with me? I probably deserved it. Eventually a message popped up.

MiSsWoRld: are you ok?

SpaceMama: no

MiSsWoRld: don't worry

MiSsWoRld: we can fix this

MiSsWoRld: I'll find him

MiSsWoRld: I'll let you know when I do

. . .

I know I did stuff in the next twenty-four hours, but I don't remember any of it.

What I remember is pulling up to our house, Thursday after school, and seeing a car that shouldn't have been there. It was covered with stickers, but I didn't make the connection. Even when I saw Jenna standing in the front yard with my dad, I didn't connect her to the car. My brain had stopped putting the pieces together. Maybe because it knew what was coming.

I dropped my bike in the yard. Dad looked like he looked when he told us Mom was dead. I needed to grab onto something, but there was nothing to grab onto. Jenna's face was red, puffy. Dark mascara lined her cheeks.

"It's Shane," she said. "It's bad. Real bad."

AFTER

OCTOBER 1998

CHAPTER FOURTEEN

I don't remember much about the drive to Fort Collins, except that Jenna never stopped smoking—just lit one cigarette after another—and that her little Honda rattled pretty bad once it hit eighty. I didn't care. I just wanted to get there, so that I could know Shane was okay. I kept thinking: if I can see him, he'll be okay.

All we knew was that Shane had been badly hurt and taken to Presbyterian Hospital in Fort Collins. Jenna had learned this much from a guy from the Pride Alliance who worked part-time as an orderly and who called when Shane was brought in. When Jenna called to get more information, they confirmed Shane was a patient there, but couldn't say anything about his condition.

I was surprised Dad let me go. I'd lied to him so many times. But he must have seen on Jenna's face what I saw—a sense that something terrible was happening.

"Call me as soon as you get to the hospital," he said. "And I need you back here by eight o'clock. It's a school night."

When Jenna and I got to the hospital, they wouldn't let us see him, said we had to be family. I checked in with Dad and then joined Jenna in an alcove on the edge of the lobby. We just sat there, not knowing what else to do, listening to the drone of the TVs that hung everywhere. It was cold in the lobby, but I was sweating, my heart racing. I closed my eyes, took a deep breath and held it, trying not to hear the blood pulsing in my ears.

I'd been here before. Not in this hospital, but one just like it, sitting in a cold lobby, waiting for my mom to die. I felt it in my body all over again, something deep inside me forming into a tight ball of fear and panic.

"Who's this?" Jenna asked.

I opened my eyes and saw two guys coming toward us, one maybe Shane's age, the other older, maybe fifty. They stopped right in front of us.

"Are you Ash?" the younger guy asked.

He was short, just a couple of inches taller than Shane, and his blond hair was gelled into spikes, with frosted tips, like maybe he thought he was in the Backstreet Boys. He was out of breath, like he'd run here.

"Do I know you?" I asked.

"I'm Kevin. This is Brian, my social worker."

"I'm not his social worker," the older guy said, shaking hands with me, then Jenna. His voice was calmer than Kevin's, but something in his eyes suggested panic.

"Did you see Shane?" Kevin asked.

"How do you know Shane?" Jenna asked.

"From Denver," Kevin said. I remembered now. This was the guy Cal mentioned.

"And how do you know me?" I asked.

"Shane talked about you. Skinny kid, dark hair. I took a guess. Answer the damn question! Did you see him?"

"They wouldn't let us," Jenna said.

"Mind if we join you?" Brian asked, as he and Kevin took the chairs opposite us. The television above us murmured something about a snowstorm.

Brian had his hand on the back of Kevin's neck. I found myself staring at Kevin. It was his eyes, which were too big for his face. He reminded me of a nature show I'd seen about lemurs, whose eyes are all out of proportion to the rest of their bodies.

"So you know Shane from Denver?" Jenna asked.

"That's right," Brian said. "I met him soon after he moved there, I guess about a year ago. It was at this totally shady place, Mr. Bill's. A bar where he shouldn't have been. A bar where nobody should be, really."

"Then why were *you* there?" Jenna asked. "I mean, if it was so shady." She wasn't even trying to keep the edge out of her voice.

"I was trying to get this one away from there," he said, nodding his head toward Kevin.

"What'd I tell you?" Kevin said. "Total social worker."

"I'm not a social worker," Brian said. "I teach social work at MSU."

"Same thing," Kevin said.

I remembered Shane mentioning a Brian, some older professor who helped him out of his money jam with Cal.

"And how'd you know Shane was here?" Jenna asked.

"I've got a friend who works at the *Casper Star-Tribune*," Brian said. "He called me this afternoon, said a police bulletin had just come over the fax."

"What did it say?" I asked.

"Not much," Brian said. "Just that Shane Deerfield had been assaulted and brought here."

"Assaulted?" I asked. Somehow I'd managed to believe that Shane had just been in an accident.

"Yes," Brian said.

"Do they know who did it?" Jenna asked.

"No mention of suspects yet," Brian said.

"Why would someone do this?" I asked. "Shane wouldn't hurt a fly. He couldn't, even if he wanted to."

Kevin looked right at me, his big eyes suddenly narrow.

"What are you, an idiot?" he said.

"Hey!" Jenna said.

"No, seriously," Kevin said. "What fucking rock are you living under?

Gay guy, five foot nothing. Gets the shit beat out of him. In Juniper. Because he was picking a fight? Hell no. It was because some asshole went fag hunting."

We looked over at Brian.

"It's the only thing that makes sense," he said. "You know Shane. Can you imagine him starting a fight?"

I couldn't. But I could imagine him pissing the wrong person off. I remembered the story he told me about getting punched on that camping trip with his parents. I swatted the thought away and said nothing.

Just then the lighting in the lobby changed. Shards of bright light danced across the furniture. After a second, the light stabilized, and I tracked it to its source.

There was a woman standing in the hospital driveway, in a pool of light, her back to the lobby. In the glare, I could just make out a guy with a camera on his shoulder.

"Turn that up," Jenna said, pointing to the television. On the screen, we could see the flip side of what was happening outside, a reporter standing in front of the hospital entrance. Under her, the caption read "Local Man Injured in Assault." Brian reached up to boost the volume.

> *I'm standing outside Presbyterian Hospital, in Fort Collins, where a Juniper man, identified by police as college student Shane Deerfield, has been brought with serious injuries suffered during an alleged assault. According to initial reports, Deerfield was found beaten on the east side of Juniper, near the new Walmart Supercenter. One person briefed on the situation said that Deerfield was tied to a fence, almost like, and I quote, "he had been crucified." We'll bring you more on this story as soon as we have it.*

"Motherfuckers," Kevin said.

It was like I was about to fall off a cliff, even though I was sitting down. I felt dizzy and put my head between my knees. The image stamped itself on my brain. Shane, tied to a fence, his arms outstretched, his bloodied head lolling to one side. I blinked, and blinked again, thinking I could shut it out. I couldn't.

I looked up at Brian. His face was bloodless, clenched. "I've got to make some calls," he said, heading over to a bank of phones on the far side of the lobby.

I kept seeing that image, Shane tied to the fence. I was crying now, and I looked over at Jenna, hoping to see something that might reassure me. Jenna, who always knew what to do. But what I saw only made things worse. Tears streamed down her cheeks, and her mouth was twisted and contorted, like somebody was jabbing her with hot needles.

"Sons of bitches," Kevin muttered, wringing his hands. "Fucking sons of bitches."

Nobody said anything. At some point, Brian returned from making his calls.

A door clanged open behind us. Two cops, their hands locked on the arms of a third man, were pulling him through the lobby. He was short, the third man, and his head was bandaged and bloody. Relief surged through me. It was Shane, up and walking.

"Look," I said, grabbing Jenna's arm. "Look!"

She turned to see what I was seeing, and she gasped, which meant she had seen him too. Shane, up on his feet. Shane, not dying.

But then my head cleared, and it all fell apart.

"Oh my God," Jenna said. "J-Town."

"Wait," Brian said. "You know that guy?"

"Yeah. He was a source for an article on the local drug trade I'm working on for the campus paper."

"Did Shane ever mention him?" Brian asked.

"Never."

"What about you?" I said, looking at Kevin, who was conspicuously quiet. "Do you know this J-Town dickwad?" His eyes roamed the lobby, looking everywhere but at me.

"Why would I know him?" he asked.

"That's not an answer."

"No," he said, his gaze finally on me. "I never saw him before in my life."

Brian was staring at Kevin. Not saying anything. Just staring.

"What?" Kevin said.

"Nothing," Brian said. "Nothing."

CHAPTER FIFTEEN

"I don't know about those guys," Jenna said, once we were in her car.

We were back on the road, heading to Juniper. With Jenna's lead foot, we had a good shot at delivering on my promise to be home by eight o'clock.

"I don't know," I said. I still felt shaky, like I couldn't trust the car I was sitting in to hold me up. "Brian seems nice."

"A little too nice, maybe," Jenna said. "Did you see the way he was all handsy with Kevin? He's old enough to be that kid's father."

"Maybe it's like Kevin said. He's kind of like a social worker."

"Yeah, and J-Town was at the hospital because he's a candy striper."

"You think J-Town had something to do with what happened to Shane?"

"I don't know. I mean, it could be a coincidence. I'm guessing this isn't J-Town's first visit to a hospital with a bandage on his head. You've met him. Imagine how many people probably want to punch him on a daily basis."

"Right," I said.

"Still," she said. "If it's a coincidence, it's a weird one."

We were both quiet after that, and with no conversation to distract me, the image of Shane tied to a fence came flooding in. I tried to Photoshop the image, taking the blood away, bringing his outstretched arms down to his side, removing the fence entirely, just leaving Shane, at peace, on the wide-open prairie he loved. But I couldn't make it stick.

When had I left him that message? This was Thursday evening. Jenna had picked me up at my house, what, earlier that day? It felt like so much longer than that. And when had I called Shane? It was late Tuesday night—actually early Wednesday morning, sometime around three in the morning. Jenna said she'd seen him earlier that night at the Pride Alliance meeting, and that he'd wanted her to go with him to Lucky's, but she didn't go. And then he must have gotten home late, passed out, and heard my message the next morning.

Which means the last thing he'd heard from me were the words I left on that voicemail. As Jenna's car wheezed toward Juniper, those words clanged in my head like a church bell.

Have a nice life.

Have a nice life.

Have a nice life.

. . .

I got home to find Dad sitting at the kitchen table. He told me to sit, and he put a bowl of chili and a glass of water in front of me.

"I saw the news," he said.

The smell of the chili made me think I had an appetite, but when I took a bite, I almost gagged. I pushed the bowl to the side.

"Is he going to be okay?" Dad asked.

"I don't know."

"I'm sorry, Ash. I really am."

"For what?"

"For your friend."

"That's all?"

"I don't know what you want me to say."

"That maybe you're sorry for keeping me from him? That maybe you realize this is all your fault! That none of this would have happened if I had just been able to see him!"

My voice was ragged, laced with sudden tears.

"You're just like whoever did this to him!" I shouted. "One look at him and you think he's the wrong kind of person! You have no idea who he is!"

I got up from the table, knocking over my water glass. I had to get away from him, quick, before he could see in my eyes what I was starting to know.

This wasn't his fault. It was mine.

. . .

What little sleep I got that night came in fits. I kept waking up, each time having forgotten, and then remembering, what was happening. At some point I woke to find Dad standing in the doorway. A gray light seeped through the curtains. Seeing Dad there, I was suddenly grateful for him. Despite the terrible things I'd said to him last night, he was still there, looking out for me.

"I'm sorry," I said, unable to even look at him.

"I know you are, Ash."

"I didn't mean it. I was just—"

"Don't worry about it. Grab a shower. I'll make you some eggs. Maybe you should take a day off school."

"Thanks," I said.

I needed the shower. Not just because I reeked, but because I needed to be alone, surrounded by nothing but hot water and white noise. In a shower, you can shut everything else out, and the world shrinks down to just a few feet. For a small sliver of time, I could pretend that none of this was happening. That I was just taking a shower, getting ready to go to school on a normal Friday. That Shane was fine.

When I got out, Dad had the local news on, some story about how to make stuffed kittens out of socks and yarn. I managed to eat half the eggs, which felt like sawdust in my mouth.

The sock kittens eventually gave way to a live shot, and we saw the reporter from yesterday, standing in front of the hospital, her hair and collar flaked with snow. I turned the volume up.

I'm standing outside Presbyterian Hospital, where Shane Deerfield remains in critical condition. According to the Washburn County Sheriff's Office, Deerfield was found beaten and tied to a fence on the east side of Juniper around 6:00 p.m. Wednesday. He was last seen at Lucky's Lounge in Juniper just after midnight Tuesday.

Police are questioning two Juniper residents, Jared Townsend and Nick Crenshaw, both twenty-one, as persons of interest. At the moment, we have no indications of a motive. Back to you in the studio.

They'd left out the part about Shane looking like he was crucified, but that image kept flooding my brain. Shane, bloodied, arms outstretched, left for dead. I felt the eggs coming back up.

"Do you know either of those guys?" Dad asked.

"Jenna knows that Townsend guy," I said, swallowing hard and leaving out the part about having met him myself.

I replayed in my mind what the reporter said about the timeline. If nobody saw Shane between midnight Tuesday and 6:00 p.m. Wednesday, where was he? How long had he been tied to that fence before somebody found him?

I remembered waking up in the middle of the night Tuesday, thinking maybe Shane was throwing pebbles against my window. Was he already on the fence by then? Was he there when I called him, his phone ringing just out of reach? For a moment, I hoped he was. Because that would mean he never heard my message. He wouldn't have had my words in his head as he hung there, beaten and bloodied and alone in the frigid night air.

"Jenna's coming over," I said. "We're going to the hospital."

"They're not going to let you see him."

"I don't care. I just have to be there."

I expected Dad to resist, but he just nodded.

. . .

Back at Presbyterian Hospital, bunches of flowers and cards were piling up just outside the entrance, dotted by the occasional stuffed animal. A few candles struggled to stay lit under the light snow. It's weird, but it took me a minute to connect all this to Shane. What was happening to Shane was happening publicly. Jenna lingered to read the cards, but I headed into the lobby. I knew I'd lose it if I read the things people were saying.

In the lobby, small groups of people were scattered about, noticeably younger than your average hospital visitor. I recognized some of them from the play, including Patrick, who was standing by himself in a corner. I'd heard that the weekend performances had already been cancelled.

Jenna came in and led me over to a group of people she knew from the Pride Alliance and introduced me as Shane's boyfriend. I had this sudden urge to explain that I'd broken up with Shane and didn't deserve the title, but I kept quiet. A couple of girls hugged me. Their tears threatened to unleash my own, but I fought them off. I really didn't want to start crying. I had this sense that if I started, I'd never stop.

Nothing changed until five o'clock, when the local news came back with an update. The reporter who had been at the hospital was now outside the Washburn County Courthouse in Juniper.

This afternoon, Jared Townsend and Nick Crenshaw were arraigned on charges of attempted first-degree murder, aggravated robbery, and kidnapping in the case involving Shane Deerfield, who remains in a coma at Presbyterian Hospital. The two men's girlfriends, Leanne Henson and Becca Chandler, have been charged as accessories after the fact.

The Juniper police described the motive as robbery, though they said Mr. Deerfield's homosexuality may have been a factor. According to members of the local gay community who were in the courtroom today, Deerfield was open about his sexuality and apparently met Townsend and Crenshaw at Lucky's Lounge in Juniper late Tuesday evening.

Brian Cavanaugh is a professor of Social Work at Metropolitan State University and a friend of Deerfield's:

"According to people I've talked to in the gay community, Shane was at the bar, minding his own business, when these two guys started talking to him. They said they were gay, and he said he was too. Now he's in a coma."

Friends of Deerfield say he had no previous acquaintance with Townsend and Crenshaw.

We'll bring you more on this story once we have it.

The crowd at the hospital soon grew, overflowing the lobby and taking over a chunk of the parking lot, despite the falling temps and increasingly heavy snow. Food arrived—pizzas, coffee. The mound of flowers outside was growing so fast it seemed like it was alive.

But the biggest shift was in the media presence. It went from one local station to more than we could count. Hospital security roped off a section of the parking lot just to the side of the main entrance. With all the spotlights, it was like night had become day. Almost lost in the cluster of local reporters, their mics bearing their station call letters, was a more familiar logo. CNN. The story had gone national.

Around eight o'clock, I called Dad, told him I wasn't coming home yet. Jenna and I found a couple of seats in the lobby. I slouched into my chair and fell into a dead sleep.

. . .

"Wake up," Jenna said, nudging my shoulder. I clawed my way out of sleep, disoriented. I couldn't tell if I'd been out for ten minutes or ten hours.

"What?"

"It's Shane's mother. Let's go."

Groggy, I followed Jenna through the sliding doors into the parking lot.

"That's her," Jenna said, pointing toward a woman off to the side, anonymous under a wool hat.

"How do you know?"

"I heard a security guard point her out."

The crowd had grown since I dozed off, numbering probably a hundred now. Lots of people held candles. Others held signs. Signs with Shane's picture on them. Hand-drawn signs that claimed, "Hate Is Not a Wyoming Value."

There was something moving about all of this. People were coming together to demand justice, to say that Shane's life mattered, that their lives mattered. But as one speaker after another took the megaphone, something about this began to feel dirty. These people didn't know Shane. They'd probably never heard his name until just a few hours before. How quickly they'd taken him and made him their own, shaping him toward their own needs, their own politics. Somewhere in that hospital the real Shane Deerfield was fighting for his life, and yet he had already become a symbol, a name to be shouted from a tinny megaphone by people who didn't know the first thing about him.

I looked over at Mrs. Deerfield, alone on the fringe of the crowd. She turned toward me, and our eyes locked. I wanted her to know that I understood, that I wasn't like these people, but she broke the eye contact and, with her head down, slipped away from the crowd, back into the hospital.

"Come on," I said to Jenna.

We followed Mrs. Deerfield into the lobby. I called her name, but she didn't stop. I called out again, "Mrs. Deerfield, please!" and this time she stopped and turned around, waiting as Jenna and I approached.

Standing in front of her, I was suddenly paralyzed. I didn't know how to introduce myself. Could I even call myself Shane's boyfriend?

"I'm Ash," I said, finally, and as I struggled with what to say next, there was a flicker of recognition on her face.

"Ash," she said. "Shane told me about you."

I was suddenly crying, the sobs coming quick and heavy.

"Oh, sweetheart," she said. "Come here." She wrapped me in her arms, and we rocked together, holding each other up. When I got my breathing under control, I introduced Jenna.

"Jenna," Mrs. Deerfield said, and there was a gleam in her eye, the first thing I'd seen that broke the sadness in her face. "I know about you too, dear. Thank you for being such a good friend to my Shane."

Jenna, ever the reporter, sidestepped the emotion and asked how Shane was doing.

Mrs. Deerfield was quiet for a moment, like she couldn't trust herself to get the words out.

"Not good," she said, finally.

"They won't let us see him," I blurted. "And I have to see him." I tried to line up more words in my head, words that might explain why I couldn't be with those people outside, but I was exhausted, and the words wouldn't come. Our eyes met and locked, as they had in the parking lot. She took both my hands in hers.

"I understand," she said. "Come with me. Both of you."

. . .

Time moved differently in the ICU. There were no windows, so there was no night, no day. Just the beeping and whirring of machines. I'd heard those sounds before, the sounds of people being kept alive, people like my mom. At some point I stepped out to call Dad. I told him we were with Shane's parents, and that I wanted to stay. He made me promise to keep in touch.

Mr. and Mrs. Deerfield stayed by Shane's side, behind a curtain in another room, replaced occasionally by Shane's aunt and uncle, or by his brother, who looked to be about sixteen. Jenna and I held back, being careful not to intrude. But at some point—it must have been three or four o'clock, Saturday morning—Mrs. Deerfield asked us if we'd like to spend some time with him.

"You go," Jenna said.

"Are you sure?"

"Yes. I'll come in in a bit."

I thought I was prepared for what I was going to see when I pulled that curtain aside, but I wasn't. Shane's face was swollen, purple like an eggplant. There were stitches everywhere, bloody X-marks holding his face together. His left ear was stitched up, but the stitches weren't holding. Fresh blood trickled from his earlobe, pooling in the crevice of his collarbone.

Something pulled my eye up from the pool of blood, back to the ear. That little bump at the top of his left ear. How many times had my fingers drifted over it, that cute little protrusion, one of the hundred tiny things that made him Shane. Bile rose in my throat. I swallowed it down. I looked back at his face, drawn toward his one partially opened eye, a blazing blue reflecting the bright light over the bed. There was no life behind the eye. It may as well have been a marble, just as hard, just as dead.

My vision blurred and everything got louder. The beeps of the machinery, the whoosh of the thing that was breathing for him. My throat tightened, and I worried that I wouldn't be able to find my next breath.

I wiped my eyes clear and glanced at the screen beside his bed. It was filled with a bunch of numbers I didn't understand, but one that I did. Temp: 106. That's not possible, I thought. That must be a mistake.

I crept to the side of the bed. His hands were bent and curled into tight fists. It was the first sign that he was alive, and that he was suffering.

I sat down by the bed and put my hand on his balled-up fist. I whispered how sorry I was. That I didn't mean what I said on the voicemail. That he was still mine, and I was his, and that this would always be true.

. . .

When I got back to the waiting area, Shane's mom pulled me aside.

"Can we talk?" she asked.

We found a corner of the ICU away from the bustle.

"I don't know how to say this, Ash, but you need to know. Shane was—is—HIV positive. The doctor just told us. It showed up in the bloodwork."

I didn't know what to say. Normally this news would be shocking, and I guess it was, but it didn't matter. Not when so much else was broken.

"Did you know?" she asked.

I shook my head.

"Maybe this is none of my business," she said, "but I don't really care anymore about what is and isn't my business. You should get tested, sweetie. If you haven't already."

Even as her son lay in a coma, she was worried about me.

"That's not really necessary," I said. "Shane and I . . . we never . . . I never . . ." I found it strangely embarrassing to have to admit to Shane's mother that we'd never had sex. It was like admitting some sort of failure.

"Really?"

"Really. I wanted to, but he said we should go slow. I didn't understand it. I thought maybe he just didn't want to. But now . . ."

Her eyes brightened, glistened.

"He was protecting you," she said.

All I could do was nod.

"That's Shane," she said. "That's Shane to a T." She squeezed my hand. "I'm so glad I got to meet you, Ash. I hope we can stay in touch. After." She choked back a sob. "There's so much I want to know."

. . .

Around six in the morning, I stepped away to call Dad. When I got back to the ICU, the family was gathered around Shane's bed.

"What's happening?" I asked Jenna.

"He's failing," she said.

Jenna and I stood at the window to Shane's room and held hands. We couldn't hear what was being said, but we watched as Shane's family took turns saying goodbye. Kissing him, touching him. We watched as they held one another's hand, forming a protective circle around Shane's bed. We watched as the nurse took the tube out of his throat. We watched as he started to choke. We watched as his brother collapsed, wailing, to the ground.

We watched as Shane became perfectly still.

CHAPTER
SIXTEEN

Jenna and I stumbled out of the hospital just as dawn was breaking. The parking lot was full of people, but eerily quiet. The silence was thick, broken only by the occasional sob. People held candles, their flames diminished by the growing light of day. I felt empty, hollowed out.

"I can't be here," I said.

"Me neither," Jenna said.

We were quiet on the drive north, not saying a word. Nothing felt real. I couldn't believe this was actually happening. That Shane was dead. It seemed only yesterday that I'd watched him sleep, the morning sun bouncing off his chest. How could he be gone?

I must have drifted off, lulled to sleep by the tinny racket of Jenna's car. When I woke up, we were parked outside my house. I tried to work up the energy to say something, but nothing came. I was out of the car and halfway up the walk before Jenna called after me.

"Ash!" she yelled. "Don't you fucking disappear on me!"

How did she know that to disappear was all I wanted?

"I won't," I said.

When I got inside, I found my dad sitting at the table in the too-bright light of the kitchen, drinking coffee. He stood up when he saw me, not saying anything, not moving.

"He's gone," I said.

"I know. I heard it on the news."

We both just stood there, neither of us knowing how to bridge the space between us. But then he said my name.

That was all it took. I rushed forward and collapsed into him, desperate for something that felt permanent.

. . .

Dad said I could take a couple of days off from school if I wanted. Except for the occasional trip to the bathroom, I stayed in bed for forty-eight hours. All I wanted was to be still and quiet in a dark room.

This was exactly what happened after Mom died. I retreated to my bed and refused to leave. Dad would leave bits of food by my bed, a glass of water. Occasionally he would try to lure me into the rest of the house, but I'd just roll over and pull the blankets over my head.

Now it was all happening again, even down to the plates of food. I woke once to find a bagel, another time to find the bagel replaced by a chocolate doughnut. A glass of water sat untouched. To the extent that I registered sound—a door shutting, a pot rattling in the kitchen—it seemed to be coming from some distant world, sound waves traveling through murk before reaching my ears.

At some point, I felt a presence in the room and remembered the morning Shane showed up to take me to breakfast. I didn't want to open my eyes, because I knew that, if I did, he wouldn't be there. When I finally opened them, I saw Jenna, perched on a chair by my bed.

"You're cute when you sleep," she said.

"What?"

"You're cute when you sleep. You bunch the blanket under your chin, and you get all scrunchy, like a baby monkey. It's adorable."

Her voice sounded strange, like she was trying to sound like herself, but failing.

"What day is it?" I asked.

"Monday. Your dad called me at the paper. Said you'd been sleeping ever since I dropped you off. I told him just to let you sleep, but he was worried about you. So, here I am. I'm supposed to, like, fix you. Or whatever."

She got up and threw open the curtains. Even the gray morning was too bright for my light-deprived eyes, and I pulled the blankets over my head.

"You missed Brian and Kevin on *Larry King* last night," she said, sitting back down.

"What?" I said, still shielding myself with the blankets.

"On CNN. It's weird seeing people you know on television. It's like they're suddenly different people. Kevin was wearing a tie, which made him look like a kid whose mom had dressed him for the school picture. He didn't say much. Brian did most of the talking."

"What did he say?"

"That what happened to Shane was a hate crime, and that it was indicative of a larger culture of violence against gay people. He was good. I mean, he was obviously torn up about what happened, but he managed to make it mean something."

I wasn't sorry I missed it. I was sure Brian was good, but I wasn't ready for Shane's death to mean anything. It was the most meaningless thing I could imagine.

"Oh," she said, "and Clinton issued a statement."

"Who?"

"Bill Clinton. The President."

This took me longer than it should have to process. Why would the President of the United States issue a statement about Shane?

"He said what happened to Shane is all the more reason for Congress to pass his hate crimes bill. Which was nice, I guess, except for the fact that he's clearly using Shane to distract from the blowjob he got from that intern. It's so gross."

I needed her to stop talking. The last thing I wanted to think about was a presidential blowjob.

"Come on," she said. "I told your dad I'd get you out into the world again. Nothing too difficult yet. Maybe just a bowl of cereal on the couch. We'll do the harder stuff later."

. . .

Jenna was surfing from one overly cheerful morning talk show to another when Christopher emerged from his room. He hovered for a minute before sitting next to me on the couch. I'd managed to avoid him since that day he admitted he'd sold Shane drugs. Or maybe he'd managed to avoid me.

He was breathing heavy, like he always did in the morning, his nasal passages full of gunk. He kept clearing his throat, and the rattle of phlegm made my stomach turn.

"Listen," he said. "I'm sorry about your friend."

His voice sounded different, less hard.

"Even though he was a faggot?" I asked. It was satisfying to throw that word back at him, the same word he'd flung at me. At Shane.

He sighed.

"Nobody deserves what happened to him," he said. "I don't care who you are. Or what you've done."

At the top of the hour, the talk shows gave way to hard news, and Jenna held the channel on a report about Shane. They ran a long segment on the attack and the investigation. J-Town and that Crenshaw guy, as well as their idiot girlfriends, had spilled their entire guts while I was sleeping. Their statements, along with various police reports and interviews, added up to a detailed account of what happened.

Shane arrived at Lucky's around 10 p.m. Tuesday. He had been drinking earlier in the day at The Old Brick, using a fake ID, and then had attended the Pride Alliance meeting on campus. When he got to Lucky's, he took a seat near the end of the bar. The bartender had seen him there four or five times before. Shane ordered a beer, and he and the bartender exchanged small talk. The bartender noted that Shane stood out in the crowd because he was so neatly dressed and polite. He was also a good tipper. After the beer, he ordered a Jack and Coke, and then another beer.

J-Town and Nick Crenshaw arrived around eleven thirty. In contrast to Shane, they were grungily dressed. They ordered a pitcher of beer and sat four or five stools down from Shane. Crenshaw paid for the pitcher by dumping handfuls of coins on the counter.

The two men spent twenty or so minutes chatting up the girls next to them, but they weren't getting anywhere. They eventually went to the back of the bar and hung out near the pool table. At some point, witnesses saw Shane go over and talk to J-Town. According to statements from both J-Town and his girlfriend, Leanne, Shane was hitting on him, suggesting they hook up. When Shane went to the bathroom, J-Town and Crenshaw hatched a plan to rob him. They would pretend they were gay, suggest a hookup, and then, once they had lured Shane out of the bar, take whatever money he had.

The three men were seen leaving the bar together shortly after midnight. They got into a black pickup. Crenshaw got in the driver's seat, J-Town on the passenger's side. Shane sat between them. It took them four or five minutes to get to the east side of town, near the new Walmart. It was around here, J-Town told the police, that Shane grabbed J-Town's crotch and licked his ear. This is when J-Town said, "Guess what. We're not gay. And you're getting jacked." J-Town hit Shane in the head, though he couldn't remember whether he used his fist or the butt of his .357 Magnum. He ordered Shane to hand over his wallet, which Shane did. It contained just twenty dollars.

Crenshaw kept driving, while J-Town continued to beat Shane, punching him four or five more times. When asked why he kept beating Shane, even after he realized he wasn't worth robbing, J-Town said he wanted to teach him a lesson not to come on to straight people.

They drove through Crescent Heights and then turned onto Prairie View Drive. At the dead end, Crenshaw steered the truck down a dirt path, going about four hundred yards before he ran up against a dip in the land and a split rail fence. He turned off the truck.

Crenshaw watched as J-Town started to drag Shane out of the right-side door. Shane fought back, but he was already weak and wounded. When J-Town got him on the ground, he continued to slam his head with the butt of the gun and to kick him. Crenshaw stood to the side, laughing. Shane screamed for mercy, begging for his life. He told them he had $150 back at his apartment, which they could have if they just left him alone.

J-Town ordered Crenshaw to get some rope out of the truck and then told him to tie Shane to the fence. Crenshaw did as he was told, but when J-Town starting punching Shane again, Crenshaw told him to stop, at which point J-Town struck Crenshaw in the mouth with the butt of the gun, opening a serious gash on his lip.

J-Town took Shane's shoes off, throwing one into the brush and the other toward the truck. He asked Shane if he could read the truck's license plate. He wanted to find out if he would be able to identify them later. Shane read the numbers to him. This made J-Town even angrier. He slammed Shane in the head with the gun three more times, caving in his skull just behind his left ear.

Leaving Shane there, unconscious, but still breathing, Crenshaw and J-Town drove back into Juniper. Near the intersection of 19th and Locust, they ran into two guys who were vandalizing a car. Crenshaw challenged the men, calling them wetbacks. One of them pulled out a knife, the other a small club. J-Town sprinted back to the truck and got the .357 Magnum. He rushed one of the men and slammed the gun into his head. The man managed to clip J-Town in the side of the head with his club. This is the wound that would land J-Town in the same hospital as Shane.

The cops arrived, and J-Town and Crenshaw ran off in opposite directions. The cops caught Crenshaw, and when they walked him back to the truck, they saw the gun, covered in blood. Shining a light inside the cab, they saw a small brown loafer.

J-Town managed to get away, making his way back to Leanne's apartment.

Meanwhile, Shane remained tied to the fence. He was there for eighteen hours. It would have been longer, but around 6:00 p.m., a college student lost control of his mountain bike and fell off. When he got up, he saw something that looked like blood on a face about fifteen feet away. At first he thought it was a scarecrow, but when he got closer, he found Shane, struggling to breathe through the one nostril that remained partly open.

The cyclist ran to a nearby house, and the homeowner called the police. The officer responding, Brenda McGovern, thought she had found a thirteen-year-old boy, given how small he was. After she untied him, she cradled him in her arms.

"Little boy," she said, "don't die, please don't die."

We were quiet as the channel went to commercial. I tried to focus on the images on the screen. A lady in a white dress, running through a field of yellow flowers, chased by a small dog. It was a commercial for allergy medication, and it gave me all I wanted. A pretty lady. A beautiful day. A happy dog. Maybe if I just kept my attention focused on this, I wouldn't have to think about everything I'd just heard.

But then the allergy commercial gave way to one about trucks, and I was right back in it. Shane's last conscious moments. That image of him tied to the fence was seared into my brain, but I hadn't let myself see the rest of it. Shane in a bar, being friendly, thinking he was safe. Shane in that truck, suddenly aware that he was in trouble, but unable to do anything about it. Shane, being dragged, and beaten, and tied up. Begging for his life.

It took me a minute to realize I was shivering. I tried to stop, but that only made it worse. When my teeth started to chatter, Jenna put her arms around me. For a moment, I thought Christopher might do the same, but he just got up and went into his room.

Jenna and I sat like that for a long time. Me shaking so bad I might fly to pieces. Jenna trying to hold me together.

CHAPTER SEVENTEEN

I stayed home again on Tuesday, replaying the news report over and over in my mind. So much of it made a painful kind of sense. Shane, drinking alone in a bar, maybe hitting on a straight guy, touching someone who didn't want to be touched by him. When I thought back to the trouble he got himself into in Cody, all of that was plausible.

But there was something about the whole thing that seemed off. Why would Shane have agreed to leave with *both* of them? Let's say he was trying to pick up J-Town. When J-Town said, 'My boy Crenshaw's coming with,' wouldn't that have set off all sorts of alarm bells? Shane might have been drunk, but he wasn't stupid. He had to know that was a recipe for something other than a hookup. Especially with guys he'd never met.

Which left me with a question: why did he get in that truck?

. . .

I wanted to stay home again Wednesday, but Dad had cut me all the slack he was willing to cut.

"You have to go back to school sometime," he said. "Maybe it will do you good. Get your mind off things."

It's weird the things parents think.

It started on the bus. I avoided taking the bus to school whenever I could, opting for the fifteen-minute bike ride instead. But as the weather got colder and the winds harsher, the bus was really the only option.

At first it was just a slight buzzing, something a little behind me, maybe on the far periphery. By the time I got to school and was walking through the main lobby, the buzzing had become visual. You could see it in people's faces, an interest that wasn't there before.

People knew.

My scalp itched, like tiny birds were pecking at my head. I tallied up the people who knew about me and Shane. Dad, Jenna, Brian, Kevin, Christopher. I guess Brian could have tipped someone off, given the way he was working the media. But who would he know at Juniper High? Could it have been Christopher? But he probably didn't want his brother to be publicly connected to anything remotely gay. Then I remembered meeting those kids from the Pride Alliance at the hospital, being introduced as Shane's boyfriend. It could have been any of them, maybe someone with a brother or sister at Juniper High. Ultimately, the source didn't really matter. In Juniper, information, once it's out, travels like the wind, quick and unbroken across the flat prairie. Especially if it involves a newly visible queer.

So, yeah, the morning was full of buzzing, but nobody said anything. At least not to me. They just stared, pointing at me with their eyes instead of their hands. It took until lunch for someone to include me in the conversation that was whirling all around me. I was sitting by myself, hunched into my hoodie, sopping up pizza grease with a too-thin napkin, when I felt a presence.

"What's up, Ash?"

It was Ryan.

"Mind if I sit down?" he asked, not waiting for an answer. He did a quick scan of the cafeteria, like he was checking to see if anybody was watching. They were.

"So," he said. "Is it true?"

I thought about lying. What right did he have—what right did anybody have—to know what had happened between me and Shane? As Shane was becoming more of a public figure by the hour, it seemed even more important to keep some piece of him to myself. But then I remembered the rumors that fly like the wind and thought, what's the point?

"Probably," I said.

"Probably?"

"Well, I don't really know what you're asking."

I waited as he worked up the nerve to say the actual words.

"Is it true that Shane Deerfield was your boyfriend?"

Why did every question have to be so complicated? I mean, yes, he was, but then he wasn't, but only if he got my breakup voicemail, which he probably didn't, because when I left it, he was tied to a fence with his skull crushed in.

"Yes," I said.

Ryan gave the cafeteria another scan before turning his attention back to me. "I'm sorry," he said.

"For what?"

"For your loss."

That's all it took for the tears to come spilling out. I did what I could to staunch the flow, to suck up the snot that was unleashed with the tears. It wasn't pretty.

Ryan looked like he'd started a fire and didn't know how to put it out.

"I'm sorry," I said, pulling myself together. "I didn't know that was going to happen."

"It's cool," he said, handing me a napkin. "How long were you guys together?"

And there it was, the question I didn't realize I'd been dreading. Because the answer wasn't what I wanted it to be. I wanted to be able to say things like: "We'd just celebrated our one-year anniversary," or "God, I don't even know anymore. It feels like it's been forever." But I didn't have answers like that. Also, I didn't even know how to do the math. When did we start being "together"? That shirtless day on the rock when I kissed him? That night on the swings, when he was about to kiss me, but didn't?

"Six weeks," I said. It had been six weeks since I first saw Shane, on a big fake horse, singing about corn. And that was the beginning of everything, even if neither of us knew it.

"So," Ryan said. "Not that long."

Tell it to my heart, asshole. My face must have done something because he started to backpedal.

"No. I just meant that, I don't know, maybe . . . fuck, I don't know what I meant. Six weeks is long enough, right? I mean, I guess. I've never really dated anybody. I don't know what it would be like. To, you know, lose them."

If I had tried to explain it, it wouldn't have made sense. I could have rambled on and on about Einstein and the theory of relativity, but even that wouldn't have explained anything. I mean, how is it that those six weeks felt like a lifetime? How can you be that shattered by someone so quickly?

Maybe it was because six weeks was exactly six weeks longer than I'd ever thought I'd get. Being a gay kid in Juniper didn't exactly allow for dreaming.

"It sucks," was all I could say.

The bell rang for the end of lunch.

"Listen," Ryan said. "I know I've been an asshole. But if you ever want to talk? Just let me know."

He took his tray and left before the tears started up again.

. . .

After lunch, I found myself heading to Mr. Lindquist's classroom. I hadn't planned on seeing him, but I guess some part of me sensed that a conversation about the nature of reality might be a welcome distraction.

He was writing on the board, a string of numbers and letters, and a bunch of symbols I didn't recognize.

"Do you know what this is?" he asked, eyes still on the board, his face bright with excitement.

"No idea."

"It's Einstein's equation for the theory of relativity. See, on the right side you have the energy of the universe, including dark energy. The left side decribes the shape of the universe, its geometry. But that equal sign is where the action is. It's what explains how the Sun warps space-time, and why the Earth orbits the Sun. That equal sign is where gravity comes from. It's elegant. Beautiful, actually."

"Is this for our class?" I asked, suddenly worried that the one class I loved was about to turn into just another version of calculus.

"Oh, heavens no," he said, still staring at the equation. "This is for Physics II. You should take it next semester. I think you'd like it."

"I'm not so good at math," I said.

He turned away from the board, seeming to register my presence for the first time.

"Math is just another language for the concepts you're already thinking about in my class. It's a language you can learn, just like Spanish."

"I kind of suck at Spanish too."

He put the chalk down in the tray, wiping the dust on his khakis. Then he picked the chalk up again, stared at it for a second, put it back in the tray, and wiped his hands again.

"I try not to put too much stock in rumors," he said, his eyes meeting mine for the first time. "All kinds of things get said about people in this town. Most of them don't contain a shred of truth."

I could have agreed, could have said, yeah, whatever you're hearing? That's a pack of lies. But he seemed to be offering me something, something I might need.

"And then sometimes they're true," I said.

He sighed, looked down at his shoes, and then back up at me.

"How are you, Ash?"

I thought about it for a moment.

"I don't know."

"That makes sense," he said, sitting down at his desk. "People think grief is an actual emotion, but in fact, it's really just confusion. The mind and the body don't know what to think, what to do."

He seemed on the verge of saying something else but stopped himself. He fidgeted with the things on his desk, moving the stapler from one side of the desk to the other, and then moving it back.

"I should probably get going," I said. Talking to the gay kid about his dead boyfriend was more than he'd signed up for. I was halfway toward the door before he said anything.

"What are your college plans?" he asked. I turned around, surprised by the question, though I shouldn't have been. I mean, it was my senior year, and I knew I was supposed to be obsessing over college brochures and applications.

"I'll probably just go to the university," I said. "My dad works there, so I'd get a big break on tuition."

"It's a perfectly good school," he said. "And they have a fine physics department. There's just one problem."

"What's that?"

"It's in Juniper." I chuckled, thinking he was making a joke, but he wasn't smiling.

"You don't like Juniper?" I asked.

He was about to move the stapler again but didn't. He just clutched his right hand with his left, trying to keep it still.

"I've made a life here. But it's not the life I might have made somewhere else."

"What do you mean?"

He sighed.

"Guys like us? We're maybe not such a good fit for small towns."

"Guys like us?"

He didn't say anything.

"You mean physics nerds?" I asked.

He looked up from his desk.

"We have more things in common than physics, Ash."

I suddenly got it, the thing he wanted to say, but couldn't. Because you couldn't be a gay high school teacher in Juniper. And if you were, you certainly couldn't tell anybody. And if you did tell somebody, it absolutely couldn't be your only gay student. People would automatically assume you were up to something pervy and you'd lose your job.

"I'm just saying," he continued, "it's a big world out there. You ought to go see some of it."

As much as I hated Juniper, I'd never actually thought about leaving. That's the thing about small towns. They narrow your vision—make it hard to imagine other ways of living.

I wanted to keep talking, to let him know that I understood, but I could tell this was as far as he could go—as far as we could go.

"I'll think about it," I said.

"See you tomorrow," he said. He went back to rearranging his desk. Afraid, perhaps, that he'd said too much, even though he'd said almost nothing.

I turned to leave. "Mr. Lindquist?" I said, with one hand on the door frame.

"Yes, Ash?"

"Thanks."

"Of course," he said, returning his face to its public setting, cheery and unassuming. Whatever door had been opened was shut again. "Of course."

. . .

The buzzing followed me the rest of the day, and it was still with me when I trudged up the steps of the bus. It surrounded me as I took my regular seat in the back. Maybe because I was distracted by the buzzing, I found myself getting off at 11th Street, before the stop for my house, but just a five-minute walk from Shane's apartment.

Once I realized where I was, I couldn't stop myself. I wanted to see Shane's apartment. It was more than that, actually. I wanted to crawl through the window Jenna had pushed me through just weeks before, and I wanted to land on Shane's bed, and I wanted to smell him. I wanted to smell his sheets, and his clothes, and the general Shane-ness of his apartment. I wanted to take his molecules inside me, because that's what smelling is, right? I mean, it's gross, but when you smell something, you're literally taking the particles of that thing—a flower, a dead squirrel, shit—into your nostrils. I wanted to find whatever pieces of Shane remained, and I wanted to take them inside me.

It was too late when I saw the van out front, the big red CNN logo on its side. A woman with a microphone came at me, trailed by a camera guy. I recognized the woman. I'd seen her on television during floods and tornadoes.

"Are you Ash?" she said, pointing the mic in my face. "Can we ask you a few questions?"

She was perky and eager in a way that felt absolutely wrong, given the circumstances.

"What are you doing here?" I asked.

"We were hoping to speak with the parents. We got a tip that they'd be here later. But we'd love to talk to you. Can you tell us about Shane? You're the boyfriend, right?"

I was suddenly aware of my heart beating, and I struggled to catch my next breath.

"I don't really want to talk to you," I said, turning around, but the camera followed me, and so did the reporter's microphone.

"I know this is hard," she said, "and I'm so sorry for your loss. But maybe you can tell us something about the real Shane, the Shane only you knew."

She made it sound so simple, like you could somehow capture the essence of a person by finding the right words. But when I finally opened my mouth, the only words I could find were the kinds of things you could say about anyone.

"He was kind," I said, trying to slow my breathing. "He was generous. He was thoughtful."

The reporter looked disappointed, but she thanked me for my time.

As I was leaving, I noticed a face peeking out of an upstairs window. The old lady. I wondered if she understood that the CNN van outside her apartment was somehow related to the fact that she no longer received sweet little notes filled with bad poetry and smiley faces.

. . .

The phone was ringing when I walked into the house. Dad was in the kitchen, staring at it. After a few more rings, he took the phone out of its cradle and hung it back up. It was quiet for a minute, then rang again. Dad lifted the handset, hung it back up. When it rang again, he yanked the cord out of the wall.

"Word's out," he said.

"Yeah," I said. "I know."

I told him about school and about being ambushed by the CNN crew.

"This is going to be a circus," he said, "and there's nothing that says you have to be part of it. Maybe you should talk to Jenna about how to handle these idiots."

"Good idea."

"In the meantime, don't answer the door. And we'll leave the phone unplugged for a while."

I headed toward my room, but Dad called me back.

"What?" All I wanted was the quiet isolation of my bedroom.

"You know you're going to feel better, right? At some point? There's going to come a time when you won't feel what you're feeling."

I knew he was trying to reassure me, but it had the opposite effect. If I wasn't feeling *this*, what would I feel instead? At least the loss was tangible evidence of what Shane and I had.

"When your mom died," he continued, "I didn't think I could go on.

I mean, I literally couldn't imagine it. And that was terrifying. Because there were you and your brother to take care of."

I couldn't believe we were talking about this. We never talked about this.

"So how'd you do it?" I asked.

"I just did," he said. "I don't remember much about those first few days and weeks, but I—we—got through it. We just kept going. That's what I discovered, Ash. People are enormously resilient. If you had told me I'd have to live the rest of my life without your mom, I would have said, no way. That would be impossible. But then we lost her, and I kept going. It's just what happens."

Something opened up inside me.

"I think about her every day," I said. "But it hurts to think about her."

"I know. Me too. But it's going to hurt less and less. Eventually, our memories of her will bring us comfort rather than pain."

I tried to call up a memory of Mom that didn't hurt. Nothing came at first. My brain was too crammed with images of her in a hospital bed, tubes everywhere. But, with a little more effort, I was able to see her in that ridiculous apron she used to wear, the one that said, "No Bitchin' in my Kitchen."

I remembered the day she tried to teach me how to make homemade pasta. This was a problem since she didn't have the first clue about how to make homemade pasta. But that didn't matter. What she brought to the process—what she brought to everything—was enthusiasm. By the end of the afternoon, we were both covered in flour and dough, and there was pasta everywhere. Long wobbly strands hanging from cabinet knobs. Misshapen lumps (they were supposed to be ravioli) scattered across the counter. I found an ill-advised attempt at tortellini in my hair.

We ended up ordering pizza.

I waited for the memory to hurt, but it mostly didn't. Progress, I guess.

But with Shane? Every single thing I remembered about him hurt.

I couldn't imagine a time when it wouldn't.

"By the way, this came for you," Dad said, handing me an envelope.

"What is it?'

"Tickets to Shane's memorial service. For you and Jenna."

"Wait, you need a ticket?"

"They're expecting thousands. They needed some way to make sure the folks that mattered most to Shane will be able to get in."

CHAPTER EIGHTEEN

The morning of Shane's memorial, I woke to a cold rain. By the time I was out of the shower, the rain had turned to snow—a big, lumpy wet snow. The weather lady said this was going to be a bad one.

I felt stupid in my itchy dress shirt and a tie I hadn't worn since Mom's funeral. Jenna was wearing a leather skirt, and she'd swapped out her usual T-shirt and army jacket for a brown suede jacket over a fuzzy top, the fuzz poofing out of the jacket. She'd also turned up the volume on her makeup. Her lips were the brightest shade of red I'd ever seen on lips. She caught me staring.

"Shane would have wanted this," she said.

The memorial was in Casper, where Shane had grown up, and the two-and-a-half-hour drive was clearly going to take longer, given the weather. Once we were on the road, Jenna's tin can of a Honda struggled against the snow, which was coming at us sideways, especially near Medicine Bow, where the wind was absolutely crazy. But Jenna was undaunted, gripping the wheel and leaning forward. She said we'd be fine, as long as I didn't talk to her.

That pathetic CNN interview with me had been airing nonstop over the last twenty-four hours. It was actually worse than I thought it would be, not because of the stupid things I said, but because of the caption at the bottom, which described me as a "friend of Deerfield." I had been worried about the wrong thing. I thought being outed in front of millions of people was the worst thing that could happen. Turns out being erased was. It was like losing Shane all over again.

When we got closer to the church, I noticed green and yellow ribbons in storefront windows, the same ribbons that had sprung up on campus shortly after Shane's death. We were off the highway, so I figured it was safe to talk to Jenna again.

"Why green and yellow?" I asked.

"The green stands for peace," she said. "The yellow for tolerance."

"That's nice."

"Is it really? Is that what you're hoping for? To be tolerated?"

I thought about it for a minute.

"It's better than being killed."

It was snowing harder now. We found a parking space a few blocks away and headed toward the church, trying to keep each other from falling on the increasingly slippery sidewalk. We were a couple of blocks away when we heard shouting.

"God hates fags! God hates fags! God hates fags!"

"Shit," Jenna said.

"What is that?" I asked.

We passed a row of news vans, their satellite dishes catching the snow. We followed the lights from the TV crews to the park across the street from the church. The chanting got louder as we pushed our way through the crowd.

"It's Fred Phelps," Jenna said.

"Who's Fred Phelps?"

"Reverend Fred Phelps, of the Westboro Baptist Church. They're from somewhere in Kansas."

"What're they doing here?"

"They protest gay funerals. Mostly AIDS victims."

There were maybe fourteen or fifteen people in a roped-off area of the park, surrounded by press. A much larger group of people was trying to drown out the chanting. The chanters were all holding signs: "No Tears for Queers," "No Fags in Heaven," "God Hates Fags," "No Special Laws for Fags," "AIDS Cures Fags." Some in the crowd were children. One girl, looking no more than ten, held up a sign showing two stick figures engaged in anal sex. The text read "Fag Sin." In the middle of the group was a tall, thin man wearing a cowboy hat and a red, white, and blue jacket. He was holding up a board with a huge picture of Shane on it, cartoon flames licking the edges. "Shane in Hell" was written in bold letters at the bottom.

"That's Phelps in the middle," Jenna said. "The asshole with the cowboy hat."

The chanting died down, only to start up again.

"Faggot Shane, burn in hell! Faggot Shane, burn in hell! Faggot Shane, burn in hell!"

I was trembling. I wanted to smash things.

"We have to go," Jenna said.

We fought our way through the crowd and crossed the street. A line of police officers stood in front of the church, several of them with dogs on leashes. We presented our tickets to the ushers at the door, one of whom led us to seats about halfway to the front. The sanctuary was packed. There were flowers everywhere, more than I'd ever seen in one place, and their fragrance filled the air.

I was still shaking from the scene outside. I closed my eyes and tried to focus on the sweet smell of the flowers.

There was a bustle down front. The family was being seated. I caught a glimpse of Shane's mom's face before she was obscured by the rows of people behind her. Gone was the strength I'd come to rely on at the hospital. In its place, only brokenness.

I wish I could remember everything people said about Shane during the service. I'm sure it was nice. To be honest, though, I heard very little of it. People spoke, but I couldn't get myself to focus on the actual words. My brain was too full of the hateful words I'd heard outside.

When the priest called people to the front for communion, I stood.

Jenna looked at me like I was crazy.

"The urn," I said. I wanted to see the urn containing Shane's ashes, to get as close to it—to Shane—as possible. She took my hand, and we joined the others in line.

"I'm not sure we're supposed to be doing this," she said. "I haven't been baptized."

"I have. You can be my plus one."

When our turn came, we took the cracker, avoiding eye contact with the priest. We were more focused on the urn, which was sitting on a cloth-draped table just in front of the altar. It was beautiful, a soft blue that called to mind a Wyoming sky. It caught what little light bled through the upper windows from the snow-blanketed day, and it seemed to glow. We watched as people paused in front of it. Some of them touched it. Others couldn't bring themselves to do more than lay their hands on the cloth it sat on.

When Jenna and I took our place in front of the urn, she placed her hand on it. Her fingers lingered there, in a caress. She looked at me, but I couldn't make myself touch it. The urn suddenly seemed so wrong, a feeble attempt to cover up the truth of what had happened. Shane shouldn't have been cremated, his mangled body hidden in this beautiful piece of ceramic. He should be laid out here, open casket, for everyone to see. Wounds and blood and all. People should have to see what they did to him.

I glanced over my shoulder and caught a glimpse of Shane's mom, her face crumpled in grief. I immediately regretted what I had been thinking. No mother should have to see the bloodied body of her murdered son. The urn was for her, not for me.

"Let's go," I said to Jenna, head down, unable to look Shane's mom in the eye.

. . .

When we got back to the house, I invited Jenna in for hot chocolate. I didn't want to be alone.

Dad was out somewhere, probably at the university. Sometimes the landscaping crew got called in during a heavy storm to plow the roads. Christopher was in the kitchen drinking coffee, and Jenna sat with him while I made the hot chocolate. It was that time of early evening when the shocking brightness of the kitchen was a welcome defense against the coming darkness.

Jenna was telling Christopher about Phelps and his band of haters.

"What a bunch of idiots," Christopher said.

I should have left it alone. We were sitting there, drinking hot chocolate, and Christopher was acting decent. If I had kept quiet, maybe everything would have been different. But I couldn't. I could still hear the slurs Christopher hurled at me that night Shane came over, the things he said.

"Seems it wasn't too long ago you didn't think twice about calling me a faggot," I snarled. "So that makes you an idiot too, I guess."

"Fuck you," he said. "I'm not like those rednecks from Kansas."

"What makes you any different?" I asked.

"Well, for one, I'm not stupid enough to stand in a snowstorm and protest a memorial service."

"Maybe you're just lazy," I said. "Hateful and lazy might be worse than Phelps and his crew. At least they were doing something."

"Ash," Jenna said, a warning in her voice. "It's been a long day. Can we not?"

It had been a long day. And there were so many long days to come.

"I don't think either of you knows what it's like to be gay in this town," I said, my voice breaking. "Whatever it was that got Shane killed, it's still here."

"J-Town and that Crenshaw kid are in jail," Christopher said. "They're going to be there for a long time."

"I'm not talking about individual people," I said. "I'm talking about something in the air I have to breathe every single day. It's thick with hatred for people like me. For people like Shane. And now everybody knows

I'm a faggot, which is apparently enough to get you killed." I remembered the buzzing that followed me around at school on Wednesday. It would be so easy for that buzzing to turn into violence.

"So you don't need to tell me it's been a long day," I said. "I know it's been a long day. Tomorrow's going to be another one. And so's the day after that."

"Don't be a little pussy," Christopher snapped. "You don't have anything to worry about. Nobody's gonna hurt you."

"God! How stupid can you be?!" I yelled. "They killed Shane!"

Christopher didn't say anything, and I thought maybe he was going to retreat.

"You think you know what's happening here," he said. "You're certain of it."

"What's your point?"

"I'm just saying you might want to be a little less certain. There's a lot you don't know."

"Like what?"

He paused again, like he was deciding how much to say.

"That story about Shane at Lucky's?" he said. "Running into J-Town and Crenshaw, guys he'd never met before, and getting into that truck with them? Does that make sense to you?"

"Why wouldn't it?" Jenna asked. "People do stupid shit in bars all the time."

"You know what a small town this is, right?" Christopher said. "Well, there's an even smaller part of it, filled with people who spend every waking minute looking for meth. And in that world, everybody knows everybody. No exceptions."

"You're saying Shane knew those guys?" I asked. "That they knew him?"

"I'm not saying anything," Christopher said. "Just that you don't have anything to be afraid of."

He got up from the table and put his mug in the sink.

"If you're smart," he said, "you'll forget every bit of this. Shane, J-Town, the whole damn thing. Don't go looking into corners.

"But whatever you end up doing," he said, heading toward his bedroom, "keep me the fuck out of it."

. . .

It took me forever to fall asleep. Phelps, the memorial, that conversation with Christopher, all of it had my brain whirring. When I finally did nod off, it was a fitful sleep, troubled by a vivid dream of Shane, as Curly, covered in stage blood. I jolted awake from the dream in a cold sweat. It was still dark out. I spent the rest of the night, sleepless, wondering what Christopher wasn't telling us.

CHAPTER NINETEEN

Jenna and I had agreed to meet for lunch Saturday at the Friendly Grill. The sky was clear, which made it even colder, and the wind was brutal, whipping right into my face as I turned the corner at Elm Street. The ten-minute walk was enough to numb my ears, and I thought about what Shane had endured, left in the cold for eighteen hours. I wanted to believe the doctors, who insisted that Shane was unconscious after the beating, but in my mind he was always alert, his eyes bright with fear.

I found Jenna in a corner booth hovering over an omelet. I ordered a burger and a coffee.

"You look like shit," she said.

"Thanks."

"No sleep?"

"Not much."

"Me neither."

Jenna shook hot sauce on her omelet and scooped up a big bite.

"I've been thinking about what Christopher told us," she said, her mouth half full of eggs. "About Shane maybe knowing J-Town and Crenshaw."

"Me too."

I took a big slurp of coffee, trying to warm myself after the walk.

"J-Town told the cops that he and Crenshaw didn't know Shane," I said. "They just pretended to be gay so they could rob him. But why would J-Town make up a story that makes him a gay-bashing robber? How does that help him?"

"I know. It doesn't make sense."

"So, if we believe Christopher, everybody's lying. J-Town. Crenshaw. Shane's friends, all of whom said Shane didn't know these guys."

"Right," she said.

"He never said anything to you about J-Town?"

"Not once."

"So maybe Christopher's just blowing smoke. He hated Shane, so now he's trying to make Shane something other than the poor gay victim."

"Maybe," Jenna said.

I took a bite of my burger, and another, and then I scarfed down the whole thing. When I looked back up, Jenna seemed lost in thought.

"What?" I asked.

"It's just, Christopher was right about one thing. The meth world around here? It's super tight. People know each other."

"Okay, but that still doesn't explain why J-Town told us he didn't know Shane."

"Meth heads lie," she said. "It's the only thing they know how to do. Also, remember how tweaked out J-Town was? He literally didn't know what day it was. We can't trust a thing that guy says."

"Including what he told the police about that night?"

Jenna thought for a minute, pushing the last bites of her omelet around on her plate.

"Probably."

"So, you think Christopher's right? They knew each other?"

"I don't know. But I'm not sure he's wrong."

I remembered my last AIM exchange with Shane.

"Shane was weird the last time I messaged with him," I said. "He said something about not being able to escape his past. Do you think maybe Shane owed somebody money?"

Jenna signaled the waitress for the check.

"I don't know, but we need to make a trip to Denver."

"Why? To see Brian?"

"No, not Brian. We need someone down in the muck."

"Kevin?"

"Yeah, Kevin."

"How do we find him? We don't even have his number."

"Mr. Bill's. That bar where Brian said he and Kevin met."

"I don't have a fake. How will I get in?"

"Oh, they'll welcome you with open arms at this place," she said, laughing. "Trust me."

"But what about my dad? He's not going to let me go to some bar in Denver."

"Leave him to me," she said.

. . .

"It's kind of a memorial," Jenna said when she came to pick me up.

"Another memorial?" Dad asked.

"This one's less official. No church, no family. Just some of Shane's closest friends. We're going to stay up all night and just tell stories. About Shane. We really want Ash to be there. It'd be weird without him."

"And this will be . . ."

"At my apartment," Jenna said. "I'll take good care of him. I promise."

I could tell he was struggling with this, and I felt bad about lying. It must be hard to be a parent if you have to do it all by yourself. He didn't have my mom to help him know how tight to hold the reins, when to let them go, and here I was, making things worse. But it was too late to turn back now. Jenna and I were in this thing. We had to see it through.

"Okay," Dad said, finally. "I'll see you tomorrow."

. . .

Mr. Bill's was on Broadway, just south of the Capitol. Jenna said there were a few gay bars along that stretch, conveniently located for the closeted state senators passing anti-gay laws just up the street. As for Mr. Bill's, she was right. I didn't have any trouble getting in, unless you counted the pervy look the guy at the door gave me and the way he winked when he called me "sweetheart." It was Jenna who had the difficulty.

"Not exactly your crowd, darling," the guy said.

"I'm just here to make sure my friend doesn't get into too much trouble."

"Define 'too much,'" he said, laughing.

Inside, it was packed and smoky. We wedged into a space at the bar, and Jenna ordered us beers. I figured I could nurse mine, at least look like I belonged in a bar. Going slow would be easy, since my first sip tasted like dirty water. How did people drink this stuff?

It didn't take long to realize there was something weird about the crowd. It was split between really young guys and really old guys. The old guys, mostly in their fifties or sixties, were scattered about, some at the bar, others sitting by themselves at small round tables. The young guys—most of whom looked barely older than me—drifted from old guy to old guy, casually dropping a hand on a thigh as they leaned in close to murmur into an ear. Usually the older guy would shake his head, and the boy would move on, but every now and then the older guy would leave with the boy. They'd come back ten or fifteen minutes later, the older guy looking sheepish and ordering another drink, the younger guy finding another old guy to murmur at.

"What kind of place is this?" I asked.

"It's a hustler bar," Jenna said.

"Hustlers? As in—"

"Basically escorts, but ghetto."

I scanned the crowd again, accidentally locking eyes with a big burly lumberjack-looking guy at one of the tables. He was staring a hole through me. My cheeks burned hot.

"How do they know I'm not working?" I asked.

"They don't. There's probably an easy twenty bucks in it for you if you're interested."

"Gross," I said.

Jenna scanned the room.

"I don't see him," she said. "Let's check the back."

The back room contained a pool table, surrounded by five or six young guys, all skinny, tight-jeaned. We recognized Kevin immediately, with his big lemur eyes, sitting on a stool in the corner. His eyes got even bigger when he saw us.

"What're you guys doing here?"

"We were actually looking for you," Jenna said. "And look, here you are. Right where Brian said you shouldn't be."

At the mention of Brian's name, Kevin's face turned sour.

"He's not my dad."

"Or your daddy?" Jenna asked, with a smirk.

"Definitely not," Kevin said. He looked like he'd smelled something rotten.

"What're you drinking?" Jenna asked.

"Jack and Coke."

Jenna headed to the bar, leaving me alone with Kevin. There were so many things I wanted to know. Was he, like, for sale? Did he ever come here with Shane? And what was his deal with Shane? Were they friends? More?

Kevin shook a cigarette out of a pack, offering me one. I shook him off.

"I thought you'd be taller," he said, lighting his cigarette.

"What?"

"From the way Shane described you, I thought you'd be, like, really tall. Like a giant."

"I guess Shane considered everyone tall."

"Yeah, he was one little dude. He was right about your eyes, though."

"What'd he say about my eyes?"

"That they were like little pools of oil." I didn't know if this was a compliment—it didn't exactly sound like one—but I blushed anyway.

"What're you, fifteen?" Kevin asked, taking a long drag on his cigarette. The cigarette made him look ridiculous. Lemurs shouldn't smoke.

"Seventeen."

"Huh."

"What?"

"Nothing. I just thought Shane's type was, like, older."

Jenna returned with his drink.

"What're you boys chatting about?"

"Just girl talk," Kevin said, with a glint in his eye. Jenna didn't react, just studied him.

"You know," Jenna said, "your name came up when I was researching that article about the local meth trade."

I knew she was lying. She would have told me if she knew about Kevin before we met him.

Kevin's face was still.

"I don't know any meth dealers," he said. "Somebody say I did?"

"J-Town," Jenna said.

The bare hint of a smile spread across Kevin's face.

"You know him, right?" Jenna asked. I told myself never to play poker with this girl. She could bluff the pants off anybody.

Kevin took a long swig from his drink, which didn't seem to be his first of the night. His eyes were kind of glazed, and I'd noticed a slurring of his speech.

"Yeah," he said. "I know him. Everybody knows him."

"And what about Crenshaw?" Jenna asked.

"I've seen him around. Mostly with J-Town. Wherever J-Town was, there was Crenshaw. He followed him around like a puppy."

He was about to take another swig of his drink when he froze, the glass halfway to his mouth. His eyes were looking past me, and when I turned around, I saw a tall, older guy. Black jeans, black shirt, caterpillar mustache. Cal.

"Kevin!" he shouted. "What a surprise to find you in this unseemly establishment. What brings you here? And who, pray tell, are your friends?"

Kevin had recovered enough to take a gulp of his drink and was about to introduce us when Cal stopped him.

"Wait, I know this one," he said, laying his meaty paw on my shoulder. "Ash, right? The adorable friend of our poor Shane."

"Yeah," I said, trying, and failing, to pull away from his grip.

"And who's this?" he asked, nodding at Jenna and working his fingers into my shoulder.

"I was in your car once," Jenna said. "With Shane. You drove us to Fort Collins."

"Darling, there have been many, many people in my car."

"Jenna," she said.

"It's a pleasure to make your acquaintance. I see empty glasses! This won't do at all. Kevin, be a peach and fetch us another round of libations."

Kevin got up from his stool, waiting for Cal to cough up cash for the drinks. When none appeared, he bit his lip and shuffled off to the bar.

"It's such a shame what happened to Shane," Cal said. "What kind of sick, depraved person could do such a thing?"

"Do you know them?" Jenna asked.

"The perpetrators? No, I don't believe I've had the pleasure."

"I just thought, maybe in your line of work, with the limo and all, that your paths might have crossed."

Cal's mouth formed a tight grin.

"Are you familiar with the name of my company, darling?" he asked.

"I'm not."

Cal reached into his shirt pocket, pulling out a business card and handing it to Jenna.

"Cal's Class Act Limousine Service," Jenna said. "Nice."

"According to reputable sources," Cal said, "those two young men were not class acts."

Kevin returned with our drinks, handing me something that looked like Coke, and Cal proposed a toast.

"To Shane. A soul too fine for this fallen world."

"To Shane," we said.

Cal downed his drink in one tilt. I took a sip of mine. It was definitely Coke, but it wasn't only Coke. Something else burned the back of my throat.

"I've an idea," Cal said. "Why don't we take this party on the road? I've got a little place, just up the highway, and my driver is outside. I decided to give myself the night off, you see, so I'm feeling quite liberated."

I caught Jenna's eye, silently pleading with her to get us out of this.

"That sounds like fun," she said.

"You guys will have to have fun without me," Kevin said. "I'm supposed to meet somebody."

"I don't believe that for a minute," Cal said, smiling. "Anyway, it wouldn't be the same without you."

I expected Kevin to resist, but he didn't. He just sank back onto his stool. The part of me that knew getting into Cal's limo was a bad idea started vibrating harder.

"Drink up, my friends," Cal said. "Our chariot awaits!"

As we were leaving, I excused myself to go to the bathroom and gave Jenna a look that said she had to come with me.

"What are we doing?" I asked when we were safely out of view of the others.

"This is our way in," Jenna said.

"Into what?"

"Into whatever it was Shane was involved in."

"So you think he was involved in something?"

"Maybe. And if he was, J-Town is at the center of it. And since we can't get to J-Town, Kevin's the next best thing. And so is Cal. If you can't smell the stink on that guy, your nose is broken. There's something here, Ash. Something I need to know."

"As Shane's friend? Or as a journalist?"

She thought about this for a moment.

"Both," she said. "But also as Jesse's sister. Whatever Shane was doing with J-Town involved drugs, and if drugs were involved, maybe this leads us back to Jesse."

Maybe she was right, but all of this felt wrong. Like maybe we were on the cusp of learning things we wouldn't be able to unlearn. What we already knew was bad enough. What if there was something worse?

CHAPTER TWENTY

When I climbed into Cal's limo, the first thing I noticed was the smell—or smells, actually. A mixture of cigarette smoke, mold, and puke. The upholstery was a shabby peach, dotted with cigarette burns and stains made by God-knows-what bodily fluids.

"Home, James!" Cal shouted to the driver.

"His name's not really James," he said to us in a stage whisper. "It's Petey. But what kind of name is Petey for a chauffeur?"

I'd made sure to sit as far away from Cal as possible, but it didn't matter. He took up so much space that it was like he was right on top of me, his arms and legs reaching into every corner of the car. He made us drinks as soon as we hit the road, cranberry juice with vodka. It tasted like metal, but I drank it. The Coke-and-whatever back at the bar had taken some of the edge off. I figured the vodka could only help.

"What's the Lincoln Escort Service?" Jenna asked, reading off a flier she'd fished out of the door pocket.

"One of my many businesses," Cal said. "I'm something of a serial entrepreneur, you see. I have several balls up in the air at any given moment."

"What's your clientele like?" Jenna asked.

"Mostly wide-load truckers."

Jenna laughed.

"I'm sorry," she said. "What?"

"Yes," Cal said. "I arrange for drivers to escort big trucks with heavy loads on the interstate."

Jenna's eyebrows climbed to the top of her forehead.

"My dear," Cal said. "Did you think this was something more lurid? Something sexual?"

The way he said "sexual," dragging the word out as if he were licking it, turned my stomach.

"Of course not," Jenna said. "I know you only associate yourself with class acts."

After about a half hour and another round of drinks, Petey swung the limo onto a small dirt road, untamed brush narrowing our passage. The limo bounced over ruts and holes, passing a sign for "Cal's Western Village" and a dilapidated warehouse before emerging onto what looked like a clichéd movie set of a frontier town. There was a saloon and a post office and raised wooden sidewalks. I half expected to see a tumbleweed blow through. The limo ground to a halt outside of a building that had a Sheriff sign hanging off the front.

Climbing out of the car, I stumbled, lightheaded from the vodka. Jenna put her hand on my arm to steady me.

"What is this place?" she asked.

"Another of my business ventures," Cal said. "This one has been a bit slower to bear fruit, but its day will come. People are hungry for a chance to relive the glory of the frontier. The modern world is so terrible. People crave escape."

He led us into a low-slung building with shuttered windows. We stumbled through a dark hallway and into a bedroom. Across from a large bed stood a bank of video monitors and computer screens. The monitors showed black-and-white images of the limo we'd just gotten out of.

"I like to see who's coming," Cal said.

He guided us through the bedroom and into a lounge-type space full of overstuffed couches and fluffy rugs with a big stone fireplace anchoring the room. In the corner was a semicircular booth, tricked out in red vinyl, the kind you'd see in a restaurant. Off the lounge was a kitchen, where Cal was pouring drinks.

"We have a welcome ritual here at Cal's Western Village," he said. "A shot of tequila to smooth the soul and soothe the spirit." He passed the small glasses around. "To new friends!" he shouted.

The tequila burned, but not as much as it would have an hour ago, before the other drinks had blazed the trail. I felt it immediately, like it had found some sort of fast track to my central nervous system. I was beginning to see the appeal of alcohol.

Cal poured us another round and pointed us toward the booth, and I found myself sitting between Jenna and Kevin. Maybe it was the tequila, but being next to Kevin felt good, the casual pressure of his knee against mine. I found myself staring at his hands, which seemed bigger than they ought to be on his small frame. It took me a minute to realize that Jenna and Cal were talking. I made myself focus.

"Porn?" Jenna was saying. "Really? You?"

"I know it's hard to believe," Cal said, laughing, "but I wasn't always the wrinkled figure you see before you. In my twenties, I was considered quite the hot ticket. And believe me, in LA in those days, all you needed was the right look. A pretty face could open just about any door. To directors. Hollywood starlets. Guys with cameras hoping to break into the industry."

"And now?" Jenna said. "You're the guy behind the camera, instead of in front of it?"

We followed Jenna's gaze to the far corner of the room, where a video camera sat mounted on a tripod.

"Oh, that thing?" Cal said, laughing. "That hasn't worked in years. It's just part of the décor now. An homage to Old Hollywood."

Jenna laughed, harder and louder than she should have. Cal's eyes narrowed, his smile melting away.

"You're a curious girl, Jenna," he said.

"Curious as in odd?" she asked. "Or inquisitive?"

"More the latter."

"Comes from being a journalist."

"You're a journalist?" Cal asked, raising an eyebrow.

"I guess. I write for the campus paper."

"Interesting," Cal said.

"It is," Jenna said, downing her tequila. "Always."

"Kevin," Cal said, keeping his gaze on Jenna. "Why don't you pour us another round? And then maybe give Ash a tour of the place. I'm sure he'd enjoy that. I want to talk some more with Lois Lane here."

The part of me that would normally have said, "No thanks, I'd prefer not to wander off alone with Kevin," was no longer working. Instead, I found myself taking another shot from Kevin and following him down a dark hallway.

The hallway led to other hallways. The walls were painted black, lit only by dim naked light bulbs on the ceiling. Kevin led me through twists and turns, past several small bedrooms. I was completely disoriented, from the tequila, from the labyrinth of hallways, from the weird lighting. I kept one hand on the wall to steady myself.

"This is my room," Kevin said, opening a door at the end of yet another hallway.

"You live here?"

"No, but I'm here often enough to earn my own guest suite."

His "suite" was just another bedroom, slightly bigger than the ones we passed, sparsely furnished. Just a bed, a dresser, a couple of bedside tables. A table lamp sat on the floor, and when Kevin turned it on, it cast an orange glow across a thick shag carpet. He kicked his shoes off and sat cross-legged on the bed.

"Join me," he said.

He had been drinking as fast as the rest of us, but he seemed to be getting more sober, not less. I was clearly going in the other direction, which I guess is why I took my shoes off and joined him on the bed. He scooched in until our knees were touching.

Everything was vibrating and blurry. The room, the air, Kevin, sitting across from me, leaning in now, his face inches away from mine. He nodded at my drink. I downed it. He took the empty glass and placed it on the table beside him. His face swam through the murky air, and his lips, warm and soft, found mine. He tasted like tequila, but just underneath the tequila was something strange, earthy, like dirt flecked with metal. His tongue lapped against my teeth, and I sucked it in. He pushed me back on the bed until he was on top of me, grinding his pelvis against mine. I had my arms around him, and I was pulling him to me, tighter and tighter, like maybe if I pulled hard enough he would pass right through me. I shivered as his hand crawled under my shirt, the fingers of his other hand slipping beneath my waistband. I was hard, and when he took me in his hand I gasped.

This was what I had wanted, back in those blissful days of lying entangled with Shane, hungry for the kind of touch that Kevin was offering me now, his hand wrapped tight around my dick. But it suddenly felt wrong. So wrong. That should be Shane's hand. That should be Shane's weight on top of me. That should be Shane's breath, hot and urgent against my neck. What little sense remained struggled up through the tequila, fought off the increasingly frantic motion of Kevin's hand on me, and found the strength to push him off.

"What the fuck!" Kevin hissed.

"I don't want to do this," I said, buttoning up my jeans.

"Seems to me you do." He nodded at my crotch and moved his hand toward it.

"Get off!" I yelled, swatting his hand away and lurching off the bed.

"Don't be a fucking pussy," he said. "You know you want this."

"Not from you."

"Oh, what, you'll only give it up for your precious little Shane?" He was standing up now, moving toward me. "I suggest you reconsider. Cal can be a good friend to have. And a bad friend not to have, if you know what I'm saying."

"What's Cal got to do with this?" I asked, putting my hand on his chest to keep him from coming closer.

"Jesus, you really are an idiot, aren't you? Cal runs the show, asshole. And he wants you in it. Says you have the look. Personally, I don't see it. You're no Shane. But Cal's the boss."

"Wait," I said, trying to piece things together in my alcohol-fuzzed brain. "Shane was working for Cal?"

Kevin laughed.

"I wouldn't call it working. Cal described it as a 'relationship of mutual need and benefit.' The same relationship Cal had with J-Town. The same relationship Shane had with J-Town."

The adrenaline surging through me was an antidote to the tequila. My brain cleared, and I remembered why Jenna and I were there.

"So Shane did know J-Town."

"I guess you could say that," Kevin said. "He was fucking him."

There was a sudden ringing in my ears. The room pitched sideways.

"I don't believe you," I said, swallowing the bile that was beginning to rise.

"What, you think Shane was able to pay cash for all the drugs he was doing? Must be nice to live in a world of unicorns and leprechauns. Shane was needy. Too much was never enough with that kid. Cal knew it. J-Town knew it. The question is, how come you didn't know it? I mean, he was *your* boyfriend, right?"

I would have lunged at him, but I was suddenly puking my guts out, painting the shag carpet with streams of tequila and cranberry.

. . .

The next thing I knew, Jenna was shaking me awake. I was in Kevin's bed, fully clothed. It felt like an elephant was sitting on my head, with its trunk jammed down my throat. I moaned, rolled over, but Jenna kept shaking me.

"Come on!" she said. "We have to go. Cal's driving us back to Denver to get my car."

I put my feet on the floor and managed to stand up. I was weak, shaky. I caught an image from the night before—Kevin on top me—and I shook my head to fight it off.

"What time is it?"

"Almost noon," Jenna said.

She handed me my sneakers and led me through the tangle of hallways to the kitchen. Cal and Kevin were sitting at the counter, eating powdered doughnuts.

"He's alive!" Cal shouted. "Come nourish yourself, my boy!"

The thought of a dry, sugary doughnut made me gag. "I just need some water," I said.

"Kevin," Cal said, "fetch the lad some water. He's had a rough night."

Seeing Kevin brought more fragments. His lips on mine. His hand in my pants. Me pushing him off.

"Dude, I have *never* seen someone puke like that," he said, handing me the water. "That was some *Exorcist*-level shit. I thought your head was going to spin around."

"I remember puking. But what happened after?"

"James was kind enough to get you cleaned up," Cal said.

"James?"

"Petey. My driver. He's an expert at such situations. He's a one-man HAZMAT detail. I trust you're feeling better now?"

"A little," I said, but the minute I said it, a wave of nausea passed through me. More memories from last night crowded my brain. I could see it again, Kevin telling me about Shane and J-Town having sex. I felt a stab of jealousy, tried to shake it off, but it lingered, terrible and insistent.

"Excellent," Cal said. "Because we need to get you and Jenna back to her car. But first, Jenna, Kevin, would you be so kind as to wait for us in the limo? I need a word alone with Ash."

"I'll just wait over here," Jenna said, heading toward a big ugly lounge chair on the far side of the room. "Just pretend I'm not here."

"We wouldn't have to pretend," Cal said, his voice almost a growl, "if you weren't actually here." And then he just stared at her.

Jenna held his stare for a minute, but then she caved.

"I'll be just outside if you need anything, Ash," she said. When she and Kevin were gone, Cal took another doughnut from the bag, keeping his eyes locked on mine as he popped it in his mouth.

"Sit," he said, pointing to the stool beside him. "I hear you and Kevin didn't exactly hit it off last night."

He was smiling, but I detected something less friendly underneath the smile. His mustache was clotted with sugar from the doughnuts. My stomach churned, and I tasted something acidic.

"Kevin's nice," I said. "It's just that I'm not really looking to date right now."

Cal chuckled.

"That's so cute," he said.

"What?"

"That you think Kevin's nice. He's not. Also, dating? How quaint."

"I just think I need some time," I said. "You know. After Shane."

"Oh, I understand. It's a kick in the tenders. Believe me, I know. I've lost people over the years. Too many people. I just thought you and Kevin might have some fun together, that's all. There's nothing wrong with fun, is there?"

His questions sounded like threats, like he was daring me to disagree.

"No," I said.

"Good, good. Because I like you, Ash. I've liked you since the moment we met. 'That boy's got grit,' I said. 'He knows the 4-1-1,' as the kids say."

There was nothing I could say to this. I was pretty sure I lacked grit.

And I definitely didn't know the 4-1-1.

"But I worry," Cal continued, "that you might leave here under a misapprehension. And that's not something I can allow."

His face was tighter now, and I could see the faint outlines of what he must have looked like as a younger man.

"I don't think I have a misapprehension," I said.

"Are you sure? Because there's something you should know about Kevin. You get a few drinks in him, and he's liable to say anything. He'll just make shit up out of thin air. He's going to have to learn to control himself, that boy."

"Kevin didn't—"

"Now is not the time for you to speak, Ash," he said, holding his hand up. "Now is the time for listening. Do you understand?"

Even the air between us felt menacing. I nodded.

"Excellent. So, you just forget whatever Kevin told you. Put it right out of your mind. Also—and I can't stress this enough—I'm counting on you not to say anything to your journalist friend." He leaned in so close I could smell the sugar on him. He put his hand on my knee. "I'm going to be honest with you, Ash. I don't like her. I've known women like her all my life. Nasty women. Deficient, you might say, in a certain delicacy. Lacking—I'm sorry to have to say this—class."

"You don't have to worry—"

"No, no," he said, his hand massaging my knee. "You're listening now. Just listening. You see, I can't have questions being asked, Ash. People poking their noses where noses ought never to be. I'm a businessman, and my enterprises require a certain amount of discretion, which means I require the same discretion from the people around me. And you're around me, now, Ash. You're right here with me."

He gave my knee one more squeeze before removing his hand and leaning away from me.

"But that grit of yours," he said. "It worries me. It's a tricky business, grit. In the right proportions, it serves to fortify. To strengthen. But too much grit? Well, it can gum up the works. You don't want to gum up the works, now, do you, Ash?"

What I wanted was to get as far away from this guy as possible and never see him again.

"No," I said.

"No what?"

"No. I don't want to gum up the works."

"Then we have an understanding?"

"We do."

"Excellent," he said, and just like that, he was all smiles, the threat entirely gone from his face. He turned the empty doughnut bag upside down and shook the powdered sugar into his meaty palm. When he lapped at it with his tongue, I thought I was going to empty my guts all over again.

"Did I ever tell you about the last time I saw Shane?" he asked, wiping his hands on his jeans.

I shook my head.

"We were at Subway, having a sandwich. We'd been talking for hours. He told me things I don't think he'd ever told anybody. Anyway, as we were leaving, he said, real serious-like, 'I'm gonna die one of these days, Cal.' I asked him what he was talking about. 'Somebody's going to kill me,' he said. 'Because I'm gay.'"

The hairs on my arms shot straight up.

"And you know what I did, Ash, when he said that?"

"What?"

"I laughed. I laughed right in his face. 'In Juniper?' I said. 'That kind of thing doesn't happen in Juniper.'"

He dipped a napkin in my water glass and blotted the white streaks he'd left on his jeans.

"Shows how much I know," he said. "Anyway, we need to get you home, sweetheart. You look like shit."

CHAPTER TWENTY-ONE

"But you said meth heads lie. That it's all they know how to do."

Jenna and I were back in her car, on the road to Juniper. We'd been quiet on the ride from Cal's place to Denver—hadn't wanted to risk Cal overhearing us, even though there was a glass panel between us and him. But the minute we were alone in her car, I told her everything I remembered from the night before. I thought she'd say we couldn't believe a word Kevin said, but that's not what happened. Which is why I was reminding her of the First Law of Meth Heads: they lie.

"They do," she said, "but mostly when it serves their own interests. How did what Kevin told you serve his interests?"

"He wanted to hurt me. I wouldn't have sex with him, and that pissed him off. So he decided to make up stuff about Shane. To, like, destroy my image of him."

"Maybe, but it sounds like he was the one who was hurt. I'm guessing he liked Shane, but Shane chose you. So, yeah, maybe he wanted to inflict some damage, but only because he was already damaged. And people who are hurting? It's like meth heads, but in reverse. They tend to tell the truth."

"But if Kevin's job was to recruit me for whatever shady outfit Cal's running, then how did telling me about Shane make that more likely?"

"You said it yourself," she said. "He needed to destroy this idealized image you have of Shane. And yeah, he was doing it to hurt you. But he was also doing it because it was the smart play. A person with no illusions? That's exactly the kind of person Cal wants working for him."

"So you believe Kevin? Shane was so desperate for meth that he was, what, trading J-Town sex for drugs?"

That was the hardest part of this for me to believe. Not so much the drugs. Shane had told me about the drugs. But sex with J-Town? No. Absolutely not.

"It makes sense, Ash. Face it, there's a lot we never knew about Shane. And what we did know, well, it raised a lot of questions. Questions we never really wanted to ask."

"But then the whole hate-crime story goes out the window. I mean, if J-Town and Shane were already hooking up, nothing J-Town told the cops makes sense."

"Right."

"So what made J-Town go crazy on Shane? I mean, you don't beat someone like that if you're just looking for money."

She was quiet for a minute, her fingers dancing on the steering wheel.

"I'm thinking about something Cal told me last night," she said, "when he was running his mouth while Kevin had his hand down your pants. He said Shane was HIV positive."

She waited for me to react.

"You knew?" she asked when I didn't say anything.

"Yeah. Shane's mom told me. In the hospital."

"You didn't know before?"

I heard the accusation in her words, the suggestion that Shane had done something wrong.

"There was no need to."

It took her a moment to realize what I was telling her.

"Oh," she said.

"But what's this got to do with J-Town beating Shane to death?" I asked.

"According to Cal, Shane told him about his HIV just a week or so before he was attacked. And if Cal knew, it's likely others knew. For all his hush-hush vibe, that asshole just loves to talk."

"So you think J-Town knew?"

"Maybe," she said. "And maybe he was pissed off that Shane exposed him to HIV."

"Pissed off enough to kill him?"

"If he was high, sure. Or even if he was coming down and was out of dope. Meth rage is a real thing. It's super weird that the cops aren't talking about it as a possible factor in Shane's murder. Makes me wonder what else they're covering up."

I was quiet for a moment, trying to wrap my head around what Jenna was telling me.

"There's still something I don't get," I said.

"What?"

"That confession. The story that J-Town and Crenshaw killed Shane because he came on to them, and they were disgusted, or whatever. I mean, it doesn't make sense. They say they told Shane at the bar that they were gay and suggested they hook up. This was their stupid plan to rob him, right? So, they said, 'Hey, let's hook up,' and then they were surprised when Shane made a pass at them? Of course Shane made a pass at them. That was the whole point of them being in the truck together."

"Yeah," she said. "I've been thinking about that. That confession is a pack of lies."

"But why *those* lies?"

"Think about it," she said. "They knew they were going to spend the rest of their lives in prison. That was a given. Nothing they said was going to keep that from happening. So, *how* did they want to go to prison? As drug snitches who ratted out an interstate drug-trafficking ring? Or as fag-hating tough guys who would kill anybody who came onto them? If you're going to prison, the fag-hating story is a much better one. Not only might it keep you from becoming someone's bitch, but it might keep you from being jacked by members of that same drug-trafficking ring who were maybe doing time in the same place. It was all about protecting the network, which had the added benefit of protecting them.

"On top of that," she said, "J-Town had been having sex with Shane, and probably with lots of other guys. If the true story comes out, all that becomes public. What better way for J-Town to maintain his closet than to become a guy who hates queers so much that he killed one?

"It's weird," she continued. "J-Town and Crenshaw are obviously idiots, but this story they came up with? It was pretty fucking smart."

The more Jenna talked, the less I knew what to feel. I'd taken some weird comfort in the hate-crime version of events. It kept Shane innocent. It made him an easy victim to rally behind. And the anger that came with the hate-crime story was invigorating. It gave me—us, everybody—a villain. But now things were murkier. Shane didn't deserve what happened to him, whether J-Town killed him because of the HIV thing or because of a drug deal gone bad. But what Jenna was saying made the whole thing more complicated than I wanted it to be.

I told Jenna what Cal told me that morning, about Shane predicting that he'd be killed because he was gay.

"Did you believe him?" she asked.

"At first I did. It was so eerie, you know? But now, I don't know. It's like Cal's already writing the screenplay, and that was the scene with the creepy foreshadowing. Doesn't it seem just a little too perfect? Like maybe Cal's trying to throw us off the scent of what really happened?"

She didn't say anything for a while, just kept her eyes on the road.

"When can you make another trip to Denver?" she asked.

"I don't know. Maybe Friday afternoon? Why?"

"I think we need to talk to Brian."

"But he's totally convinced this was a straight-up hate crime. I mean, he's been on television talking about it."

"Right," she said. "Seems he's clinging to that version of events pretty hard. Just like Cal. I want to know why."

. . .

When I entered the main lobby of the high school Monday morning, there were green and yellow ribbons everywhere, hanging from the ceiling, plastered on the walls, festooning the armbands that everybody was wearing. Everybody but me. I had forgotten. Monday had been declared a "Day of Remembrance, to honor Shane's memory and to mourn his loss."

Peace and tolerance. That's what Jenna said the green and yellow represented. What a brave move, all these kids standing up for peace and tolerance, two things that nobody could disagree with.

"Ash!" someone yelled. It was Lucy Vintner, student body president, full-time organizer, and all-around do-gooder. She and two other girls were sitting at a table in front of the trophy case, stacks of armbands in front of them.

"Ash!" she yelled again. "Come here!" She couldn't have picked me out of a lineup before Shane died.

"Here," she said, handing me an armband as I approached the table. "We noticed you didn't have one."

I reached out to take it, but my hand stopped halfway. I knew it would be easier just to go along, to pledge my allegiance to peace and tolerance. But I couldn't do it. I didn't want to lump myself in with these people, people for whom Shane's death was just an opportunity to prove how open-minded they were. They wouldn't have had anything to do with Shane when he was alive. Shane, who was just a little too—much. A little too light in the loafers, limp in the wrist. No, it was dead Shane they needed, dead Shane they were comfortable with.

"No thanks," I said. The heat of their judgment burned my back as I walked away.

. . .

I felt the same thing in homeroom when Principal Hoggins came on the PA system. His theme was "Things like this don't happen in Juniper," which only pissed me off more. I mean, a thing like this had *just* happened in Juniper. He went on and on about how hate isn't a Wyoming value, how we're a live-and-let-live state. He actually said that. "Live and let live." But everybody was lapping it up, nodding along. Jocks fought back tears when Hoggins played "Candle in the Wind," the song that had brought the whole world to tears when Elton John sang it at Princess Di's funeral the year before. That, at least—Elton and the weeping football players—Shane would have appreciated. It was probably the gayest thing that'd ever happened at Juniper High.

For the rest of the day, I felt hypervisible and invisible at the same time. In the space of a week, I'd gone from being stared at because I was queer to being stared at because I wasn't sufficiently queer-positive. It was especially bad at lunch, where the difference between people sitting with friends and people sitting alone had always been stark. So I was grateful when Ryan joined me, less grateful when neither of us knew what to say. I hadn't seen him since the week before, and I didn't know how to follow up on his invitation to talk. So we just sat there in an awkward silence, until he finally broke it.

"It's cool, huh?"

"What?"

"This," he said, gesturing vaguely at the rest of the cafeteria. "All these kids showing their support. For Shane."

I laughed. This was the person who had called me a faggot because I maybe sat too close to him on the couch. And now he was wearing one of those stupid armbands.

"What," he said. "You don't think so?"

"It's just all so fake. None of these kids even knew Shane. So what is it that they're honoring? Other than some enlightened version of themselves that isn't the least bit real."

His eyes widened behind his thick glasses, and he leaned back, like I'd sucker-punched him.

"I don't know," he said. "I mean, people change, right?"

"Do they?" I asked, my face suddenly hot, my eyes locked on his.

He looked down, then back up.

"It's just," he continued, his eyes back on mine, "you're right. I didn't know Shane. But this thing really hit me, you know? That could have been you on that fence."

He was quiet for a minute. When he spoke again, it was in a whisper. I had to strain to hear him above the noise of the cafeteria.

"It could have been me," he said.

"No, it couldn't have!" I said, louder than I meant to, my voice breaking. "But that's so typical, a straight guy finding a way to make this all about himself. I'm sick of it."

"That's the thing, though," he said. "That's what I'm trying to tell you. What happened to Shane? It kind of made me deal with some stuff I hadn't been dealing with."

He glanced around the cafeteria and then leaned in closer, his voice still barely above a whisper.

"It's funny. Now seems like the absolute worst time to do this. I mean, Shane died because he was openly gay. But it also seems like the right time, you know?"

"The right time to do what?" I asked.

He studied the table for a minute before looking back up at me.

"To come out."

I must have looked like a confused puppy, head cocked to the side.

"I'm sorry. What?"

"I take it you didn't know," he said, chuckling.

I didn't understand what was happening. I thought maybe I was going insane.

"I just want to make sure we're on the same page here," I said. "You're gay."

"Yes."

"But I thought . . . I mean . . ."

"I guess all that verbal gay-bashing worked. Really threw people off the scent."

"Well, you were really good at it," I said, dizzy from what I was hearing.

"Yeah, I'm so sorry about that. For what it's worth, I was just scared. Though I know that's not an excuse."

"How long have you known?"

He scanned the cafeteria again, feeling all the eyes on us, but his voice was no longer a whisper.

"I don't know," he said. "Somewhere between forever and two weeks? I mean, I guess I've always known, but I never let myself know it, you know? And then Shane was killed, and yeah, I never even knew him, but we had this thing in common, right? What kind of coward would I be if I didn't acknowledge that?

"Like, maybe," he continued, "we all have a responsibility now. A responsibility to Shane."

I wondered what Ryan would think if he knew what I was beginning to know. That the perfectly innocent boy-next-door image the media was painting was a lie. That Shane had maybe been trading sex for drugs. That he was part of whatever sleazy operation Cal was running out of his "Western Village." Would it matter? Would we even be having this conversation if he knew? Would any of these people be wearing those armbands?

"What?" he asked, sensing that I'd drifted off someplace.

"Nothing. Just . . . I'm glad you told me."

He smiled.

"So am I," he said.

CHAPTER
TWENTY-TWO

Jenna and I were sitting on a wobbly bench outside a classroom at Metropolitan State in downtown Denver. It was Friday after school, and I'd somehow made it through the week. It helped that Ryan and I had fallen into a rhythm of having lunch together. We were picking up where we left off, but now with the gay stuff added. I periodically checked myself for any indication that I was in the process of re-crushing my earlier crush, but that wasn't happening. Shane was still so present, even though he was gone. Being into another guy was the last thing I could imagine.

"What do you think he knows?" I asked Jenna.

We were waiting for Brian to get out of class. Jenna had gotten the room number from someone in the department office.

"I don't know. But I'm guessing more than he's told us."

There was an increasing chatter from inside the classroom, and people began filing out. We waited until the stream slowed and made our way inside. Brian was standing behind a lectern, putting papers and books into his bag. When he saw us, it took him a moment to smile. Before the smile there was something else, some hint that he wished we weren't there.

"What are you guys doing here?" he asked.

"We wanted to talk to you about Shane," Jenna said. "Is now a good time?"

He made a show of looking at his watch and scrunching up his face.

"It won't take long," Jenna said.

"Sure. But let's get out of here. I hate this building. It's a tomb."

It was beautiful outside, clear blue sky, low sixties. It was amazing the difference being two hours south of Juniper could make, especially once you lost the wind. It was crazy that we were in a snowstorm just a week before.

Brian led us to a park just a few blocks away, though I'm not sure "park" is the best way to describe it. It was more like we'd entered a time warp, some passage back to the nineteenth century. It looked like the kind of scene you'd see in a black-and-white photograph. Old, ornate houses. Wrought-iron fences. Bricked sidewalks. Streetlights that looked like they should be powered by gas rather than electricity. Benches sat in front of the houses, each looking onto an expanse of green grass. I half expected a horse and carriage to appear. Men in top hats, women in hoop skirts.

"This was one of Shane's favorite places," Brian said, leading us to a bench. "He said it looked like a painting you could walk into."

"You guys came here a lot?" Jenna asked.

"Not so much since he moved to Juniper. But yeah, when he was still living here."

We sat on the bench and were quiet for a minute, feeling the sun on our faces, listening to the chatter of birds and squirrels. I was wondering how Jenna was going to begin her interrogation when Brian beat her to it.

"I hear you've been spending time with Cal," he said.

"You know Cal?" Jenna asked.

"Not personally."

"Who told you we'd seen him?"

"Kevin."

"Right," Jenna said. "Kevin. So what's your deal with him, anyway?" She laughed, trying to lighten the tension that cloaked the three of us.

"My deal?"

"Yeah. The nature of your relationship."

"I wouldn't call it a relationship," he said, chuckling. "My research focuses on at-risk LGBT youth, and my fieldwork often takes me into places I wouldn't otherwise venture. Places like Mr. Bill's."

He looked at me and smiled.

"I hear you've been there recently, Ash," he said.

"Where'd you hear that?" I asked.

"Denver's a small town. The gays talk.

"Anyway," he continued, "I met Shane there, who introduced me to Kevin, and they led me to Cal. Well, not literally. I'd rather not be in the same room with Cal. But Shane and Kevin told me a great deal about him, and I've been able to fill in the rest. Cal's an interesting figure. I imagine you've already gleaned something of the nature of his so-called 'business ventures.' It's textbook, actually. Older man, pretends to be interested in the welfare of troubled gay teens, but it's all just an excuse to have pretty boys around."

Jenna gave him an accusatory raised eyebrow.

"Cal and I are very different people," he said, in response to the eyebrow. "Though I guess you could say we do have something in common. We're both interested in damaged human beings. Me, so I can help them. Cal, so he can exploit them. He smells damage on a person and turns it to his advantage."

I remembered what Kevin told me, that Cal said I had "the look." What if he really sensed something else? Not so much a look, but a wound.

"He smelled it on Shane?" Jenna asked. "Damage?"

"He did."

"And what about J-Town?" Jenna asked. "What kind of damage did Cal smell on him?"

"I can only guess since I've never met him. I know some people are speculating that his violent attack against Shane was just a projection of his own self-loathing."

He must have seen the confusion on my face.

"You know," he said, "the theory that the worst homophobes are themselves gay, but can't admit it? It makes a certain amount of sense, but I don't think that's the case here. It wasn't some secret queer desire that made J-Town kill Shane. It was heterosexuality."

"What do you mean?" I asked.

"Heterosexuality is this incredibly powerful force, but it's also incredibly fragile, especially for young men. Any perceived threat to it can result in a disproportionate response. As a straight man, J-Town had to work hard to live up to the expectations of heterosexual masculinity. You know, physical domination. A lack of emotion. A refusal to empathize. Shane subverted those expectations just by being himself. This triggered an anxiety in J-Town, an anxiety that led to rage. To violence. To murder."

"But what about Crenshaw?" Jenna asked. "He was there too."

"Crenshaw doesn't matter. He's a follower, a go-along guy. He was only there because J-Town was there."

"How do you know that?" she asked.

"Things I've read. People I've talked to."

"So this was all J-Town?" I asked.

"It was."

"You sound pretty certain," Jenna said.

"You'll have to forgive me. You caught me just after class, where I get to go on and on to a captive audience. But yes, I'm pretty certain. With J-Town, there's clearly some sort of psychosexual dynamic at work."

"Your theory assumes," Jenna said, "that J-Town is straight."

"That's right."

"What if he isn't?" she asked.

"Well, as I've said, there is a competing theory. You know, closeted gay man, refuses to acknowledge his homosexuality, lashes out at an openly gay man. You know the rest."

"But what if he wasn't refusing to acknowledge it?" Jenna asked. "What if he was acting on it?"

"What are you getting at?" Brian asked.

"Shane and J-Town knew each other," Jenna said. "They were having sex. Shane couldn't always afford the meth he needed. J-Town accepted other forms of payment. J-Town's gay. Or at least bi."

Brian's face fell, the professorial certainty seeping out of it.

"That's not true," he said. "Who told you that?"

"I can't say," Jenna said.

"Ah, right. You're a journalist. Have to protect your sources. No matter how scummy or misguided they may be."

"Confidentiality doesn't just apply to good people," Jenna said.

They were both quiet for a moment, registering this new dynamic between them.

"So," Brian said. "You think you have a scoop, something that undermines the official theory of the case. J-Town and Shane knew each other. They had a sexual history. What is it you hope to accomplish by making this public? I mean, besides making a career for yourself."

"This has nothing to do with my career," Jenna said. "It's about telling the truth."

"Ah," Brian said, laughing. "The almighty truth. Our great salvation."

"You don't think the truth matters?" Jenna asked.

"It's not that the truth doesn't matter. It's that the truth doesn't exist. What people call 'the truth' is merely the result of certain forms of power colliding. It's the byproduct of a complex web of narratives and counternarratives."

"Bullshit," Jenna snapped. "That's the kind of thing that passes for wisdom in philosophy departments. I didn't think it had made its way down to social work. I thought you people believed in reality."

"We do," Brian said. "We very much do."

He turned away from us, staring out over the perfectly manicured grass. He didn't say anything for a bit, and neither did we.

"You say you want the truth," he said, finally, turning back to Jenna. "How much of it do you want?"

"What do you mean?"

"I'm just wondering if there's a line somewhere. This much truth is fine. But too much is a problem. Is there a point where you'd say, 'No thanks, I have all the truth I can stand'?"

"Journalists don't get to decide that," Jenna said.

"I see. It must be nice, not having to worry about such things. Most of us don't have the luxury of simply telling the world everything we know, and not worrying about the consequences."

Jenna started to respond, but Brian stopped her.

"I'm going to tell you some things. Things that perhaps I shouldn't tell you."

"I'm all ears," Jenna said, but I felt something behind the bravado, a faint sense that maybe she didn't want to hear what he was about to tell her.

"Did Shane tell you what happened in Cody?" Brian asked.

"He did," Jenna said.

"So you know he filed a false police report, one claiming he'd been raped?"

"Yes."

"What about Morocco? Did he tell you what happened to him in Morocco?"

"No," Jenna said.

"What about you, Ash?"

I shook my head

"This was a few years ago, spring of 'ninety-five, I believe. You know Shane was attending boarding school in Germany, right?"

We nodded.

"Well, the school allowed students to plan their own spring break, unchaperoned, and Shane and a group of friends decided to go to Morocco. Marrakesh, to be precise. On their second day there, after a long day of sightseeing, they went back to their hotel, but Shane, being Shane, wasn't tired yet. He wanted to see more, do more, talk to more people. So, he went out on his own, in the early morning hours. He met a group of German tourists and had coffee with them at a café. And then, on his way back to the hotel, he was overtaken by a group of local men and raped. Repeatedly. Six times."

I felt like I was falling, like the bench below me had suddenly dissolved. I replayed Brian's words in my head to make sure I'd heard him correctly.

"They raped him," he continued, "and they took his shirt, and they took his shoes. Doc Martens. He made a point of telling me they were Doc Martens. They must have meant a great deal to him."

My heart was racing, and I thought I might throw up. The image flooded my brain in bright, vibrating waves. Shane alone in the streets of a foreign city, pummeled and sexually assaulted by a gang of men, every one of whom was probably twice his size. But it was the shoes I fixated on. When J-Town and Crenshaw took Shane's shoes, that wasn't the first time that had happened. This must have added to Shane's terror as J-Town and Crenshaw attacked him, that he found himself in a repeating nightmare, where men beat him bloody and then took his shoes.

"Marrakesh was fairly well known for these sorts of male-on-male encounters," Brian continued. "Encounters, you can imagine, that were rarely taken seriously by the local authorities. Or if they were, it was the victim who was blamed. But in this case, Shane received a good deal of police cooperation. They liked him, I guess, like everybody liked him, and they were very kind. They believed him, and they investigated. But they never caught the guys who raped him. Never found any evidence of the attack."

"Wait," Jenna said. "What are you implying?"

"What do you think I'm implying?"

"It sounds like you believe Shane made up the Morocco story. Just like he made up the Cody story."

"Not at all. I believed him. You would have too if you had heard him tell it. And I know about the trauma he suffered afterward. The sleepless nights. The nightmares. But what do you think other people will think once they know about Cody? I think they'll make the connection you just made. That maybe Cody wasn't the first time he lied about being raped."

"That's ridiculous," I said.

"Of course it is," Brian said. "But that won't matter. The truth that Jenna has put so much faith in? It won't mean a damn thing."

We were quiet for a moment, Brian maybe tired of talking, Jenna and I certainly tired of listening. It was too much to take in. But eventually Brian started up again.

"Let me tell you another story. Did Shane tell either of you that he had a record?"

We shook our heads, resigning ourselves to more bad news.

"When he was fifteen, Shane was arrested for molesting two eight-year-old boys. This was in Casper. Shortly afterward, he attempted suicide and was hospitalized. He received counseling, and the arrest record was sealed."

I needed him to stop talking. I didn't think I could take anymore.

"If the record was sealed," Jenna said, "how—"

"He told me himself," Brian said.

"Okay," she said, "but still, what's your point?"

"If this gets out—and it will—the rest of it won't matter."

"What's the rest of it?" Jenna asked.

"That Shane was himself a victim of sexual abuse, both as a boy and a teenager."

At some point, you hear so many terrible things that I guess you just go numb. The words swim toward you, invade you, and you just sit there, defenseless against them.

"He told me this back in the summer, just before he moved to Juniper. He even identified the perpetrators. Three adult males, over the course of several years. One was even a member of his church.

"We know that victims of abuse are more likely to become abusers, so this information might serve to partially explain whatever Shane did to those little boys. But the backstory won't matter. All that will matter is that Shane was arrested for sexually abusing children."

"But none of this has anything to do with Shane being killed," Jenna pleaded, her voice laced with frustration. "It's irrelevant."

"So there is a line," Brian said.

"What do you mean?"

"A line where there's suddenly too much truth."

"That's not what I'm saying. I'm saying it's not relevant to Shane's murder. He was the victim here. And now you're putting him on trial."

"If you publish this story, Shane *is* going to be put on trial. The defense attorneys will use all of it to try to keep J-Town and Crenshaw off death row. It doesn't need to be relevant. It simply needs to muddy the waters."

Jenna was about to respond, but Brian held his hand up.

"There's just one more thing," he said. "Then I'll leave you alone. Did you know that Shane was HIV positive?"

"We did," Jenna said, proud, finally, not to be blindsided.

"Good. So, let's sum up, shall we? A drug-using, HIV-positive gay man with a history of sexually abusing children, who makes up stories about being raped, and who may have been trading sex for drugs, gets killed. There's your headline. There's your truth. Because believe me. This isn't just about whether J-Town did or didn't know Shane. If you pull on one little string, this terrible knotty mess will come with it. Is that what you want?"

"But even if this muddies the waters," Jenna said, "it won't change the outcome. Are you actually worried that J-Town and Crenshaw will get off? That they won't go to prison?"

"Oh, they're going to prison. For a long time. That's not in doubt."

"Then what are you even saying?" she asked.

"I'm saying that if you publish your scoop, we'll lose the Shane Deerfield we need. A symbol of things that happen to us—to gay men and lesbians—every fucking day. A symbol of the ways in which we're beaten, and abused, and killed, just for being gay. We'll lose him in the fight for better hate crimes legislation. We'll lose him in the fight for gay marriage, for a nondiscrimination bill. We'll lose him as a shining example of how all us queers are just normal, well-behaved American citizens who deserve equal protection under the law.

"And I don't know about you," he said, looking just at me now. "Maybe you're too young to feel it. But my generation of gay men? We're fucking tired of it. We're fucking exhausted. And the only thing that keeps us from giving up is the rage. And then this terrible thing happens, and it turns out there's a silver lining. The country is so in love with Shane Deerfield that maybe they're finally willing to see the rest of us as human beings. I'm old enough to know that opportunities like this don't come along every day."

I could see the anger in his face, quivering just below the surface, something he probably had to suppress every day of his life. And I remembered that moment at the memorial, watching Phelps and his band of haters, when I felt my grief turning into anger. The anger felt better than the grief. The anger was something I could use.

I realized why I didn't want to know the things Jenna and I were discovering. Those things threatened to turn the anger back into sadness. The story of Shane being killed because he was gay? That was easy to be angry about. It was a clean, righteous anger. But the things we were learning? It just made me unspeakably sad. It was like Shane was a magnet, and all the terrible stuff in the world was made of iron.

"But what about the person?" I asked, my voice barely above a whisper.

"I'm sorry?"

"You said we'll lose Shane Deerfield as a symbol. What about Shane the person?"

My voice quavered, and I had to choke down whatever it was I was feeling. Anger, yes, but also confusion, and a sadness so heavy I could barely move.

"We've already lost the person, Ash," Brian said. "He's gone."

The sun was setting over the roofs of the old houses, and a chill had crept into the air. I could see why Shane loved this spot. There was something unreal about it. Maybe that's what he needed. An escape from the real.

"So, I'm begging you," Brian said, turning to Jenna, his face catching the last of the afternoon light. "Leave it alone. All of it. Let people love Shane. Let them try to love us."

CHAPTER TWENTY-THREE

I didn't sleep at all that night. I couldn't stop thinking about the terrible things Brian had told us. Shane being sexually abused as a young boy. His attempted suicide. The gang rape in Morocco. How could anyone survive all of that?

But that's the thing, right? He didn't.

And then there was whatever it was he did to those two little boys. I literally couldn't think about that, couldn't reconcile it with the person I knew.

I thought about calling Jenna, but when I picked up the phone to dial her number, I realized I didn't want to talk about any of this. Talking about it would just make it more real. More terrible.

Maybe Brian was right. Maybe there was such a thing as too much truth.

I remembered something Mom said. I was eight, maybe nine, and I'd gotten in trouble at school. This girl, Mary Beth Wilkerson, asked, "Am I fat?" And I said, without giving it a second thought, "Yes." Because she was. She was clearly fat.

She burst into tears, and various administrators got involved, and next thing you know, I'm carrying a note home to my parents describing my "cruel and insensitive behavior." Mom said she couldn't believe how mean I had been, that I knew better than that, but I didn't understand. Mary Beth asked me a question. I answered truthfully. What was the problem?

But Mom said Mary Beth's question wasn't really a question. It was a plea for someone to make her feel better about herself.

"Ashley," Mom said, "I'm going to tell you something that not a lot of people will admit. The truth is overrated, and lying gets a bad rap. A part of living with other people is learning to tell when they want to know the truth, and when they don't. And when they don't, it doesn't make you a bad person to lie just a little. It makes you a kind person."

And yeah, I know, I'm chasing a ridiculous comparison here. There's a huge difference between telling the truth about Mary Beth Wilkerson and telling the truth about Shane. But isn't it basically the same question? If Mrs. Deerfield asked me if her son was a meth-addicted hustler, would I be able to say, as I did with Mary Beth, "Yes"? And should I? Because however noble and high-minded Brian's argument was, isn't this what it boiled down to? Telling Shane's mom things about her dead son that would break her heart more than it was already broken.

. . .

Saturday afternoon Jenna showed up and tossed a bunch of pages on my bed.

"What's this?" I asked.

"A draft of my article," she said, flopping down on the beanbag in the corner. "I want you to read it."

"What's in it?"

"Everything."

She was right. Everything was there. Shane's drug use. His HIV status. His history of being sexually abused and his arrest as a sexual abuser. She told what happened in Morocco and Cody. But the big news, of course, was that, contrary to everything people thought they knew about the case, Shane and J-Town knew each other. They'd had an ongoing sexual relationship, one possibly related to drug payments.

She had to play a bit fast-and-loose with sourcing, since no one had been willing to go on the record, but she made a persuasive case. The article's takeaway wasn't that Shane was a low-life drug-user who we shouldn't care about, but that he was a profoundly wounded person, whose various wounds led him to a night when he was brutally murdered. That murder, Jenna wrote, was no less tragic for the complexity that lay behind it. It was actually more so.

So, yes. It was well written, generous, and true.

And I hated it.

"You can't publish this," I said, throwing the pages down on my bed.

"Why not?"

"You know why not."

"Actually, I don't," she said, her voice rising. "I've been thinking about everything Brian said, and I get where he's coming from. But it's not my job to be a gay rights activist. I'm a reporter. My job is to tell the truth."

I was about to say that being a journalist was making her a terrible friend when Christopher swung the door open, no knock, no nothing.

"Good," he said, shutting the door behind him. "You're both here."

He pulled the chair from my desk and sat down, straddling the back of it. He was wearing a sleeveless T-shirt, which he should never do. Didn't have the arms for it. He locked eyes with me, and I held his stare, which I never did. It felt too intimate, especially given how distant our relationship was. But his look carried a challenge, and I wanted to meet it.

"You two have a lot to learn about minding your own business," he said.

"What are you talking about?" I asked.

"I hear you're still sniffing around this Shane thing."

"Who'd you hear that from?" Jenna asked.

"I heard it from Cal, who heard it from Kevin, who heard it from some Brian guy. Cal strongly suggests that you—how did he put it?—curtail your investigative impulses."

"And if we don't?" Jenna asked.

Christopher's eyes narrowed, the bones in his face suddenly visible.

"Don't get cute," he said. "This isn't complicated. Just leave it alone. Whatever it is you think you know, forget it."

I looked over at Jenna, ashamed to find myself on Christopher's side.

"I don't think I can do that," she said.

"Of course you can," Christopher said.

"As a journalist—"

"Yeah, Cal said you'd pull some journalism crap. Something about Woodward and Bernstein, whoever the fuck they are. He said you had delusions of grandeur. I'm here to remind you that you're not that special. You're just a bullshit reporter for a bullshit college newspaper who doesn't know half as much as she thinks she knows."

"Fair enough," Jenna said. "But I'm still going to publish. This is news."

Christopher exhaled, pushing his chair closer to us. His eyes were bloodshot, with heavy bags underneath.

"Do you have any idea what's going to happen if you publish this shit?" he asked.

"I do," she said. "Isn't that why you're here?"

"No. I'm here to tell you the rest of it. You think, what, your precious little Shane was involved in a few low-rent drug buys with small-town dealers? Picking up a little meth here and there, either by cash or by ass. Please. Shane was part of an interstate network responsible for keeping Juniper, as well as the whole damn university, knee-deep in meth.

"Now, think for a minute what that means, where he must have ranked in the food chain. There were people below him, people like J-Town. People like me. But there were plenty of people above him. Cal, of course, but it's not really Cal you need to worry about. I'm here because the guy above Cal got wind of your activities, a guy whose name I will not even mention. And let's just say he wasn't happy. Interstate drug trafficking is a federal crime, and with weights like what we're talking about, it pretty much guarantees life in prison, no parole. Also, the product Shane was moving? It came from farther south. Like, *Mexico* south. So that's a whole 'nuther aspect you don't want to have to deal with.

"Shane's dead, so he's got nothing to worry about. But this guy? He's more than a little worried. And he doesn't like to be worried. So stop playing big-time reporter and wake the fuck up."

"What if I just go to the cops?" Jenna asked.

Christopher laughed.

"You think this kind of business happens without the cops having a piece of it? Why do you think this ridiculous hate-crime story caught on so fast? Any story that focuses attention somewhere other than drugs is a good story, even if it makes Juniper the fag-bashing capital of the country. The hate-crime story is good for Juniper, good for the police, good for Cal and everybody up and down the chain. So, that's the story. It's already out there, and everybody likes it. Leave it the fuck alone."

Christopher's words hung in the air. It was Jenna who finally broke the silence.

"And if I don't?" she asked.

"That question suggests you still don't get it," he said. "There is no 'if.'"

He stood up, shoving the chair back under the desk.

"You're a college girl," he said, as he was leaving. "Act like you got some damn sense."

There was something I still needed to know.

"Christopher," I said. "Wait."

He turned around.

"Why are you doing this?" I asked.

"Doing what?"

"Working for Cal. Dealing drugs. All of it."

He was quiet for a minute. When he spoke, his voice was mostly air.

"Why do you care?" he asked.

It was a good question, one that made me wonder if I had failed him in the same ways he had failed me. Had I ever really tried to understand him, to imagine what Mom's death had done to him? Maybe if Mom hadn't died, and if Christopher hadn't been working at The Old Brick, he never would have found himself doing things he had to know were wrong.

Maybe he wanted out. Maybe he needed someone to care enough to help him find a way. I played the only card I had.

"What do you think Mom would have said?" I asked.

There was movement in his face, a slight flinch, and then a softness that wasn't there before.

"I don't know," he said, turning to leave. "I guess we'll never find out."

. . .

I didn't want to be the first to speak. I was hoping Christopher had said enough, that Jenna would finally recognize not only that there was nothing to be gained from publishing her article, but that she'd be putting herself—and maybe me—in serious danger. So we were both quiet for a while, letting this new information hover in the air between us.

Eventually she hoisted herself out of the beanbag and gathered her pages from the bed.

"Where are you going?" I asked.

"To campus. I've got revisions to do."

For a second, I thought this was good news, that maybe she was going to take out all the bad stuff about Shane, but the look in her eye was more determined than ever.

"What kind of revisions?" I asked.

"You heard your brother. Shane wasn't just using meth. He was *dealing*. He was part of whatever network was bringing drugs into Juniper. This is part of the story. It might even be the most important part."

I couldn't believe it. I'd only known Jenna for a couple of months, but I thought I had some sense of who she was. We'd been through so much together. I'd come to depend on her instincts and her courage. But now both of those things were leading her into some bad territory.

"Jenna."

"What?"

"Think about what you're doing."

"What am I doing?"

"You're ruining Shane's reputation, which will have national implications. You're heaping more pain on Shane's family, like they don't already have enough. And you're going to put yourself in the sights of a criminal network that isn't just Cal and his ridiculous boys, but serious guys. Dangerous guys. Forget all the other stuff, but are you really willing to do *that*? To maybe put a bullseye on your back?"

She waited before she answered, like maybe she was considering my question. But she wasn't. She'd already made up her mind.

"You still don't get it, do you?" she asked. She was standing at the foot of my bed, rolling and unrolling her article.

"Get what?"

"That this is bigger than Shane, bigger than me. Meth's destroyed so many lives, Ash. Most of them just kids. These kids are turning to it because it's cheaper than crack, more potent than weed or alcohol, and they're doing it because their lives suck, so why not? They're just sad, depressed. So they turn to this cheap high, and then that's it. All they care about is scoring the next hit.

"When are they going to put Jesse's face on the cover of a magazine?" she asked. Her face was red, her voice shaky. "Where are the rallies and marches for him? This is a fucking national emergency, and no one's paying attention. Instead, we get distracted by shiny objects, stories about a poor defenseless kid who got killed because he was gay. And we get to say, 'Well, I don't really approve of queers, but I wouldn't have killed him,' and then we get to feel more enlightened. Meanwhile, the kid wasn't killed because he was gay. He was killed because of meth. Because he was using it. Because he was dealing it. Maybe because the sex he was having to pay for it got him infected with HIV, and he told the wrong person. We'll probably never know what happened in that truck. But we do know that Shane wouldn't have been there if it wasn't for meth. That's the fucking story, and I'm in a position to make people see it."

Something was bubbling up in me, had been ever since she started talking. I wasn't sure I had the words for it, but I had to try.

"Sometimes it's like he's still alive," I said, my voice quavering. "And I can protect him. I couldn't protect him from J-Town and Crenshaw, but I can protect him now.

"That's what this feels like," I said, my voice stronger now. "I just want to keep him safe."

Jenna sat down on the bed beside me, leaning her shoulder into mine.

"But you can't," she said. "You know that, right?"

I nodded, sniffing away a tear.

"And you know it's not your fault that Shane was murdered?"

I could still hear my voice on that voicemail, telling Shane to have a nice life when he was slowly dying. Not a day went by when I didn't regret that message. It didn't matter that Shane never heard the things I'd said. What mattered was that I'd said them. But Jenna was right. I wasn't responsible for Shane's death.

I nodded again.

"Here's the thing, though," she said. "There are kids out there who still need protecting. Because the meth that killed my brother? The meth that killed Shane? That didn't just fall out of the sky. It flowed to them through a network that included Cal and that asshole Christopher was talking about. And they're still out there, selling that shit.

"Jesse's gone. Shane's gone. Lots of other kids are gone. But those assholes are still in business."

"And you think you can actually do something about that?" I asked.

"I think *we* can do something about that."

"We?"

"We're in this together, Ash. I lost Jesse. You lost Shane."

"We both lost Shane," I said.

"True. But you're the one who made him happy. You know that, right? For a short time, you made him happy."

I sat with this for a moment, letting myself believe it.

"If we're in this together," I said, "I should get a say in what happens next. This can't just be your call. I'm sorry about your brother. I really am. But Shane matters too."

I turned toward her, looking her in the eye.

"I matter."

She didn't say anything. Just stared at me. After a long minute, she stood up and walked toward the door.

"I'll send you the revision when I'm done," she said, not even looking at me as she left the room.

CHAPTER TWENTY-FOUR

On Monday, I moved through the day like I was stuck in an extended out-of-body experience. I watched myself doing my usual things. Taking a shower. Brushing my teeth. Eating a piece of cinnamon toast. Getting on the bus. I walked the halls and went from class to class. But it was like it was all happening to someone else. While this Ash-shaped person was going about his normal routine, the actual me was stuck in a repeating tape loop in my brain. I kept replaying the arguments, over and over: Jenna's, Brian's, Christopher's.

My dad always said that, when facing a difficult decision, I should figure out what I want the result to be, and then work backward from there. So I asked myself: what do I want to happen? And the only answer I could come up with was this: I want nothing bad ever to have happened to Shane Deerfield. I want him to have lived a life free of pain and abuse and trauma.

Of course, I had no way of making that real, which made the whole "What do I want to happen?" exercise a complete waste of time. What did the result matter if you had no way of achieving it? I couldn't save Shane from what happened to him in Morocco. I couldn't undo what Shane did to those two little boys. I couldn't erase the meth that Shane had apparently helped spread through Juniper.

Which is why I kept coming back to Jenna's argument, which was about the future, not the past. Maybe publishing the article was the only way to make things better going forward.

I became vaguely conscious of the world around me only at lunchtime, when I expected to see Ryan waiting for me in what had become our usual spot. He wasn't there. Which made it all the more surprising that he was sitting on my front stoop when I got home from school.

It was that time of day in late October when the temperature drops fast, a reminder that winter is coming. Ryan was sitting in the last patch of sun to strike the stoop, his face turned toward the warmth.

"Hey," I said.

"Hi."

He was wearing his clunky glasses, new Chuck Taylors the color of a pumpkin, a tight-fitting cranberry sweater. I was struck again by what I had found attractive about him in the past, some sense that he always looked exactly like himself.

"Where were you today?" I asked.

"I decided against school."

"What, you just didn't go?"

"That's right. My parents have this thing where, twice a year, if I don't feel like going to school, I can just not go. It's called a 'mental health day.' They like it because it keeps me from faking sick."

"So, today your mental health was . . ."

"A little shaky."

"Do you want to come inside?"

"Can we just maybe sit here? The sun feels so good."

"Sure," I said, plopping down next to him.

He just sat there, staring out at the street, where there was nothing worth staring at. His knee was bouncing.

I thought about telling him about the things Jenna and I had learned about Shane. Maybe he could help me figure out what to do. But that thought only lasted a second, since it just raised the whole problem over again. For him to be able to help me, he'd have to know what Jenna and I knew, and I wasn't sure I wanted anybody to know those things, especially Ryan. His whole coming out was based on a version of Shane that was turning out to be false. Did I really want to rob him of the thing that had allowed him finally to be himself? So I just sat there and let him fidget, waiting for him to say something. When he finally did, it was a doozy.

"I like you, Ash. Like, I *really* like you."

The words must have given him the courage he was looking for, because he turned away from the street, looked right at me, and just kept going.

"I guess I always have. Even back when we were playing video games. I had such a crush on you, but I told myself it was just normal, you know. Just a buddy thing.

"But then I got the sense that maybe you liked me too, and instead of making me happy, that just terrified me. I guess that's why I blew up at you that time, why me and the other guys cut you out. Being around you was too dangerous. I couldn't risk it."

He looked back at the street.

"So I made a deal with myself. I could have the feelings. You can't stop feelings. But I would never, ever act on them."

He chuckled, like he couldn't believe what a bad deal he'd made.

"And I went along like that for a while. You know, quietly miserable, but safe. But then Shane died, and I felt like such a coward."

He took a deep, shaky breath.

"And you and I started talking again, and all those feelings came rushing back, but stronger."

He turned back toward me. His face was lit up, by the sun, by everything he was feeling.

"I don't even think you know the effect you have on people," he said. "You're kind and sweet and brave, and you're way cute. And I know this is the worst possible time to tell you this. It's stupid, and I'm sorry. I don't expect you to, like, like me back. But I had to tell you."

His knee, which had been bouncing the whole time, was finally still.

"I've kept stuff bottled up for so long," he said. "I just had to tell you."

I'd actually dreamed of this moment. A year ago, it was all I thought about. And now here he was, saying the things I'd been dying for him to say, and all I felt was . . . sick. Sick and confused and angry. Not at him, but at the universe, which finally gave me what I wanted at the precise moment when I didn't want it.

Because all I wanted was Shane. The part of me that might want somebody else? That part was dead. I didn't know how to say all that, so I said the only thing I was sure of.

"I'm such a mess, Ryan."

He put his hand on my shoulder, pulling it back when I flinched.

"If you'd told me this a year ago," I said, "I would have been so happy. You were right. I was totally crushed out on you. And it kills me to know that we liked each other but were too scared to do anything about it."

"But that's the thing," he said. "We can start over. We—"

"I can't, Ryan. I just can't. I'm sorry."

The air went out of him like he was a balloon, and I'd popped it.

"Because of Shane? Or because you don't feel that way about me anymore."

"I don't even know. That's the thing. I don't know anything anymore. Yes, because of Shane, but what does that even mean? I'm starting to wonder if I even knew who he was. If what we had was real.

"And until I can figure that out," I said, "I'm not going to be much good to anybody."

I didn't want to say this next part, because it's what everybody says when they're rejecting somebody. But I had to say it.

"I think what I need right now is a friend. The world makes that so hard, you know? You spend your whole life denying you're gay, and then so much time obsessing about getting the perfect boyfriend when maybe what you really needed was a friend. A gay friend. Someone who's going through the same stuff. Someone who gets it.

"I'll understand," I continued, "if that doesn't work for you. But I'm really hoping it does."

He was quiet for a moment. I didn't know I'd been leaning against him until he pulled away from me, and I felt the loss of contact immediately. I was going to lose him too. But then the weight of his shoulder returned.

"I'm not promising I won't occasionally be weird or bummed," he said. "But I'm willing to give this gay friend thing a shot."

Relief coursed through me. I felt like I could breathe again.

"But can we start gay friending tomorrow?" he asked. "I have to get home. I'm supposed to chop vegetables. My parents are trying to teach me how to cook. I think so they don't have to."

I could tell he was hurt and that he was trying to hide it. I wanted to hug him, but I held myself back.

"But we're good?" I asked.

"We're good," he said, grabbing his backpack and standing up. He was halfway down the walkway before he turned around.

"I've been meaning to ask you," he said. "Have you ever been? You know, to the place where it happened?"

The sick feeling I'd had moments before returned.

"No," I said.

"I'm not saying it won't be hard. I was a mess when I went, and I didn't even know Shane. But you might want to try it. There's something clarifying about being there."

Clarity. That would be most welcome.

"Thanks," I said. "I'll think about it."

CHAPTER TWENTY-FIVE

I couldn't imagine going without Jenna, but whenever I thought about calling her, my stomach got tied in knots. She'd sent me the revision, in which she'd laid out in even more detail the connections between Shane's death and the meth trade. And though Shane was still the story's victim, it was hard not to sense him becoming, if only slightly, its villain as well. Jenna captured the tragic irony of a kid so addicted to meth that he became one of its primary movers. In Shane, Jenna wrote, we have a perfect microcosm of an American tragedy.

I finally worked up my nerve and called Jenna late Monday night. I told her that there was something I wanted to show her. We agreed that she'd pick me up the next day at 3:30.

Monday's warmth was nowhere to be found on Tuesday. It was overcast, temps in the midforties and falling by the time Jenna picked me up. She asked where we were going. I told her just to drive to the high school. Neither of us said much, just small talk, anything to avoid dealing with the real stuff that hovered between us.

When Jenna slowed down to take the right onto Grove Street, I told her to keep going straight. She gave me a weird look but did it. My heart was racing. It took her less than a minute to realize where we were going.

"No," she said, her voice thick with something. Anger. Maybe fear. "Absolutely not." She swerved the car into a parking lot.

"How fucking dare you!" she growled, slamming on the brakes.

"I can't believe you would do this."

"I'm sorry. But I have to do this, and I can't do it without you. And if I'd told you where we were going, you wouldn't have come."

"Damn right I wouldn't have come! You knew that, and you brought me out here anyway?" Her voice broke, the muscles in her face rigid.

She was staring straight ahead, her hands tight on the steering wheel.

"I think we both need to do this," I said.

She sat there for another minute, saying nothing, the anger rising off her like steam.

"Fuck," she said, putting the car into gear. "Goddamn it."

She swung the car toward the exit and took a right onto Central, heading not toward town, but toward Prairie View Drive. Toward the fence.

A part of me wished she'd turned back toward town. I didn't believe in ghosts, but I did believe that places have a kind of memory. That the things that happen in a place—especially terrible things—leave a trace.

The news reports were detailed about the location, so we knew where to go. When Prairie View Drive dead-ended, we followed a dirt road full of ruts and potholes that eventually became rocky, too rocky for Jenna's poor Honda. She stopped the car, and we got out and walked, navigating the rocks and the cactus that littered the terrain. I stubbed my toe on a rock and realized why they took Shane's shoes. Anybody who tried to walk across this field barefoot would cut their feet to shreds.

There was another hour until sunset, but it was already cold, the wind whipping unobstructed across the high plains. We walked a ways, a couple of football fields, maybe, until we came to a slight crest. On the other side of the crest was a gulley, just a slight depression in the landscape. And there it was, the fence.

It was a simple log fence, split rail, the horizontal slats tucked into a series of cross-hatched supports. It wasn't even a whole fence, really. It only ran twenty feet or so and seemed designed to mark private property, not to keep anybody out of it. It was draped with flowers, some dead, some still in bloom. There were a few burnt-out candles beneath it, a couple of stuffed animals. Cards littered the ground. "Rest in peace, Shane." "You were loved." "May God hold and keep you."

From where we were standing, it looked just like it did in the photos I'd seen in the press. It conveyed a sense of utter isolation, and I winced at the thought of Shane being so alone. But when I turned around, trying to see what Shane would have seen, the view was different. You could see Aspen Court, a development of new, fancy houses, less than half a mile away. You could just make out the sign for the new Walmart. You could hear the hum of cars and trucks on I-80. If you took a deep breath, you could catch a whiff of the cement plant off to the west. And now it wasn't the isolation that was so terrifying. It was the proximity. Shane was close to so many people, which must have given him hope. Surely someone would wander by.

The proximity made a terrible kind of sense. J-Town and Crenshaw didn't do this at some far-off place, remote from the town. No, this happened where we lived. This place was as connected to Juniper as the high school, the churches, the university.

Jenna walked up to the fence and laid her hands on the cross slats. She turned around and looked at me, and then lowered herself to the ground, sitting cross-legged, her back leaning against a fence post. I went over and sat beside her.

We didn't say anything for a long time, each of us taking in the place, trying to figure out what it could tell us. I closed my eyes, trying to feel what had happened there. I pictured Shane, exactly where we were, but with his hands tied behind his back. I imagined the blood that caked his face. I tried to feel the brutal winds, to see the dark, dark night.

"It's just a place," I said, finally.

"What do you mean?"

"Just a stupid fence in a stupid field near some big, stupid houses. There's no magic here."

We were quiet again. I cinched my jacket tighter against the wind.

"So," Jenna said. "What do you want to do about the article?"

It had been overcast all day, but as the sun was going down it found a patch of clear sky, low to the horizon in the west. It didn't bring any heat, but it brightened the landscape with that soft autumn light, oranges and yellows mixed with delicate streaks of pink and purple.

I missed Shane. I missed my mom. I missed them both with an ache deep in my bones. I wished they'd had a chance to meet. They would have liked each other.

I knew what my mom would have said about the article. And I was pretty sure I knew what Shane would have wanted.

"Everything you said makes total sense," I said. "About Jesse. About meth. About all the kids out there who need people to pay attention. I mean, there's nothing I can say to that. You're right." I stopped talking, not knowing how to say the next part.

"I feel a 'but' coming on," she said.

"You can't publish it. It's just not the right thing to do." I tried to line up a better argument in my head, but I didn't have one.

I braced myself for her disappointment.

"You're right," Jenna said.

I wasn't sure I'd heard her correctly.

"I am?"

"Yeah. The more I thought about it, the more I began to question my own motives. I've been so obsessed with what happened to my brother that I think I was trying to force all that onto what happened to Shane. It was like I couldn't really see either of them because I could only see both of them. I don't know. I think I was just missing my brother."

She gasped, like she'd told herself something she didn't know.

"I miss him so much." She was crying now, and I put my arm around her.

"It's been two years," she said, "but it feels like it was yesterday. How long am I supposed to feel like this?"

I didn't have an answer, just a fear that I might be asking the same question in two years.

"Anyway," she said, shaking my arm off and wiping her nose, "it wouldn't be fair to Jesse to make this about Shane, and it wouldn't be fair to Shane to make this about Jesse. Shane's life was hard enough. Why make his death even harder?

"But I'm going to keep investigating the drug stuff," she said. "That story needs to be told. If you care about your brother at all, you should maybe give him a heads-up. He's not smart enough to avoid jail time when all this comes out."

I would have to let Christopher know, if only for Dad's sake. Dad had been through enough. He didn't need to see Christopher go to prison.

"What about Cal," I asked, "and that other guy?"

"Fuck them. I will *not* be afraid of those assholes. Too many people are dying. Somebody needs to stop them."

"This is a terrible idea. You're going to get hurt. Or worse."

"Don't worry about me," she said. "I'll be careful. It's just a matter of finding people willing to go on the record. I'm betting there are plenty of people who'd like to see those scumbags taken down and put away for a good long time. I'll find them."

She stood up, stretched, and looked back to the east, over the prairie.

"It's funny," she said. "When I first started working on my article, I just wanted to find out who was responsible for my brother's death. But now? I'm thinking being a reporter might be what I want to do with my life. I think I can be good at it. I just need to find the right way to do it. There has to be a way to tell the truth without hurting innocent people."

She turned toward me.

"I've already filled out the paperwork to change my major."

I stood up, stiff from the ground and the cold, and leaned against the fence.

"What about the cows?" I asked.

She chuckled.

"I can still hang out with them. I know people at the cattle barns on campus. But that cow-grudge thing turned out to be bullshit. Apparently, they're just grumpy sometimes. Can't really blame them, I guess. I mean with the slaughtering and all.

"Anyway," she said. "We should get going. I have a shit-ton of work to do."

"I think I want to stay a bit," I said.

"Are you sure? How will you get back?"

"There's a bus that leaves from in front of the Walmart. I'll be okay."

There was so much I wanted to say to her. I wouldn't have met Shane if it wasn't for her. And I wouldn't have lost him. And I wouldn't have found him again, even though the Shane I found wasn't the Shane I'd lost. It was all too much for words.

"Thank you," I said.

"For what?"

"For everything."

She wrapped me in her arms, hugging me so tight I could hardly breathe.

"See you Thursday," she said, finally pushing me away.

"What's Thursday?"

"The Pride Alliance. We've made you an honorary member. Eight o'clock. Student Union."

I was about to thank her for that too, but she was already gone, picking her way through the rocks and cactus.

. . .

The sun ran out of clear sky, disappearing once again behind the clouds. The temperature was dropping fast, but I couldn't make myself leave just yet. I remembered what Shane said on that first morning when he took me to breakfast, how he loved the smell of sagebrush and pine trees coming off the Snowy Range. He even loved the wind, he said, the way it pushed one season out, another season in.

But when I inhaled, all I got was the acrid smell of chemicals coming off the cement plant. And the wind? It was just annoying. Juniper would have been a lot more tolerable if the wind would just stop.

I looked off to the east, away from town. I remembered what Mr. Lindquist said about the world being a big place, that I ought to see some of it. Maybe he was right. Maybe there was another life out there somewhere.

I was glad Jenna wasn't going to publish her article, but just at the edge of my thinking was doubt. Maybe I was wrong. Maybe the only way to honor Shane was to let the whole truth come out, no matter how ugly, no matter how incriminating. To let him be the complicated person he was.

Just then the sun found one more gap in the clouds before hitting the horizon, and it lit everything up in oranges and reds, like someone had suddenly turned on stage lights.

And there he was again, vivid as an autumn morning. Shane, on a horse. Not a fake horse this time, but a real one, majestic and strong. And there was the shimmering meadow, and the corn as tall as the sky. Shane's smile outshone the sun, and his voice leaped and danced as he sang about the beautiful morning.

That need to turn Shane into a symbol—it's so strong, so insistent. I wonder how things might have been different if I had seen him more clearly, if I hadn't been so lost in some perfect version of him.

I guess that's why I'm telling this story. I need somebody to know, somebody to see behind the image that the rest of us created out of our own desperate need. Maybe this is what it takes to keep Shane alive. Not to turn him into a symbol, but to let him be who he was. The person we loved.

But when I think about him now—and I think about him every day—the Shane I see, the Shane I need, is still on that horse, singing about corn. No clouds on the horizon. No trauma, no pain. Not a worry in the world.

That beautiful, beautiful boy.

AUTHOR'S NOTE

All the Truth I Can Stand was inspired by the murder of Matthew Shepard, a gay University of Wyoming student. On the night of October 6, 1998, Aaron McKinney and Russell Henderson met Shepard at the Fireside Lounge, a bar in Laramie, Wyoming. The three young men were seen leaving together in a black Ford pickup around midnight. McKinney and Henderson drove Shepard to the edge of town, where they beat him nearly to death. They left him there, tied to a fence, in the brutal cold. He was found unconscious eighteen hours later, when he was taken first to Ivinson Memorial Hospital in Laramie and then to Poudre Valley Hospital in Fort Collins, Colorado. He died six days later, never having regained consciousness. McKinney and Henderson are currently serving life terms in prison.

Shepard's death has had a profound impact on American law and culture. It led to the inclusion of sexual orientation in the nation's hate crimes laws, and Shepard himself has become an iconic figure, inspiring generations of Americans—gay and straight—to fight for LGBTQ+ rights.

I was thirty-one when Matthew Shepard was murdered, but when I heard the news, I flashed back to 1985, my first semester of college in a small town in Texas. I was a closeted gay man with a serious crush on a guy I'll call James. He and Shepard could have been twins—the same slight build, the same piercing blue eyes, the same hair drooping adorably across the forehead. For a while, James and I were inseparable. You couldn't call it dating, given how closeted we were, but we helped each other learn what to do with the desire that consumed us and terrified us in equal measure.

Eventually, the terror won out. My terror. I pushed James away, cruelly, desperate to deny my feelings for him. I transferred to a different college and never heard from, or about, James again. Years later, the occasional internet search turned up nothing. It was like he had simply vanished, or worse. This was, after all, the mid-1980s, a dangerous time for gay men, given the unchecked spread of HIV and a pervasive homophobia that could quickly morph into violence. Because that's the other thing about James. Like Shepard, he had an innocence about him, a trusting relation to the world. There was a good chance this innocence had put him in danger, had maybe gotten him killed.

And so, when I heard the news about Matthew Shepard and read the accounts of his brutal murder, I couldn't help but imagine this happening to James, someone I had failed so many years earlier. It was James I saw on that fence, James whose face was an illegible patchwork of blood and bruises.

By seeing James in Shepard, I was missing Shepard entirely. I was erasing the things that made him a person. The things that made him human. But I wasn't alone. This is what so many of us did, back in 1998, when we turned Matthew Shepard into a figure for our own needs.

Many years later, I discovered new reporting on what happened that terrible night in October of 1998 and what led up to it. The more I read, the more complicated Shepard's death became, and with this complication came a real sense of unease. The story I had been told—with its clear victims and villains—was turning into something messier, something much harder to live with. But in that messiness, I was reminded of a central truth: you shouldn't have to be a saint to be worthy of sympathy, respect, and love.

FACT/FICTION

All the Truth I Can Stand is best thought of as speculative historical fiction. On the most significant details, I've stayed true to the reported facts. For example, the details about Shane that Brian shares with Ash and Jenna in chapter twenty-two come from what we know about Matthew Shepard in the months and years leading up to his murder. At the same time, I've allowed myself the freedom to imagine characters and actions that might help us understand the tragic events of October 1998. Ash, Jenna, and Ryan, for example, are my own creations. And while Shepard loved theater (he was in several local productions in Casper), he never, to my knowledge, performed in *Oklahoma!*. I've fictionalized names and places as well, and I've made Shane two years younger than Shepard, who was twenty-one at the time of his death.

I have been guided by Stephen Jimenez's *The Book of Matt: Hidden Truths About the Murder of Matthew Shepard* (2013). An award-winning journalist, writer, and producer, Jimenez offers the most comprehensive account of the events leading up to Shepard's murder. Having reported this story for thirteen years and having interviewed over one hundred subjects, he documents in careful detail Shepard's acquaintance with his attackers, his difficult history of sexual abuse and trauma, and his drug use and involvement in meth trafficking. Jimenez's larger argument is that we do Shepard no favors by overlooking these more troubling aspects of his story. Rather, we have a responsibility to Shepard to take the full complexity of his humanity into account. This responsibility has shaped my own telling.

Jimenez's book was controversial, in part because it called into question what so many of us had come to believe about Shepard. Jimenez was accused of blaming the victim; of relying on unnamed sources, many of whom were involved in the drug trade; and of giving ammunition to right-wing forces arrayed against the rights of LGBTQ+ people. And right-wing forces did indeed take advantage of Jimenez's reporting, using it to argue disingenuously that hate crime legislation was unnecessary because Matthew Shepard's murder was "a complete fraud."

On the other hand, Jimenez's book has been well reviewed, and many of its allegations have since been backed up by other witnesses to the drama. Some of its staunchest defenders come from the gay press. *Lambda*

Literary Review called *The Book of Matt* "a model for journalistic inquiry." *The Advocate* praised Jimenez's "years of dogged investigation" and said the case he had built was "persuasive." Other reviewers pointed out that Jimenez, himself a gay man, had no interest in slandering a gay American icon. A collaboration with the ABC newsmagazine *20/20*, "The Matthew Shepard Story: Secrets of a Murder," garnered Jimenez a 2005 prize for investigative reporting from the Medill School of Journalism at Northwestern University and a 2006 Writers Guild Award.

Ultimately, however, my novel stands on its own. Even if readers don't accept all of Jimenez's conclusions, I trust they'll find here a sincere attempt to rethink the ways we honor and mourn those we've lost, as well as an effort to understand the lingering effects of drug abuse and drug trafficking, especially on the queer community.

METHAMPHETAMINE AND HIV

Jimenez's most valuable contribution is his focus on the role crystal methamphetamine played in this tragedy, which had gone largely unreported at the time. In the 1990s, methamphetamine quickly replaced cocaine as America's drug of choice, offering a longer-lasting high at a fraction of the cost. This was particularly the case in rural populations experiencing ongoing financial stress and despair and among some young gay men, who found in meth a release from the hatred that surrounded them and a pathway to the sexual freedom they sought.

Wyoming was at the heart of a meth trade that flowed from California and Mexico, with Laramie a central node in this trade, given its proximity to Interstate 80. Wyoming had the highest per capita rate of meth abuse in the country. Wyoming's eighth-graders used meth at rates higher than twelfth-graders nationwide. Meth-related arrests in Wyoming increased over 600 percent from 1992 to 1998; over the same period, the number of minors arrested for meth-related assaults more than doubled, from just over 200 in 1992 to more than 500 in 1998. In 2004, the

Casper Star-Tribune wrote that "Wyoming faces no greater scourge than methamphetamine."

This upsurge in meth use occurred at the same time that newly available treatments transformed HIV from a death sentence to a chronic but manageable disease. The number of Americans who died from AIDS fell by almost half from 1995 to 1997, leading to the lowest death rate from AIDS since 1987. At the same time, however, there was no decline in the number of new infections. In short, fewer people were dying, but large numbers were still being infected, and those who were infected were living longer, thus leading to more infections.

The sense that HIV was no longer a deadly disease, combined with disproportionate meth use among gay men, led to increased rates of HIV infection in the gay community. One of meth's primary effects is to reduce inhibitions, making it an extremely dangerous party drug. An early-2000s study of men in Los Angeles found that new HIV infections were three times as high among meth users as they were among nonusers. And while meth use had first surged in popularity among white gay men, it was increasingly becoming an issue among Black and Hispanic gay men.

Given this correlation of meth use and HIV, it's hard to separate Shepard's status as HIV positive from his drug use. Though some have speculated that he was infected when he was raped in Morocco in 1995, his mother said he had been periodically tested since then and had always tested negative. With the exception of his limo driver, Shepard's friends didn't know he was positive, and some speculated that even he didn't know. The infection, therefore, was likely a recent one. The media's relative silence about this piece of the story suggests a culture in denial about a drug problem that was—and is—destroying countless lives.

The relationship between meth use and HIV continues to this day. A recent study in the *Journal of Acquired Immune Deficiency Syndromes* found meth use to be "the single biggest risk factor for HIV seroconversion among gay and bisexual men." A 2020 editorial in the *New York Times* called meth use in the gay community "a crisis we are not talking about." The editorial continued, "just like during the AIDS epidemic of the 1980s and '90s, resources are paltry, government support is virtually nonexistent and an aura of denial surrounds the crisis."

As meth continues to ravage gay communities, the use of opioids (highly addictive painkillers) has recently emerged as yet another epidemic disproportionately affecting LGBTQ+ populations. A recent study found that queer men and women had an almost three times greater risk of developing opioid addiction than heterosexual men and women. As with meth use, this statistic reminds us of the ways in which members of the LGBTQ+ community find in drug use a brief if dangerous relief from the hostility and violence directed against them.

LGBTQ+ REPRESENTATION IN THE 1990s

One way to understand Matthew Shepard's transformation into an American icon is to position that transformation against the backdrop of a rapidly changing media environment. As Chuck Klosterman argues in *The Nineties: A Book* (2022), LGBTQ+ representation underwent a dramatic shift from the late eighties to the late nineties. The original title of the Beastie Boys' 1986 debut album was *Don't Be a Faggot*. The 1988 film *Crocodile Dundee II* played the sexual assault of a transgender woman for laughs. And the most popular comedian of the 1980s, Eddie Murphy, regularly mocked gay men. Much would change in the following decade.

The musical *Rent*, which featured same-sex couples, debuted in 1994, eventually becoming one of the longest-running shows on Broadway. The prime-time soap opera *Melrose Place* included a sympathetic and ongoing portrayal of a gay man. The teen drama *My So-Called Life* featured a well-drawn gay Latino character. Rock star Melissa Etheridge and her partner, Julie Cypher, graced the cover of *Newsweek* with the headline "We're Having a Baby." A lesbian couple got married on *Friends*.

Perhaps the biggest queer moment of the nineties happened in 1997, when Ellen Degeneres came out—both in real life and as her character on the very popular sitcom *Ellen*. It's hard to overstate the importance of this moment. About 44 million people (three times the usual audience) tuned in to watch the first lead character on a major network show come out. Ellen would go on to become an extremely popular talk show host, someone Americans welcomed into their homes five days a week (though her popularity dimmed considerably in 2020 amid allegations that she had created a toxic work environment).

Though not without their problems (for example, the near-total invisibility of LGBTQ+ people of color), these representations of same-sex life and love differed radically from those of just a decade earlier, and they provided a welcoming context for Matthew Shepard. Through its TV screens, America was becoming better able to identify with gay, lesbian, and bisexual figures and to view them sympathetically. Though the country was still a dangerous place for queer people, it was ready to make Matthew Shepard a tragic hero.

WESTBORO BAPTIST CHURCH

The novel's portrayal of Fred Phelps and the members of the Westboro Baptist Church is all too real. Based in Topeka, Kansas, and made up largely of members of Phelps's family, the WBC was a hate group that targeted Jews, Muslims, and atheists. Its primary vitriol, however, was reserved for gays, lesbians, and bisexuals (and later for trans folks). Its official website was godhatesfags.com, and it was well known for picketing the funerals of AIDS victims.

From a roped-off area, Phelps and the WBC protested Shepard's memorial service, holding the signs and chanting the slogans portrayed in the novel. At the trial of one of Shepard's attackers, the WBC were met by an "angel action." This involved queer activists surrounding the Phelps gang while wearing huge angel's wings. With their wings outspread, they separated the WBC from the rest of the crowd and from the media.

Phelps died in 2014. Since then, several members of his family have apologized for their role in anti-gay hatred.

MATTHEW SHEPARD'S LEGACY

Shepard's most significant legacy was perhaps the Matthew Shepard and James Byrd Jr. Hate Crimes Prevention Act, which President Barack Obama signed into law on October 28, 2009. Prior to the act's passage, federal hate crime laws only protected people based on race, color, religion, or national origin. The new law widened those protections to include gender, sexual orientation, and gender identity, marking a turning point in legal protections for queer Americans.

It's important to note the other name in the new law's title. James Byrd Jr. was a forty-nine-year-old Black man who was brutally murdered by white supremacists in Texas just four months before Shepard was killed. The fact that this bill is commonly referred to only as the Matthew Shepard Hate Crimes Prevention Act demonstrates the role race plays in the media and in the American imagination. Shepard's whiteness gave the media, and much of the country, a recognizable and sympathetic victim.

Another enduring piece of Shepard's legacy is *The Laramie Project*. In the month after Shepard's murder, writer/director Moisés Kaufman and the Tectonic Theater Project traveled to Laramie, where they conducted interviews and collected material for a play. They returned many times over the next year and a half, working to transform the archive they had collected into theater. *The Laramie Project* debuted in Denver in 2000 before moving to the Union Square Theater in New York City. HBO later commissioned a film version, which premiered in 2002. *The Laramie Project* continues to be performed throughout the world.

Shepard's parents, Dennis and Judy Shepard, have also done a great deal to ensure his legacy. In December 1998, they founded the Matthew Shepard Foundation, which is still working as a nonprofit organization dedicated to fighting violence and to ensuring the health, safety, and dignity of the LGBTQ+ community.

On October 26, 2018, Shepard's ashes were interred in the crypt of the Washington National Cathedral before an audience of more than 2,000 people in a ceremony carried live on national television. The Shepards had long been seeking a place to bury their son's ashes that wouldn't be at risk of desecration.

. . .

One of my goals in writing *All the Truth I Can Stand* was to remind us that tragic events—even those with clear victims and villains—are often more complicated than we want them to be. This is what I wanted Ash to wrestle with in my novel, and I didn't want it to be easy. I left him in doubt at the end, wondering whether he was doing the right thing in telling this story, just as I have the occasional doubt about my own telling.

At the end of the day, however, I believe that this is a story whose time has come. It's been over twenty-five years since Matthew Shepard was murdered. In that time, the queer community has made enormous strides, both at the level of equal rights (the legalization of same-sex marriage, for example) and public support (seventy-two percent of young Americans report being either "very" or "somewhat" comfortable with a close friend being LGBTQ+). We are a strong people, ready and able to face the truth.

Our ability to do so has never been more necessary. Despite significant progress, the struggle for LGBTQ+ rights continues. Florida has severely restricted instruction on gender identity and sexual orientation for grades K–12. Nationwide, books with queer content are being banned in increasing numbers. Trans folks are being denied medical treatment, the dignity of correct pronouns, and access to appropriate bathrooms.

As we resist these renewed assaults on our identities and our freedoms, we'll need to embrace our past in all its complexity—as a source of strength, a source of inspiration. This will require a clear-eyed view of everything that led to that terrible night in October of 1998, when Matthew Shepard was left to die on the cold Wyoming prairie.

We know that the dead can be flawed and still be victims. They can fail us and themselves and still be mourned.

We should be able to die as we live, fully human.

NOTE ON SOURCES

In addition to Stephen Jimenez's *The Book of Matt* (see "Author's Note"), other sources proved invaluable to me while working on *All the Truth I Can Stand*. JoAnn Wypijewski's "A Boy's Life" (*Harper's*) stands out for its willingness to ask tough questions. I also learned a great deal from Melanie Thernstrom's "The Crucifixion of Matthew Shepard" (*Vanity Fair*). *Losing Matt Shepard: Life and Politics in the Aftermath of Anti-Gay Murder*, by Beth Loffreda, is a brilliant combination of memoir and scholarship. And, of course, Judy Shepard's wrenching memoir, *The Meaning of Matthew: My Son's Murder in Laramie, and a World Transformed*, offers a moving account of the events leading up to Shepard's murder, and of the changed world that followed.

My depiction of *Oklahoma!* is indebted to the 2019 Broadway revival of the show, directed by Daniel Fish.

For information on the lynching of James Byrd Jr. and the media coverage of it, see *Murder, the Media, and the Politics of Public Feelings: Remembering Matthew Shepard and James Byrd Jr.* by Jennifer Petersen and *Hate Crime: The Story of a Dragging in Jasper, Texas* by Joyce King.

ACKNOWLEDGMENTS

Writing is a solitary endeavor made possible by lots of people. I'm lucky to know some good ones.

Thanks to my agent, Savannah Brooks, for believing in the book I wrote before this one and for sticking with me through everything that followed. I'm constantly impressed by her intelligence, her integrity, her strength, and her passion for books.

It's been a pleasure working with the talented people at Calkins Creek and Astra Books for Young Readers. Thanks to Thalia Leaf, who knew better than I did what this book could be. I benefited enormously from working with her. Thanks also to Carolyn Yoder and Suzy Krogulski, who helped make this a better book and me a better writer. Suzanne Lander and Nancy Seitz provided a meticulous copyedit; Ray Pringle offered insighful comments at a crucial stage.

Thanks to Barbara Grzeslo for the book's design and Gérard DuBois for the cover illustration. I couldn't be happier with the final product.

A book needs an audience. Thanks to Kerry McManus and Chelsea Abdullah for helping this book find one.

It's gratifying to have the support of everyone at KT Literary. In particular, thanks to Kate Testerman and Kelly Van Sant.

Jennifer Delton, Susannah Mintz, Linda Simon, and Susan Walzer have been my partners in an ongoing conversation about writing for almost thirty years. I wouldn't be the writer I am—the *person* I am—without their love and intelligence.

I owe more than I can say to my partner, John Peabody. He came into my life when I least expected it, and every day since has been a gift. This novel wouldn't exist if I didn't have John in my life and in my heart.

Finally, thanks to all the young queer folks who are finding ways to love yourselves when the world won't. I see you.